ALEXA GRACE

Profile
of
Evil

ALEXA GRACE

Copyright

This ebook is a work of fiction. Names, characters, places and incidents are products of the author's imagination or are used fictitiously.

Any resemblance to actual events or locales or persons, living or dead, is entirely coincidental.

Cover design by Christy Carlyle of Gilded Heart Design

ISBN-13: 978-1484906378

ISBN-10: 1484906373

Dedication

For Carly

This book is also for the men and women
in law enforcement who pursue sex predators
who prowl the Internet,
thus keeping real children from being abused.

CONTENTS

Acknowledgments

I extend a special thank you to Lt. Adrian Youngblood of the Seminole County Sheriff's Office, who generously gave his time to answer my questions and reviewed the book for accuracy.

My gratitude goes to Agent Kyle Worthington of the Seminole County Sheriff's Office, City/County Investigative Bureau for his wealth of information about the drug Methamphetamine, and for apprehending those who make it.

My appreciation goes to Police Chief Patrick Flannelly, of the Lafayette Police Department, who keeps me straight on law enforcement in Indiana. And to Bob Mueller and Wally Lind at Crime Scene Writers for patiently answering my questions.

Thank you also to Nate Kitts, who helped me stay accurate in the facts of computer technology. Any mistakes here are entirely mine.

A warm thank you goes to my editor and friend, Vicki Braun. And to Adele Brinkley of With Pen in Hand.

My appreciation also goes to Diana Barrios Tan and Christy Hilton-Hall, who won the use of their names in this book. And to Nancy Carlson, Gail Goodenough, and Lisa Mitton who approved the use of their names in this story.

Much appreciation goes to the Beta Reader Team who devoted their personal time to review each page of this book: Anna Coy, Sandy Galloway, Carmen Odum, Sylvia Smith, Lisa Jackson, Jo Lynn Guillory, Barrie MacLauchlin, Debbie Perry, Phoebe Weitzel, Diane T. Brennan, Barbara Vorwalske, Nate Kitts, Gail Goodenough, Melissa McGee and Sue Stiller.

Finally, I want to express my appreciation to my family, friends, readers and street team. Without their encouragement and support, this book would not have been possible.

1 CHAPTER ONE

Brody Chase, Sheriff of Shawnee County, did what he did every day. He entered the sheriff's office lobby, and stopped before the wall of photographs of fallen county police officers. Focusing on a large portrait of former sheriff, Lillian Chase, he whispered, "Morning, Mom. I'll try to make a difference today." He remembered a time, when as a child, he'd begged his mother to stay home with him. When he'd asked her why she had to go to work, she'd responded, "To make a difference, Brody. We must live each day to make a difference."

He blinked at the memory. Although seventeen years had passed since his mother's death, Brody still missed her.

Navigating the labyrinth of cubicles, he said good morning to every officer in sight. He had almost reached his office when he noticed a female deputy sitting at a desk that had been moved outside his office. Damn. He'd forgotten it was the first day of Deputy Gail Sawyer's desk duty. Scanning her face, he decided she was as happy about the prospect as he was.

"Good morning, Deputy," Brody said, as he noted the large

black medical boot she was wearing on her right leg.

"I'm reporting for desk duty, sir," Gail responded as she pasted a polite smile on her face. "Actually, I was hoping we could talk about my skipping desk duty altogether."

"You're kidding," Brody said incredulously. "Your right foot is broken."

"No, sir. I can still drive with my left foot."

"Not on my watch."

"No one would have to know. I've practiced driving my patrol car with my left foot and my driving is fine."

"*I'd* know," said Brody. "In addition to the twenty-nine officers from my team and thirty from the visiting state police team, who witnessed you dropping your gun and shooting yourself in the foot at the gun range on Saturday. Oh, and don't forget the mayor and commission president were there to witness the event."

A hot wave of embarrassment washed over Gail. "Well, there's that."

"Yeah, there's that. So count on being on desk duty until your doctor releases you."

"What are my new responsibilities while on desk duty?" Gail asked.

Brody paused a moment. He'd forgotten about her desk duty and had no clue what to assign to her. Finally he said, "You're in charge of the lobby. No one should enter the building without your knowledge. You can help me prepare for commission meetings. I'll also have some Internet research for you to do from time to time."

"Yes, sir."

"To start, I'd like you to visit every officer and detective in this office and find out what work they have for you. I'm sure they can use your help."

Brody's cell phone vibrated in his pocket. Fishing it out, he looked at the display, noting the caller was his brother and lead detective, Cameron Chase.

"Hi, Cam. What's going on?"

"We've got a car fire on Indiana State Road 32 near Perrysville!"

"So handle it. Why are you calling me?"

"You need to get here fast, Brody. There are two bodies inside the car."

Brody slammed the cell phone back in his pocket and raced to the front door. Nausea and fear filled him as he prayed the two bodies were not preadolescent females, like the two unsolved murder files on his desk. The last two years like clockwork, the body of a young girl had been found in his county. Both murders remained unsolved because of a lack of identification, but Brody knew that each girl had family members somewhere. Why in the hell hadn't anyone reported them missing?

There was either a monster living in his county, or using it as a body dump site. Both options were unsettling, and people were getting nervous. He was sick of being asked why the murders hadn't been solved, and how close he was to finding the killer. The avid crime television viewers watched every week as crimes were solved and tied up with a ribbon at the end of the hour. That it was taking two years to solve the girls' murders was unacceptable to them, and they weren't afraid to voice their opinions — to him, and to the County Commission President, Bradley Lucas, to whom Brody reported. Bradley Lucas could be a horse's ass when he wanted to be, but to his credit during this investigation, he had remained supportive as long as Brody briefed him frequently. Not that there was anything to report.

Though he hadn't voiced his theory out loud to anyone but his brother Cameron, Brody believed the two murders were related. Although two murders did not fit the definition, he thought a serial killer was at work. He hoped he was wrong. Because if he was right, the knowledge of a serial murderer at work in Shawnee County would obliterate the tranquility and security most residents had known their entire lives. Their county was still a place where people left their doors unlocked at night.

Crime had been at an all-time low since he became sheriff. If he were correct and a serial killer had set up shop in his county, the sick bastard would live to regret it, because Sheriff Brody Chase would stop him if it was the last thing he ever did.

The drive to Perrysville from his office in Morel usually took fifteen minutes, but Brody made it in ten. Gray curls of smoke in the morning sky and the flashing lights signaled the crime scene ahead as Brody drew closer. Seeing parked vehicles belonging to the coroner, fire chief, crime scene techs, and Cameron's unmarked car, Brody pulled off the road and leapt from the vehicle. One of his deputies guided him down a dirt lane with a corn field on one side and woods on the other. He lifted his hand to cover his face as the pungent smoke from the burned car and charred bodies assailed his nose.

Deputy Jim Ryder, lining the area with yellow crime scene tape, greeted him as he approached the immediate crime scene. "Sheriff, the car is over there."

Brody nodded and said, "Thanks. Make sure only law enforcement gets past you."

"Yes, sir," muttered Ryder, as he tied the yellow tape around a tree.

Following the deep tracks of the fire engine in the soft earth, Brody reached the scene where a red, late model Toyota Corolla was in the early stages of a fire that was being extinguished by a firefighter. Brody figured the fire truck must have gotten there in record time to arrive before him. Because the department was largely volunteer, it sometimes took up to an hour or more just to get the fire truck manned before it could leave the station.

With his hands clasped behind him, Brody scanned the perimeter. A new red plastic gas can lay inside some brush, and a crime scene tech took photographs of it before she stored it in an evidence bag. The car's body was charred, but the numbers and letters on the Indiana license plate were visible. He moved closer to the front of the car, where he saw a body hunched over the steering wheel in the driver's seat. He headed toward the back where Cam, Fire Chief Wayne Lansky, and a couple of crime scene techs were huddled around the open car trunk, but Brody couldn't see inside.

As he approached them, his chief detective, Cameron, moved

aside. What Brody saw in the trunk made his stomach churn as bile rushed to his throat. A small, burned body lay inside the trunk in a fetal position. The acrid smell of burning flesh nearly overwhelmed him as he moved closer to examine the body, with Cam close behind him.

Sweet Jesus, what kind of a monster could do this to a child who should be curled up and asleep in bed, not charred in the trunk of a car?

"We got lucky, Brody," said Cameron.

"I doubt the victims would agree with that."

"I meant we're lucky the car didn't burn any more than it did. We need all the evidence we can get."

"Who called it in?"

"Wally Johnson. This is his property. He saw the smoke from his farmhouse down the road around seven-thirty this morning and headed down here. Tried to put it out with a small fire extinguisher he keeps in his truck, and then called in the fire."

"You doing a background check on Mr. Johnson?" Brody asked.

"Hell, yes. What was that thing Mom used to say about never leaving a stone unturned? Besides, it wouldn't be the first time the guy who lit the match is the one who called it in."

"So what's your take on this, Cam?"

"I think it's pretty obvious. The killer tried to cover up a murder with a car fire, but I think this one is an amateur, as far as the fire goes."

Brody glanced at his brother and asked, "Why do you say that?"

"We found a piece of the rope he stuck in the gas tank that wasn't burned all the way through. The fire chief thinks he stuck the rope in the gas tank and lit the rope first before dousing the entire car with gasoline. Overkill. And who leaves his gas can at the scene?"

"Agreed. The prick's an amateur, at least as far as the fire."

"What about the killings?"

A voice behind him sounded, "That's where I come in."

"Hey, Bryan," said Brody. Dr. Bryan Pittman was the county coroner and Brody's best friend since grade school. At thirty-four, Bryan was the youngest and one of the smartest coroners in the state. "How much information can you get from these bodies, considering their condition?"

"I can get a helluva lot more information from these two, than the scatter of bones we examined two years ago. Hopefully, we'll be able to identify them. I don't want another Jane Doe lying in my morgue."

"Why do you say that?"

"The fire was put out before the bodies could burn completely. I should be able to get a good look at their internal organs. But I can give you an unofficial cause of death right now."

"How'd they die?" asked Brody, as he swept his hand over his face.

"Both took a bullet to the back of the skull. Looks execution-style to me, but I won't know for sure without further study. I estimate that the killer could have been as close as three feet from each of the victims when he fired the gun."

Brody looked at Cam, "Any shell casings?"

"We're still looking, but haven't found any yet."

Bryan said, "You may not find any. I don't think this is the primary crime scene. I think the two were killed somewhere else and dumped here with the car. This place is too close to the farmer's house. Not sure the killer could see the farmhouse through the trees. If the farmer didn't hear the first shot, he'd hear the second."

"And the car was torched to destroy the bodies and any evidence," offered Cam. "Like I said, our guy is inexperienced with using fire to hide his crimes. He probably thought the fire would burn faster and longer than it did."

Bryan joined two of his assistants as they bagged both hands of the victim and then fastened the paper bags with string to prevent contamination or loss of evidence that might be found on the fingers, palms or under the fingernails.

"Weren't the hands too burned to lift fingerprints?" asked Brody.

"A man can hope, can't he?" Bryan responded.

Bryan's two assistants carefully lifted the body from the trunk, sealed it in a body bag, and transferred it to the van. They repeated the same procedure with the body in the front seat.

Bryan turned to Brody before he got into the van. "It's a slow week, so I can do the autopsy tomorrow morning at nine. Will you and Cam be there?"

"Wouldn't miss it," said Cam; Brody just nodded.

Brody glanced at Cam and wished he shared his younger brother's enthusiasm for autopsies. To Cam, the autopsy of a human body was the equivalent of a treasure hunt. Cam always said, "You never know what will be discovered that will lead us to the killer."

Brody knew he was too empathetic to victims and their families, but he did his best to hide it. All he could think about during the autopsy was the loss of another life and the destruction of the lives of those who loved the victim. He and his brothers knew firsthand about the pain of loss caused by violence.

"What are you thinking, bro?" Cam asked.

"Do you realize that prior to the past two years, the last murder in this county was when we lost Mom seventeen years ago? We went fifteen years without a murder, and now we've got four corpses, at least two of which are still Jane Does."

"Brody, you're taking these murders too personally."

"Too personal, my ass. Some sick fuck is using our county, our home, to dump bodies. No one shits in our backyard. This is the place where we grew up, Cam. It's the same place we'll raise our own families someday. We know most of the people who live here on a first-name basis. So yes, I'm taking these murders personally."

"Sorry," said Cam. "You still think the murders are connected?"

"Don't you?"

"I can't be sure until we find some evidence that connects the girls."

"Well, find it, Cam. And find the connection before another one dies."

Cameron headed toward his vehicle and Brody walked the perimeter of the scene again. Something was off. It was like an itch he couldn't scratch, and he couldn't let go of it. He stopped and scanned the area, trying to put himself in the mind of the killer.

The killer shoots the two victims. For some reason, he decides it's not safe to leave or bury the victims where he shot them. Why? Were they shot at his home? His place of work? The killer decides to stuff the girls' bodies into this car. Is it *his* car? If only they could be that lucky. The car was probably stolen.

That's it, Brody realized. The car and how it got to the farmer's property was what was bothering him. How did the murderer get the car to the crime scene and then leave? There had to be a partner or someone who helped him. There were two cars and the partner drove one of them. Were they looking for two killers? Or were they looking for one killer and a second person who was just helping him hide the bodies?

Skidding to a stop in the gravel driveway outside his house, he turned off the ignition, yanked out his keys, and pounded his hands against the steering wheel. How could she have been so fucking stupid? She'd set a car on fire to hide the bodies of those two slaves. Really? The idea flew in the face of everything they knew about hiding crimes, yet she did it anyway. Stupid. Stupid. Stupid. He clenched his hands into fists, his rage burning as white-hot anger fired through his body.

It was all her fault. Erin, his stupid cow of a sister, needed to be punished for her idiocy, and he was just the guy to do it. Getting out of the car, he slammed the door behind him and rushed to the house.

Once inside, he called for her until she entered the kitchen, holding an ice pack to her head.

"What is it?" asked Erin guiltily, her eyes refusing to meet his.

"Are you fucking nuts?" he shouted as he slapped her soundly across the face. "They found the car on fire. They found the bodies!"

She sank to her knees, still avoiding eye contact, and began shaking.

His sister still feared him, and it was a turn-on to note her body trembling. Her fear sent a jolt of lust surging through his body. He wanted to tie her up and beat her with his fists until she was bloody—until she cried for his mercy. Just like Daddy had beaten them long ago.

"Who helped you?"

"No one! I swear. After I started the fire, I hiked through the woods until I got to a county road. I walked home."

"That's ten miles!"

"I know."

"Your little car fire was discovered before it had completely burned the car and the bodies," he snarled in a quiet, menacing tone.

Erin's brown eyes flew to his face. "What does that mean?"

He slammed his fist on the kitchen counter, and hissed, "It means that fool of a sheriff, Brody Chase, and his idiot detective brother, Cameron, might find evidence I don't want them to find, evidence that could lead to us."

She pulled herself to her feet and took a cautious step back in case he lost his temper and struck her again. Pressing against the counter, she said, "It was unavoidable. They tried to escape."

Stepping forward to look more closely at her face, he ran his thumb over bruises now turning purple on her cheeks. Long, red scratches covered her arms and one eye was nearly swollen shut. Brushing away her long bangs from her eyes, *he said, "The slaves did this?"*

"Yes. I was trying to save time because I had errands to run. After you left for work, I fed them some oatmeal," she began, whining in a high-pitched voice that unnerved him. "They'd been so docile, not trying to escape, so I thought I could put them into the shower together to save time. When I cut the duct tape from the second slave, the first one held me down while the second one beat my head against the basement floor until I lost consciousness."

"How did you prevent them from getting away?"

"When I regained consciousness, I searched the house. When I didn't find them, I went outside. I heard a noise in the barn. They were inside the red Toyota trying to hot wire it to start it. When they saw the gun, they got out of the car and got on their knees."

"Did you have to kill them?" he asked.

"Yes! Bitches! How many times did we tell them what would happen if they tried to escape? If I hadn't shot them, they would have tried to get away again, and what were we going to do if they succeeded the next time?"

He pulled out a kitchen chair for Erin, and sat across from her. "It's done. I'll keep an eye on things."

"What if they find evidence that leads to me?"

"Simple. If I think they're getting close, I'll take out Brody and Cameron Chase. I've wanted to kill those self-righteous sonofabitches for a long time. Hell, if I have to, I'll snuff out the entire sheriff's department."

What he didn't say was that he wouldn't hesitate to wipe his sister from the face of the earth if she ever made a mistake like that again.

"Should we lay low for a while?"

"No way. I've got that thirteen-year-old Indianapolis girl almost groomed.

It won't be long until I can get her here for an up-close-and-personal visit. And once I get her in that basement, there's no way out."

Bryan was true to his word, and the autopsy of the body found in the trunk of the burning car started promptly at nine o'clock the next morning. Cam was in the room holding a notepad to take notes, but Brody was nowhere in sight.

Around ten-thirty, Brody entered the room and stood near Cam, who gave him a knowing glance that Brody ignored. Obviously, his attempt to hide his disdain for autopsies was not a secret from his brother.

"He started with the body in the trunk first," Cam said.

Bryan turned off his voice recorder and said to Brody, "Here's what I've discovered thus far. Our victim is a female and is five feet one inches tall and weighs one hundred pounds. I estimate she is between eleven and thirteen years old." Noticing the grimace crossing Brody's face, Bryan paused, and continued. "Cause of death was a gunshot wound to the head by a single bullet, a nine millimeter that was lodged in the forefront of her brain. Manner of death is homicide."

"So death was immediate?" Brody asked.

"Yes, she didn't suffer, if that's what you're getting at."

"Any idea when the killing occurred?" asked Cameron.

"Yes, I just examined the stomach contents. After a meal, the stomach empties itself in approximately four to six hours, depending on the type and amount of food ingested. Our victim's stomach contains largely undigested food material that looks like oatmeal. The death likely occurred within an hour or two of the meal, which would make it around five-thirty this morning."

"So that makes time of death about two hours before the farmer discovered the fire at seven-thirty," said Cameron, jotting down the information in his notepad. "So the killer had two hours to get both bodies in the car, clean up the primary crime scene, and drive to where we found the burning car."

Bryan nodded in agreement and said, "One more thing. She's had her appendix removed. That may help you identify her. In addition, we'll enter her DNA in the Missing Persons DNA Database, as well as the FBI's CODIS DNA databases. I'll let you know if we get a match."

While Bryan and his assistants cleaned up to get ready to examine the body found in the back seat of the car, Brody and Cameron headed for the break room for coffee. Cameron got to the coffee pot first, poured some in a styrofoam cup for Brody, and got a cup for himself.

"So why are you here, Brody? We both know how much you hate autopsies. Don't you trust me to get the information to you?"

"If I didn't trust your abilities, I wouldn't have promoted you to lead detective." Brody responded.

"Just checking. Sometimes, I feel you're doing the big brother thing to me like you do to Gabe."

"If our little brother would stay out of trouble and mend his wild ways, I wouldn't have to keep track of him."

"He's twenty-seven-years-old, Brody. He's not the kid you had to parent when Mom was killed."

"Thanks for the reminder. I wish I could say he was a mature twenty-seven-years-old. Partying on a regular basis and bedding half the women in the county doesn't add up to maturity for me."

"Are you still mad at him for dropping out of the police academy?"

"I was at the time." Brody paused, and rubbed his hand over his face in frustration. "I still don't get his refusal to follow the rules. He likes to bend them too much. His going around the law to get results is going to get him into trouble. Now that he's started a private investigation business, it makes me worry that much more about him. I fear the time will come when he gets himself in legal trouble, and I won't be able to bail him out."

"It's not a bad idea to hire him to consult sometimes. Gabe's a genius with computers, and he just got his forensic computer examiner certification. We don't have that expertise on the team since Kent Fillion resigned for more money in the private sector."

"I'll keep that in mind," said Brody. He lifted his cup to finish off his coffee. "I'll be at the office. Come brief me after Bryan finishes with the second victim."

Junior high school in Indianapolis had not turned out to be the exciting, wondrous place she'd imagined. In fact, gaining weight and getting braces on her teeth had thrown thirteen-year-old Alison Brown into junior high hell. The girl who used to get perfect report cards now barely got by with passing grades.

Last week, her principal had called her mother and then hauled Alison in for a conference about how much school she'd missed since the beginning of the school year.

"You must have the wrong student. My Alison hasn't missed a day of school. I know because I work nights, the eleven-to-seven shift. When I get home in the morning, I fix her breakfast and kiss her before she leaves for school."

Clutching her books to her chest, Alison squirmed in her seat and looked down at the floor. Her large blue eyes filled with tears that streamed down her cheeks.

"I assure you, Mrs. Brown, we have the correct student. Alison has missed fourteen days of school, and her teachers tell me the absences are impacting her school work."

Hearing this information, her mother turned to her daughter and said, "Alison, what's going on?"

At that point, Alison fessed up and admitted returning to the house and sneaking back into her bedroom, while her mother slept a couple of doors down. The result was a major grounding that included no phone, no computer except for school work, and no going out. Not that the last part was a concern to Alison; her social life had been dead for months now.

Alison left the principal's office just as the bell rang for second period. She rushed to her locker, unlocked the padlock, and searched for her history book. Suddenly, her locker door slammed against her head, and a long arm appeared from nowhere to knock her books out of her hands.

"Oh, my gosh, Alison has dropped her books again," said Jody Emmit. "Could she get any clumsier?"

On her hands and knees, Alison struggled to pick up the books and all the papers that had flown out of her binder. After the lecture and punishment she'd just gotten, she dared not be late for class.

With her hands on her hips and her cheerleader friends joining her, Jody laughed and said, "Poor Alison." With that, she grabbed the books in Alison's arms and threw them down the hall like they were bowling balls. Jody's friends kicked any remaining books as they scurried away to their classes.

Alison picked up the books, tucked the papers back into her binder, and then headed for class, praying she could make it before the final bell rang.

At supper that night, Alison's mom shared the entire principal conference with her stepfather, who grunted and glared at her. To say she hated her stepfather, Raymond, was an understatement. She detested him and wished she had the guts to tell her mother all his dirty secrets. But as much as she hated him, she feared him and what he promised to do—to both her mother and her—if she told what Raymond was doing to her.

Alison loaded the dinner dishes in the dishwasher, and then went to the family room where her mother and stepfather were watching television. Her mom would leave for work in a few hours.

"Mom, I have a research project for history class, so I'll need my laptop."

Her mother nodded and reached under the sofa where she'd

hidden Alison's laptop. As she handed it to her daughter, she said, "Just use it for research and nothing else. And your light goes out at eleven, right?"

"Sure, Mom. Thanks."

Alison flew up the stairs, went to her bedroom and locked the door behind her. She placed her laptop on her desk, opened it, and entered her password. The only friend she had was waiting for her on Teen Chat, and she didn't want to disappoint him.

Moments after she logged in to the chat room, she noticed Anthony was online. Alison didn't know how she would have survived the past months without Anthony. He was nothing like the popular kids at school who made fun of her weight and braces.

Alison and Anthony had spent hours chatting online for the past couple of months, and she'd shared with him her secrets and fears. Alison had told Anthony everything about her life, and he'd understood, offering her comforting words and encouragement.

One by one, she'd lost her friends from sixth grade. In a way, she didn't blame them. They were as afraid of her bullies as she was. As long as they stayed friends with her, they risked Jody and her gang focusing on them. After seeing what was being done to her, why would they want the same? So she'd lost their friendships and had become lonelier than she thought possible.

That's when Anthony came into her life through Teen Chat. She could tell him anything and he understood. He often told her that he wished they lived closer and went to the same school. Anthony would make sure her bullies never bothered her again. But as it was,

Anthony was sixteen, attended high school, and lived near Morel, an hour and a half away from where she lived in Indianapolis.

An hour later, Alison closed her laptop for the night and put on her pajamas. She felt better about things after telling Anthony what had happened that day. He always knew the right things to say to make her feel better.

She checked the time on her clock. It was nearly ten-thirty and her mom would leave soon for work. Alison pulled the lamp off the top of her four-drawer dresser and placed it on the floor. She then pushed the dresser in front of her bedroom door. Hearing footfalls on the stairs, she turned off her lamp and got into bed. Listening, barely breathing, she waited until the footsteps stopped at her door. The knob creaked as it twisted.

"C'mon, Alison. Open up. Don't you want to talk about what happened today? I can be a good listener."

Gritting her teeth, Alison listened as her stepfather stuck something hard and metallic in the door lock. She gasped when the door opened and slammed against the dresser.

"You little bitch. Move this dresser now!" He screamed.

"Go away," she pleaded. "Please go away."

After hammering the door with his fist a couple of times, he said, "You'll pay for this. Mark my words, bitch."

Alison listened as she heard him walk away. A short time later, she heard him close his bedroom door. She was safe from him—at least for tonight.

Closing her eyes, she hoped she'd dream of Anthony.

Cameron entered Brody's office, sat in one of the guest chairs, and waited for his brother to get off the phone. Glancing at Brody's bookcase, he noticed a photo taken when he and Gabe were teenagers; they were holding fishing poles, as well as the fish they'd caught. The photo next to it was taken at his police academy graduation. Brody was all smiles and had his arm around his shoulders. Another photo was of Gabe in his high school football jersey, taken after a winning game. He focused his attention back on his oldest brother and thought of what a good father he'd make someday. He'd certainly done his best with Gabe and him when they'd lost Mom.

"So tell me about the second victim," said Brody, even before he'd hung up the phone.

Cameron opened his notepad, though most of the information was in his memory. "Bryan thinks she was closer to thirteen or fourteen, a little older than the vic in the trunk. Cause of death the same—gunshot to the back of the head. This time the bullet entered at the back of the skull and exited out the front. As you know, no casing was found at the scene."

"The killer probably killed them one after the other, using the same gun, so we're looking for a nine mil. Send the slug to ATF in Indianapolis to get an official identification."

Cameron shot Brody an incredulous glare, then continued. "Seriously? Do you really think I didn't plan to, Brody? It's not like I'm a rookie."

"Sorry, Cam."

"Do you want me to go on?"

Brody nodded, and Cameron continued, "This girl had oatmeal for breakfast, too, just like the first victim, so Bryan estimates her time of death is the same. Bryan's team is checking the Missing Persons DNA Database, as well as CODIS."

"I can tell by your expression that there's more to tell."

Cameron paused, then said, "Bryan found bruising and abrasions in a circular pattern around each girl's neck. He thinks they were both wearing some kind of collar that was too tight. Maybe even a dog collar."

"Sick."

"There's more. There was extensive vaginal tearing, abrasions and scarring that suggests they'd been raped repeatedly."

Disgusted, Brody shook his head, and asked, "Do you have the license plate number with you?"

Cameron nodded, flipped a page in his notepad and handed it to Brody.

"Let's run this baby." Brody plugged the number into the database, and then turned his computer screen so Cameron could see the results, too.

"There," said Cameron as he pointed toward the screen. "Car belongs to Tillie Bradford. She lives in Gary, Indiana."

"Yeah, and there's a note to call Detective Rodney Williams."

Brody dialed the detective's number and put his phone on speaker. As soon as Williams answered, Brody introduced himself, as well as Cameron.

"We had a 1996 red Toyota Corolla on fire here in Perrysville. When we ran the tags, we saw the note to call you."

"We've been looking for that car and the girl who took it for nine months," Detective Williams said. "The car belongs to Tillie Bradford, a single mom here in Gary. Tillie's thirteen-year-old daughter, Sophia, took the red Toyota Corolla when she ran away."

"Are you telling me a thirteen-year-old, without a driver's license, drove that car all the way to Shawnee County? That's a two and a half hour drive."

"Her mother says she's a little out of control," he responded. "I'd say a *lot* out of control. One thing though, that girl is smart or was being advised by someone who knew how to disappear. We ran into one dead end after another. It was strange."

"No kidding?"

"So are you holding Sophia? Are you sending her back to Gary?"

"There were two bodies in the car, both shot in the head at close range. I think your Sophia is one of them."

"Damn, I hate to hear that. I'd really hoped we'd find her and return her to her mom." Detective Williams paused for a second, then continued. "If you need anything for a definite identification by your forensic odontologist, I have her dental records. We collected them from Sophia's dentist."

"That would really help."

"I'll email them now. Let me know if one of the bodies is Sophia so I can tell her mom," said Detective Williams. "Since the murder took place on your turf, I'll send you my file on Sophia, and her mother's contact information. I know you'll want to talk to her."

Early the next morning, Cameron entered Dr. Bryan Pittman's office to find him with his feet up on his desk, his face covered by the report he was reading.

"What's a man got to do to get a cup of coffee around here?" Cameron asked, as he tossed a bag of muffins at Bryan's report.

"What the hell?" Bryan started to pick up the report, which now was spread across the floor. "The coffee pot is in the break room, and you know damned well it is. What's up?"

"I came bearing gifts," Cameron said as he pointed to the bag.

"Please tell me these are chocolate chip muffins from Mollie's Cafe."

"They are. Thus, the need for hot coffee."

Bryan punched a couple of numbers on his phone, "Mary Beth, would you please bring in a couple of mugs and a pot of hot coffee. I'm in a meeting with Detective Chase."

A minute later, both men were sipping coffee and devouring muffins.

"I may ask Mollie Adams to marry me just for her baking abilities," said Bryan.

"She'd be smart to say no to that proposal," teased Cameron.

"Yeah, well one of these days, I plan on dating that gorgeous female. I've just got to get her to say yes, and I'm very persistent."

"Keep dreaming, Bryan."

"Your brother was an idiot for breaking up with her."

"Seriously? That was only a million years ago. Brody was eighteen and she was sixteen. Ancient history, don't you think?"

"Just sayin'." After another bite of his muffin, Bryan said, "So what's up, Cameron?"

"I'm checking on the dental records I emailed you yesterday. Are they a match for one of the girls?"

Bryan straightened in his chair, flipped on his computer, and searched his email until he found the one from Cameron with an attachment. "Sorry, I didn't see your email until now. Let's check it out." He opened the attachment to reveal dental x-rays, and then pulled two files out of a drawer. From the first file folder, he pulled out the dental x-ray he'd made during the autopsy and held it next to the computer screen.

"This x-ray was taken of the teeth of the girl found in the trunk."

Cameron circled Bryan's desk so he could better see the comparison of the dental x-ray he was holding and the x-ray on his computer screen.

"As you can see, the teeth are different. The front teeth are a little crooked and there is a cavity in the lower molar. Doesn't match this girl. Let's check the other one." Bryan slid the x-ray back into the file folder, put it aside, pulled out the second x-ray and held it up to the screen.

"Perfect match."

"At least one of our victims has a name. Sophia Bradford, age thirteen, formerly of Gary, Indiana."

Bryan's office phone rang, and Cameron prepared to leave.

"Just a second," Bryan said to Cameron. He finished his conversation, jotting a couple of notes on a pad as he did. Finally, he placed the receiver down and turned to Cameron.

"That was Cheryl in the lab. We just got a hit on one of the victims in the Missing Persons DNA database. Our second victim is Amanda Jenkins, a thirteen-year-old runaway from Terre Haute. Her grandmother gave detectives there Amanda's hairbrush for a DNA sample." He handed Cameron a small yellow post-it note. "Here's the number for the detective in charge of her case."

Alison Brown stared at the text on her iPhone in disbelief. He loved her? Anthony Burns, the sixteen-year-old, beyond handsome, and popular football player, said he loved her. She'd been searching her whole life for someone to love her, and finding him on Teen Chat was the most amazing thing of all.

Alison re-read the text one more time, and then sat on a bench outside her school. Pulling up the photo of Anthony in his football jersey, she kissed the phone display. He loved her.

Watching the yellow school buses roll away, Alison started the trek home. As she walked, she periodically pulled out her iPhone and read Anthony's text and smiled. A warmth spread through her body as she held her phone against her small breast. This must be what it feels like when you're in love, she thought. The feeling was just like all her teen romance novels had described—all warm and fuzzy.

Alison wanted to laugh out loud and tell the world that she had a boyfriend. Not just an ordinary boyfriend, but one that was popular, handsome and athletic. Her heartbeat raced as Alison imagined what it would be like to be kissed by Anthony. She wondered how it would feel to have his strong arms wrapped around her.

Alison was so preoccupied with her thoughts that she didn't realize anyone was behind her until she was shoved so hard, she fell to the sidewalk. She scraped her arms and knees so bad they were bleeding. She looked up into the scowling face of Jody Emmit.

"Alison, you are such a klutz," Jody taunted, as her cheerleader friends giggled.

"Leave me alone, Jody," Alison said, as she pulled herself up.

Jody bent to pick something up from the grass. To Alison's horror, it was her iPhone. "Oh, looky here. Who's this hot guy?"

"None of your business. Give me my phone," Alison demanded, holding out her hand and ignoring Jody's three friends, who had formed a circle around them.

"Where'd you get this picture? Did you copy it from some magazine?"

Alison ignored Jody's questions and reached for her phone again, but Jody slapped her hand.

"I asked you a question, Alison. Are you hard of hearing, plus fat and ugly? Where did you get the photo of the hot guy?"

One of Jody's friends pushed her. "She asked you a question. Answer it, stupid."

In a whisper, Alison answered, "He's my boyfriend."

Jody glanced at the photo on the iPhone, and then back at Alison. "There is no way this smoking hot guy would have anything to do with you. Not unless he has something seriously wrong with his eyesight."

At that, Jody's friends laughed uncontrollably and called Alison names.

Gritting her teeth and trembling with fear, Alison looked at her iPhone, still in Jody's hand. Without her phone, she and Anthony wouldn't be able to exchange texts. She wouldn't be able to tell him that she loved him back. She couldn't lose communication with him. She couldn't. Alison jerked her phone out of Jody's hand and stuck it deep in her jeans pocket.

"You scratched me! I'm bleeding!" screamed Jody, as she punched Alison in the nose.

The blow nearly knocked Alison down, and blood streamed from her nose; she wiped it on her shirt sleeve. She turned and ran as fast as her legs would move, knowing the group of girls was close behind. Although Alison's immediate thought was that they would tire of chasing her, after three blocks she discovered she was wrong.

The group caught up with her near a weedy, vacant lot. One of them knocked her to the ground, and then they were dragging her through a thicket of weeds and broken glass, deeper into the vacant lot. Once the girls stopped, the kicking and hitting began. Lying on the ground Alison brought her knees to her breasts, her arms covering her head in an attempt to protect herself. The beating continued, until an old man standing on his porch saw what was happening and screamed at the girls to stop.

By the time the old man reached her, Alison was too weak to stand up. Every part of her body exploded with pain, and blood oozed from her face, arms and legs. He pulled her to her feet and said, "Are you okay? I'm calling the police."

Crying hysterically, Alison begged him not to call the police. Didn't he know that would only make things worse for her? The next time she might not be so lucky.

Once Alison reached her house, she hobbled up the stairs, threw her backpack on her bed, and got into a hot shower. Examining her wounds, she discovered a deep cut on her leg and bits of broken glass sticking out of cuts on her arms. Nearly howling with pain when the water hit her face, she looked down and saw streaks of red in the water going down the drain.

Shutting off the water, she wrapped herself in a towel and used a washcloth to wipe the steam from the mirror. Looking at her reflection, she started to cry. One of her eyes had swollen shut and her nose looked broken. Opening the medicine cabinet, she found some tweezers and began pulling out the bits of glass from her arm. Using a cotton swab and antibacterial salve, she gently wiped each wound and bandaged the deeper cuts.

In her bedroom, she slipped on a pair of sweats and a soft, knit shirt. Alison went downstairs to the kitchen to find something to eat. She was pulling out a casserole to heat up when she heard the front door slam, letting her know her jerk stepfather was home from work.

Her mother was at the hospital, so she was alone with him, and no time to get upstairs to lock herself in her room. She froze and prayed he'd go upstairs and take a shower as he sometimes did after work. Instead, with metal lunch box in hand, he walked into the kitchen and sat at the table.

"What the hell happened to you, Alison? You look like something the cat dragged in," he said, as his eyes scanned her body from the top of her head to her feet.

"Nothing much. I tripped on a sidewalk crack and fell on the way home," Alison answered. She shoved the casserole dish into the microwave and set the timer.

Her stepfather was still staring at her suspiciously. "Looks like you had more than a fall. Let me see."

He was a large man, and it wasn't hard for him to pin her small body against the kitchen counter. With a finger under her chin, he examined her face. "Your right eye looks bad. You're going to have quite a shiner tomorrow. You say you fell? What'd you do, fall flat on your face?"

"Yes," Alison responded. "I fell flat on the sidewalk."

"That's too bad, baby," he groaned as he pressed against her, rubbing her shoulders with his large hands.

Alison pushed at his chest and was able to move as far as the refrigerator, but he was too fast for her. Before she knew it, he'd pinned her up against the refrigerator, massaging her small breasts with his hands and rubbing his erection against her. His mouth slammed on hers as he slipped his tongue inside her mouth so deep she nearly choked.

Alison was so scared and sickened she nearly threw up. A Britney Spears song sounded, and she jerked her iPhone out of her sweats pocket and had it to her ear before he could stop her.

"Hi, Mom. You must be on your break. Yeah, school was fine."

Hearing his wife's voice through the phone made her stepfather step away. He moved to the table, opened his lunch box, and began going through it. Alison used the opportunity to keep her mom talking so she could get up the stairs and behind the locked doors of her bedroom.

Later, she pushed the dresser against the door. Pulling out her iPhone, she texted Anthony: *I want to hear more about how you think I could run away to be with you.*

2 CHAPTER TWO

On Friday, still pissed at his sister, Erin, over her monumental fuck-up, he watched Sheriff Brody Chase climb into his SUV and head down U.S. Route 41 toward Terre Haute. That could only mean one thing. They'd identified one of the slaves as Amanda Jenkins, from Terre Haute. He wasn't as concerned about her identification as he was about what other trace evidence Brody and his team may have found at the burning car scene that could lead them to Erin and him. The sheriff was playing detective today. So what? He didn't care who Brody Bigshot interviewed in Terre Haute, there was nothing to find. Did the sheriff really think he was a stupid amateur? He'd covered his tracks and Shawnee County Sheriff Brody Chase would find nothing.

On his lunch break, he parked outside the public library, which had free WiFi. Opening his laptop, he began trolling Facebook, MySpace, and then the teen chat rooms, looking for what he affectionately called an "O.H." — online hookup.

It wasn't that he hooked up online with any teenage girl who would communicate with him. Hell, no. He had his standards and criteria very specific to his needs. In order to qualify, his O.H. had to be a lonely, preteen girl who posted her personal information like name, age, photos, even cell number and address on more than one site. For example, she might have age, name and relationship status on Facebook, but she may also have even more information he could use on MySpace. And happy day if she was also frequenting the teen chat rooms. Game on.

The teen chat rooms were a goldmine. It was truly mind-boggling how many preteen girls, ages twelve to fifteen, would tell him the most personal and useful information in the teen chat rooms. The suckers actually believed they were talking with another teen. And when he lured them into an offline meeting, things heated up in a big way—especially when he was able to persuade his targets to send racy photos and videos. He looked down and noted he'd gotten an erection just thinking about it.

All that personal information was so easy for him to get, it was laughable. God bless the World Wide Web, where he could be anyone he wanted to be. Better yet, he could be the person his O.H. wanted him to be. To date, his most successful persona was a good-looking, muscular sixteen- year-old football player with a sympathetic ear for preteen drama.

When it came to preteen drama, the more angst the girl was experiencing, the better. Bring it on. Girls with problems with parents, school, and loneliness were by far the most gullible and compliant. If he groomed or manipulated them with enough sympathy, flattery, affection and attention, he could talk these girls into anything. Best of all, these girls were the best potential sex slaves he could persuade to join him in Morel. What preteen girl could resist a sixteen-year-old stud who claimed he loved her and would die if he couldn't touch her and be near her? Teen romance. Gotta love it.

Although he could have had Cameron assign the task to one of his detectives, Brody wanted to interview Ellen Jenkins, the grandmother of murder victim, Amanda Jenkins. Thus he drove to Terre Haute, while Cameron headed to Gary, Indiana, in the opposite direction to interview Sophia Bradford's mother, Tillie.

The drive to Terre Haute took Brody a full ninety minutes that he filled with Justin Timberlake music and thoughts of the murders. What kind of a monster snuffed out the lives of two preadolescent girls with a bullet to each of their brains? Amanda Jenkins had been missing a year and a half, and Sophia Bradford had run away nine months ago. Where did the killer have them all that time? Did he hide them somewhere in Shawnee County? Or did Shawnee County contain his favorite dump sites? Why did he kill them? What had they done to get his death sentence?

When Brody knocked on Ellen Jenkins' door, she answered it quickly, as if she'd been waiting for his arrival.

"Good morning, I'm Sheriff Brody Chase from Shawnee County," Brody said. "Are you Mrs. Jenkins?"

The older woman scanned his face with bright blue eyes that didn't seem to miss a thing. "Call me Ellen. Please come in, Sheriff Chase."

She led him into a small living room, where he sat on a worn brown sofa. Ellen Jenkins sat near him in a rocking chair by the front picture window.

"I want you to know how sorry I am about Amanda," Brody began.

"You're not nearly as sorry as I am," Ellen replied as her eyes filled with tears. She clutched a lacy handkerchief in her hand and asked, "Did she suffer?"

"No, Amanda didn't suffer," Brody assured her. "May I ask you some questions, Mrs. Jenkins?"

"Yes, of course you can. Ask me anything you want. I'll do anything to help you find the monster who killed my Amanda."

"Where are Amanda's parents? Will I be able to speak with them?"

"Amanda's mom and dad died two years ago in a car accident. That's when Amanda moved in with me," Ellen Jenkins began. "She never quite adjusted to her parents' death or her new school."

"I imagine it's not easy for a preteen to change schools," Brody offered.

"Amanda loved school. She made good grades and liked her teachers. Things were fine until a group of boys decided to pick on her. They wouldn't leave her alone, especially that boy, Troy Woods, in her English class. He seemed to make it his purpose in life to make Amanda miserable. Troy would follow her home from school, teasing her, pulling her hair and shoving her. He pushed her so hard she fell, bloodying her mouth and scraping her elbows and knees."

"I see," Brody said as he jotted down the boy's name in his notepad.

"I visited the school principal, who didn't sound like she could help much because the bullying took place outside school grounds. So I filed a harassment complaint against Troy with the police," Ellen

34

confided.

"Did it help?"

"Troy stopped trying to hurt her physically, but his verbal attacks hurt just as much. There were only few days when Amanda returned home from school and she wasn't crying."

"Who were her friends? I'd like to talk to them."

"That was another reason why Amanda was unhappy here. She hadn't made any friends."

"I understand," Brody said. "May I see Amanda's room?"

Mrs. Jenkins nodded, and led Brody to a small bedroom at the back of the house. The walls were covered with a faded wall covering, and crisp white ruffled curtains crisscrossed the single window. On a square corkboard was a photo of singer Justin Bieber that had been clipped from a magazine. Otherwise, the walls were bare. A white twin bed with a matching dresser and desk completed the room. A photo with a smiling man and woman who were probably Amanda's parents graced the desk, along with some school tablets and textbooks. Brody picked up a photo of Amanda. She was a cute freckled-faced girl with braces on her teeth. Looking put out that she had to be photographed, her smile was forced.

"May I have a copy of this photograph?" Brody asked.

"Yes, take that one. I have another."

"I don't see a computer. I know Amanda had a phone, but no computer?" Brody asked.

"Oh, she had one. I just bought her a laptop, and she'd gotten an iPhone for Christmas. I haven't been able to find the laptop anywhere, so I imagine she took it with her when she ran away."

Brody made a mental note to try tracking Amanda's phone through GPS again when he returned to Morel. The last time he tried, he met a dead end when he discovered the last ping was to a cell tower not far from Amanda's home in Terre Haute, then nothing. The cell phone had been turned off or the battery had been removed. It wouldn't hurt to try again.

"Did Amanda receive many phone calls?" asked Brody.

"Now that you mention it, she didn't receive a lot of calls, but she started getting what she called "instant messages" a month or so before she left. Typical teen, I guess, she never read the message in my presence. Always went to her room and closed the door."

"Did you ever check her iPhone or her laptop to find out who she was communicating with?"

Mrs. Jenkins shrugged her shoulders. "Both were way too technical for someone like me. I never tried to do anything like that."

"What else did she take with her?"

Mrs. Jenkins opened a closet door filled with clothes. "She only took as much as she could cram into a duffle bag and her backpack."

"One more question. Did Amanda ever mention Sophia Bradford?"

"I've never heard the name."

"Are you sure Amanda never mentioned her?"

"I'm positive. I wanted Amanda to have friends. I would remember."

Cameron Chase pulled his unmarked SUV in front of a red brick apartment complex called Lakeshore Dunes. Finding building number four, he parked and searched for apartment 4D.

As he approached the building, he noticed an attractive woman in her forties standing outside the building, smoking a cigarette. "Are you the cop from Shawnee County?" she asked.

"Yes, I'm Detective Cameron Chase. You must be Tillie Bradford."

She nodded as she ground out her cigarette with the toe of her shoe. "You said you had some questions for me about Sophia. Let's go upstairs and talk."

Once upstairs, she led him into her apartment and into a cozy, yellow kitchen, where a pot of coffee was brewing. Tillie motioned for Cameron to sit down at the kitchen table. After she filled two mugs with hot coffee, she joined him.

Before he had a chance to ask her a question, Tillie began talking. "I worked late that night. I was so tired when I got home that I went straight to bed. I always check on my girls before I go to bed, but not that night. Maybe if I'd checked on Sophia, I could have called the police sooner and she wouldn't have had such a head start." She paused for a second and crossed her arms across herself as if she were cold. "I got up the next morning, and Olivia, my oldest daughter, was making scrambled eggs with shredded cheese, just the way Sophia likes them. So I opened her bedroom door to tell her that breakfast was almost ready. That's when I saw her bed had not been slept in, and that some of her clothes were missing, along with her laptop and cell phone. I ran downstairs to the parking lot.

Olivia's red Toyota was gone. I had this horrible feeling I'd never see Sophia again. I was right."

"I'm sorry, Mrs. Bradford." Cameron loved every aspect of his job, except this one. Talking to a parent who had just lost a child was the toughest thing he had to do. It was one of the few times he felt utterly helpless. What could one say to make a parent feel better? Nothing.

"Ask me your questions, Detective Chase. Ask them and leave. I have a funeral to prepare for."

"Why did Sophia run away?"

"I don't know. We were making a new start. I'd just divorced her no-good father and things were getting better. I had a new job. I thought, as a family, we'd be much happier. But Sophia wasn't happy, and she wouldn't tell me why." Tillie got up, grabbed the coffee pot, and refilled their mugs.

"Was Sophia upset about the divorce? Did she miss her father?" Cameron asked.

"No, I don't think Sophia missed her father *or* the frequent beatings he delivered to all three of us whenever he got drunk."

"What was Sophia doing that led you to believe she wasn't happy?" Cameron asked.

"She stopped talking to her sister and me. Until a couple of months before she disappeared, Sophia was a chatterbox. That girl could talk and giggle and talk some more. You couldn't shut her up. Sophia was pretty and always had a lot of friends. Then, suddenly, she became quiet and withdrawn. She stopped getting calls on her cell. Sophia dropped her after-school activities, clubs, and friends, and came straight home to her laptop. She'd be in her bedroom on that thing for hours."

"Do you know what sites she was visiting on her laptop?"

"No, I give my kids privacy. I don't pry. One night, I walked into her bedroom unannounced and Sophia quickly folded her laptop shut so I couldn't see. Maybe I should have asked, but I gave Sophia her space."

"Do you think she was communicating to someone?"

"I think so, but I don't know for sure. There was one thing odd that happened though. I brought in the mail one day and there was a package for Sophia. She grabbed it from my hand, ran to her bedroom and locked the door."

"What was in the package?"

"I found out later it was a web cam. Sophia could never afford to buy something like that, but I never found out who sent it to her."

With her ear against her bedroom door, Alison listened for any sounds in the hallway that indicated her mother and stepfather were awake. It was four o'clock in the morning on a Saturday. No one in their right minds would be up that early. Certainly not her mother, who liked to sleep late on weekends. Moving quietly back to her bed, she checked her suitcase one more time. Satisfied she had everything packed that she'd need, she carefully put her HP laptop inside and zipped the suitcase closed.

Alison strapped on her cross-body purse, opening it one more time to make sure she'd put money in her wallet. She'd saved her weekly allowance for two full months, and if that wasn't enough, she'd emptied her stepfather's wallet. He owed her that much, if not more, for the way he treated her. Alison slipped the bus ticket Anthony had sent her into a zippered compartment, and then closed her purse. Everything was in order. It was time.

Slowly opening the door, Alison crept down the hallway with the heavy suitcase and down the stairs. At the front door, she paused momentarily. She was eager to leave her school bullies and pervert stepfather, but leaving her mom was another thing. Maybe someday, Alison and Anthony would come back to visit and her mother would be so happy to see her that she'd forgive her for running away.

Alison locked the front door and began the ten-block walk to the bus station.

By the time Brody reached Mollie's Cafe where he'd promised to meet Cameron, it was six o'clock and the dinner crowd had descended upon the small restaurant. All tables and booths were filled, so as he waited for an opening, he gazed out the window.

Mollie's Cafe had the best comfort food in town, not that Brody needed comforting, and certainly not by Mollie. He turned and spotted her back by the kitchen door and thought of a time long ago when he couldn't wait to see her.

Mollie was Cameron's best friend and a frequent guest at their home. She was a bubbly, red-haired knockout, and Brody couldn't believe his luck when she said yes to their first date. They'd dated all through his senior year. Most people thought they'd marry after high school, as did he. But then things changed.

Brody was nineteen-years-old when his mother died suddenly. As if the shock of losing her weren't enough, the child welfare people threatened to put his brothers into foster homes. With help from family friends, Brody convinced them he could care for his brothers. So they all stayed in the family home, and Brody became a stand-in mom and dad, working a full-time job and attending the police academy at night.

Brody remembered how the mountain of responsibility became heavy on his young shoulders, and time was a precious commodity he never had enough of. Soon he told Mollie he couldn't see her anymore. Who had time for movies, ball games and dances, when he had two brothers to raise? Brody knew he'd broken her heart, and suspected she'd never forgiven him.

A few years later, Mollie turned eighteen and learned she was pregnant after her high school graduation party. Cameron told Brody she was devastated. She had a college scholarship and had just been accepted at Purdue. A pregnancy didn't enter into her plans.

She married Will Destin and gave birth to a baby girl she named Hailey. Six months later, Mollie became a widow when Will's truck was hit by a freight train speeding to Chicago. She'd never remarried, and every time he saw her, Brody felt guilty that the feelings he once had for her were gone.

A light punch to his arm let him know his younger brother had arrived.

"What are you thinking about, Brody?" Cameron asked. "You look like you're in the *Twilight Zone*."

"I'm back now," Brody said with a grin.

Mollie approached them with two menus tucked under her arm. "If it isn't the handsome Chase brothers. I've got a booth over here with your names on it."

She led them to a booth and handed them each a menu. "The special tonight is meatloaf with mashed potatoes, if you're interested."

"My favorite. Sign me up," said Cameron as he returned Mollie's smile.

"Me, too," Brody agreed.

As soon as she returned to the kitchen, Brody related what he'd learned in Terre Haute. "Amanda Jenkins' grandmother, Ellen, said that the girl was having a tough time just before she ran away. Amanda had lost her parents in a traffic accident and had to move in with her grandmother and change schools. She was being bullied at school, and Ellen didn't think she'd made any friends."

"Did you ask her if Amanda had mentioned Sophia Bradford?" asked Cameron.

"Yes. Her grandmother didn't recognize the name. But that doesn't mean there isn't a connection between the two girls. We just haven't found it."

"Right. Were you able to get Amanda's computer equipment? We can learn a lot by studying where she went on the web."

Brody shook his head, "No luck. It seems she took her laptop with her, as well as her iPhone, when she left."

"I didn't have any luck with that either," Cameron added. "Sophia took her laptop with her, too."

"Damn it. I was counting on getting those laptops." Brody expelled a long, tired breath.

"I'm not sure how much good we would have gained getting the laptops. Since Kent Fillion left, we don't have anyone certified in forensic computer technology to examine them," said Cameron.

Brody rolled his eyes and said, "Here it comes."

"You know I'm right about this, Brody. You're just too stubborn to admit it. There's no one in this county who has the talent and expertise that Gabe has when it comes to computers. Ask him to consult."

"Don't we need the laptops first?"

"Don't know. Ask Gabe."

"I'll think about it," Brody said before he changed the subject. "Did Sophia's mother know why she ran away?"

"No. Tillie is one of those mothers who respects her kid's privacy a little too much. She didn't ask questions. She said Sophia was spending a lot of time on her laptop in her bedroom behind closed doors. It didn't sound like she wanted her mother to know what she was doing on it."

"Did you learn anything else?" Brody wanted to know.

"Yeah. Her mother thought that whoever Sophia was communicating with online had sent her a web cam as a gift."

"I'll call Amanda's grandmother to see if she received any gifts,"

Brody said. "You know what that sounds like."

"Online predator," Cameron answered. "It's in their DNA to want photos or videotapes of their victims."

"Damn it. Just what the county needs," Brody moaned as he scrubbed his face with his hands. "What kind of a monster snuffs out the lives of two preadolescent girls with a bullet to each of their brains? Why? What had they done to earn his death sentence?"

"We need help on this one, Brody." Cameron voiced firmly.

"I already told you. I don't want the FBI..."

"That's not what I'm suggesting," Cameron interrupted. "We could get a consultant who can identify the major personality and behavioral characteristics of our offender to pare down the list of suspects."

"You mean a profiler?"

"We need someone with experience preparing a criminal personality profile, so we can narrow down suspects and improve our chances of catching the sick bastard."

"I think Sheriff Brennan hired someone like that last year when he had all those murders in his state parks. I'll email him and get a name," said Brody.

Cameron nodded, then shot Brody a worried look and whispered, "If the killings are connected, like we think they are, that's *four* girls who were murdered."

"I keep wondering, why here?" Brody said. "Why Shawnee County?"

"I want answers to the same question," Cameron returned.

"Amanda Jenkins had been missing a year and a half, while Sophia Bradford had run away nine months ago. Where did our killer keep the girls all that time? Did he hide them in Shawnee County? Does he live here? Or does Shawnee County have his favorite dump sites?"

The discussion abruptly stopped when Mollie brought their food. "Hope you're hungry. The cook gave you extra helpings."

"Thank her for us," said Cameron, as he flashed Mollie a warm smile.

Mollie leaned toward Cameron and rubbed his shoulder affectionately. "You're very welcome."

As soon as she left, Brody said, "What was that?"

"What was what?" Cameron responded as he shoved a forkful of mashed potatoes into his mouth.

"You know what," Brody insisted as he cut his meatloaf into small squares.

Cameron shrugged and shook his head. "No, I don't."

"Bull. What's with the shoulder rub?"

Looking down at his food, Cameron grinned. "Don't know."

"You do, too. There was also a *look*."

"What?"

"You definitely gave her a look," Brody accused.

"You have an active imagination, bro," Cameron said, a flash of humor crossing his face.

"Are you and Mollie ...?"

Cameron cut him off. "How would you feel about it if we *were* involved?"

"Honestly, I'd be relieved. You don't know what it's like to carry around guilt for all these years because I hurt her."

"Why haven't you tried to get back with Mollie?"

"The feelings I once had for her aren't there anymore. I don't know what happened, but they just aren't. I'd only end up hurting her again."

"Okay, then I'll consider that an all-clear," said Cameron.

"You're kidding. Are you saying you're attracted to Mollie, but was waiting to make a move because I dated her eighteen years ago?"

Cameron just shrugged and finished off his meatloaf.

Lurking in the shadows at the Greyhound bus station was the last place on earth he should be, especially on a Saturday when the rest of the world was off work, too. Being seen here could mean the end of his career and life as he knew it, but he couldn't stay away. His urges were too strong, and there were too many things that could go wrong. He couldn't afford any more stupid mistakes. The next one could be their last. It had been too long since the last time he had the rough, handcuffed, whip-to-flesh-until-she-bled kind of sex he craved. Too damn long.

Besides, he was excited about his new thirteen-year-old slave. He felt like he did at Christmas long ago, when his daddy had promised a new bike. He was itching with eagerness. That is, until Christmas Day arrived and Mom told him that his daddy had spent the money in the jar saved for the bike on booze.

He watched as his sister, Erin, stood near the door where the passengers departing the Greyhound bus from Indianapolis would file through. She kept looking at the security camera near the door. She was such a moron. He'd told his sister a half-dozen times that old Ernie McBride was a skin-flint who wouldn't put out money on a security system if his life depended on it. Ernie had told him as much last month when he ran into him in the hardware store on Main Street.

He studied his sister. Erin had changed a lot in recent years, and not in a good way. She was only twenty-six years old, yet she looked twice that age. Twenty pounds overweight, she had a habit of choosing the plainest, loosest hanging clothes she could find, as if she were trying to blend in with her surroundings. Today she had on a black hoodie with a pair of loose gray sweats and an old pair of sneakers.

Dear old dad had done a number on his little sister when they were kids. The second he arrived home drunk, he'd head for Erin's bedroom. Her screams were so loud, he had to cover his head with his pillow so he wouldn't hear them. He wondered if his mother was doing the same. Not once did she try to stop him. Not once. When he'd moved to Indiana from Utah, he couldn't leave Erin behind, so he packed her up and brought her with him.

A bus rolled to a stop outside, and the crowd waiting for passengers moved closer to the door. Erin, holding her shoulder bag close, also inched closer.

Her mouth curved into an unconscious smile the moment Alison spotted the sign announcing Morel city limits. She'd made it. She was in Morel, Indiana, and minutes from throwing herself into Anthony's arms.

The driver slowed the bus as they drove through the Main Street downtown area, the tires bumping as it navigated the brick-lined street. Colorful renovated shops and restaurants lined the street, and Alison examined both sides. A red-striped awning graced the front of a floral shop. Mollie's Cafe boasted a neon light in the front glass window, and the window of a women's apparel shop had a large yellow sale sign. Anthony told her that his mom owned a teen clothing shop and she could work there after school, but she didn't see it.

Alison was a bit nervous about meeting Anthony's mother and prayed she would like her. It was so kind of his mom to let her stay with them until she finished school. Anthony said his mom had spent hours fixing up a bedroom suite for her in the basement. He said Alison could decorate it any way she wanted.

Finally the bus rolled into the Greyhound station at Morel, and Alison wanted to leap from her seat and cheer. She thought the ride would never end. All she could think about was her Anthony and how much she loved him. She turned on her iPhone to gaze at his photo. He was the hottest boy she'd ever seen. None of the boys at her school even came close. She'd see him soon, for the first time, and the excitement was almost too much for her to bear. Turning off her iPhone, she threw it into her backpack per Anthony's instructions. Alison was supposed to have done this back in Indy, but she'd forgotten until now. Anthony had reminded her that her stepfather could find her through her phone's GPS, and that it was best she got rid of it.

The bus driver handed Alison her rolling blue suitcase, and she followed the others to the station. She strained her neck to see around the people in line to the ones inside the station, but didn't see Anthony. Where was he? The line moved slowly, causing her to shuffle along behind the travelers in front of her. Inching closer to the open station door, she again scanned the area looking for Anthony but still did not find him in the crowd.

Finally inside the station, she held on tightly to her suitcase, and watched as the others on her bus were greeted with hugs and pats on the back. Still she did not see Anthony. A light touch on her arm caused Alison to spin around. Anthony?

A heavy woman in a black hoodie smiled at her and asked, "Are you Alison?"

Alison looked up, confused. "Yes, my name is Alison."

"Hello, Alison. I'm Mrs. Burns. Anthony's mom," she said quickly, as if she were in a hurry. "Anthony got tied up and asked me to pick you up."

"Oh," Alison said with obvious disappointment.

"Now, now, you'll see him soon. Is this your only suitcase?"

"Yes. It's nice to meet you, Mrs. Burns," Alison offered politely.

But Mrs. Burns was already walking away, pulling Alison's suitcase behind her. Alison hurried after her. Soon they reached the door that led to a small parking lot. Alison followed Mrs. Burns to a small dark green car and helped her push the heavy suitcase into the trunk.

Once they were in the car, Alison repeated, "It's nice to meet you, Mrs. Burns. Thanks for picking me up."

Mrs. Burns gave her a little nod, and then turned the key in the ignition to start the car. She backed up the car to turn around, and headed toward Main Street.

Mrs. Burns drove in silence as Alison took in her new surroundings. They were in the outskirts of town when Mrs. Burns braked for a stop sign. Suddenly the back door ripped open, and a man in a ski mask burst inside.

"What the...?" Terrified Alison whipped around in her seat, choking back a cry. Mrs. Burns just sat in the driver's seat looking straight ahead.

"Hello, Alison. I've waited a long time to meet you."

She opened her mouth to scream just as his stun gun slammed against her neck, causing her to collapse in her seat.

"Damn it. What are you doing here? You couldn't wait until I got her home?!" Erin shouted.

"Shut the fuck up and drive. Now!" He pulled the lever at the side of Alison's seat that lowered the back. With both hands under her arms, he pulled her limp body into the back seat and yanked a roll of duct tape from his jacket.

3 CHAPTER THREE

Fat droplets of rain streamed down the window of the airport Starbucks as hurried travelers grabbed their Cafe Mochas and rushed toward their gate. Brody sipped his cappuccino and did some people-watching while Cameron read email on his laptop. The scent of newly brewed coffee and freshly baked chocolate chip cookies wafted in the air, as the friendly chatter of travelers competed with the thick whirr of the frothing machine.

Cameron was the first to break the silence. "I still can't believe you're flying to Florida to talk to some ex-FBI agent turned consultant who could very well tell you to take a hike."

"This is one of those situations where I can't take 'no' for an answer. It will go better in person." Brody's expression was serious, his eyes filled with determination. "Besides, who could refuse to help us? We've got a monster who's already killed four girls. He won't stop. Serial killers can't. There will be more murders unless he's stopped."

"How much do you know about this consultant?"

"I know he helped Tim Brennan solve a serial murder case in his county last year. Brennan recommends him. That's all I need to know."

"So Sheriff Brennan is still your mentor?"

"Yeah, he's the best. I'm one of the youngest sheriffs in the state. I got lucky when Tim Brennan took me under his wing. He's one of the smartest men I've ever met," Brody said.

Brody remembered the first time he met Tim Brennan. Tim had rushed to the hospital when he'd received word Brody's mother had been shot. The two men were in the hospital waiting room when the E.R. doctor appeared and told them she wouldn't make it. A bond between the two had taken Brody through the rough days of caring for his brothers while attending the police academy, until now, when Brody was searching for a monster.

Cameron gulped down the rest of his coffee and asked, "Brody, how the hell did you get the county commission to approve funding for a consultant? It wasn't too long ago they voted against getting laptops for patrol cars because they thought they were toys."

"It was easier than I thought it'd be. First, they're scared shitless about the murders. Second, I told them Sheriff Brennan recommended this particular consultant. It seems that was all Commission President, Bradley Lucas needed to hear. Apparently, he and Tim have been friends since grade school."

A ping sounded from Cameron's laptop. He opened the email and read it aloud to Brody, "A missing person report has been filed in Indianapolis. Thirteen-year-old Alison Brown has been missing for two days, last seen at her residence in Indianapolis. The preteen may be a runaway."

Brody scrubbed his hands over his face. "Christ, are you thinking what I'm thinking?"

"That this kid may have run away to meet our killer? Yes. I'll contact the mother for details while you're gone."

A female voice over a loud speaker announced that the AirTran flight to Orlando would leave in fifteen minutes. Brody gulped the rest of his coffee, grabbed his navy duffle bag, and threw the empty cup in a garbage bin.

"Good luck, Brody," Cameron said.

Brody gave his brother a brief hug. "Keep an eye on things until I return."

Brody pulled up in front of a two-story gray house in a nice neighborhood with palm trees lining the streets. Flicking on the interior car light, he checked the address he'd been given. It was the correct address, so he parked his rental car in the driveway. There were lights on inside the house, which was encouraging, for he had a critical need to talk to the resident.

Impatiently, he rang the doorbell several times, and then pounded his fist against the front door. Damn it. He had not come all the way from Indiana to Florida to miss talking with this guy. He had to be home. Brody desperately needed his help before another teenage girl lost her life. Sheriff Tim Brennan had written to him about how good this guy was, and if Brennan recommended him, he had to be excellent. Brody hammered at the door again, before peeking through the front window. There was no one inside, but from his position he could see open sliding glass doors leading to the backyard.

From the side yard, he opened the iron gate to the back of the house. The second he entered the backyard, he noticed a woman diving into an Olympic-sized pool. Transfixed, he watched her as she swam to the far end of the pool, and then kicked-off to swim to the other end, this time on her back. Her naked body, slick from the water, glowed in the moonlight. The tiny glittering lights surrounding the pool made her look ethereal as she sliced through the water.

He should do the gentlemanly thing and leave, but he couldn't move. His frozen legs seemed attached to the ground. He could barely breathe as she lifted herself out of the water. With long black hair as shiny as glass, she had an athletic build, with full, uplifted breasts, curved hips and endless legs. His jeans grew tighter as his arousal strained against the zipper of his jeans.

Moving to a deck chair, she wrapped a white towel around her body—then picked up a serious-looking handgun that she aimed at his chest.

"I don't know who you are or why you're in my yard, but I've got a little secret I'd like to share with you," she began. "In the past two years, I've shot two men. Neither man is here to talk about it."

Brody stiffened as a wave of apprehension hit him full-force. He'd been shot before, remembered it well, and had no desire to repeat the experience. He cleared his throat and said, "I apologize if

I frightened you. I pounded on the front door, but no one answered."

"That doesn't tell me who you are and why you are here," she returned, assuming one of the best shooting stances he'd ever seen.

He hesitated for a second, and then responded, "I'm Sheriff Brody Chase from Morel, Indiana, in Shawnee County. I'm here to see Carl Stone."

She quirked her eyebrow questioningly, and asked, "Who told you Carl Stone lived here?"

"A fellow Indiana county sheriff gave me the name and address in an email. Tim Brennan's his name," he replied.

She slowly lowered the gun. "Sounds like Sheriff Brennan made a typo. It's Carly Stone that you're looking for. Why do you want to talk to me?"

"You're Tim's consultant?" Brody asked, with an element of surprise in his voice.

"My brother, Blake Stone, is a detective on Tim's team. Last year, he and his wife, Jennifer, did all the work to track down the killer. I just gave them a kind of psychological road map."

"I need to talk to you," Brody said as he moved closer.

She held up a hand. "Not here. There's an IHOP Restaurant down the road. I'll meet you there in an hour."

Brody spotted Carly Stone as soon as she walked into the restaurant. Her dark hair was tightly pulled back into a bun, and she wore a no-nonsense, buttoned-up white blouse with a tailored denim jacket and khakis. Carly Stone looked all business. If only he could vanquish the image of her luscious nude body he'd seen back at her pool. One thing he didn't need right now was a distraction. And Ms. Carly Stone had the potential to be one hell of a distraction.

As she strode toward his table, he took in her exotic dark eyes, high cheek bones and olive skin. Carly seemed to know the waitress and chatted amiably until she reached him. He stood up next to the table to greet her.

With an outstretched hand, Brody said, "Let's start over. I'm Sheriff Brody Chase from Morel, in Shawnee County, Indiana."

Carly clasped his hand and said, "I'm Carly Stone, ex-federal agent and current consultant. Nice to meet you."

Brody politely pulled out her chair until she sat down, and then returned to his own.

"I apologize for being late. I had a couple of calls to make."

"I didn't notice. Just glad you're here," he said. This was a lie. She was exactly eleven minutes late and he had wondered if she was going to show. "I bet I can guess one of the people you called."

"Psychic?"

He ignored her remark and said, "Sheriff Tim Brennan."

"You're good." Carly said with a grin. "I called Tim Brennan and my brother, Blake Stone."

Brody's serious face broke into a smile. "What did Sheriff Brennan tell you about me?"

"Tim said he's known you for a long time and that you are a good man and an excellent sheriff who needs my help."

"Does that mean you're going to take the job?"

"Not necessarily."

"So you called Tim to make sure I was on the up and up?"

"Of course, I did. Do you really think I make a habit of meeting with Peeping Toms?"

Under her glare, Brody squirmed in his seat. "I've come all the way from Indiana because my county needs your help finding a serial killer. When you didn't answer your front door, I decided to check the back to see if you were home."

"And how long did you stand there while I was in the pool?"

Brody's embarrassment quickly turned into annoyance. Luckily a waitress arrived for their order.

"Carly, what will you have?" she asked, as she withdrew a small pad and pencil from her apron pocket.

"I'll have a cheese omelet, no hash browns, and a slice of bacon," Carly said without looking at the menu.

"So, your usual?" the waitress chided.

"Yes, Gracie, my usual, and keep the coffee coming."

Gracie turned to Brody. "You don't look like any of the men Carly's brought in here before. You're much better looking and not wearing a navy Brooks Brothers suit."

"Gracie!" It was Carly's turn to be embarrassed, and she colored fiercely.

"But I'm betting you're in law enforcement. Am I right?" Gracie paused, and then added, "Did anyone ever tell you that you look a lot like that actor on *True Blood*? I think Joe Manganiello is his name."

Brody glanced at Carly's shocked face, grinned and said, "Yes, I'm in law enforcement and I'd like scrambled eggs, bacon, hash browns, and a refill on my coffee."

"Coming right up," Gracie said with a giggle, and headed back to the kitchen.

"I am so sorry," Carly began.

"No need to apologize. It was worth it to see you blush," said Brody with a grin of amusement.

"I am *not* blushing," she insisted.

"Are too."

"Am not. Let's talk about your case. I have some questions."

"Ask away."

"Tim said you've had four murders in the past two years. Tell me about them."

"They were all preadolescent females. The first two bodies were dumped, one in a farmer's field, the other in a ditch alongside a country road."

"And the last two?" asked Carly.

Gracie arrived at their table to fill their coffee mugs, so Brody paused until she left. "We found the last two in a car that had been set on fire. They'd each been shot in the back of the head, execution-style."

"So the fire was set to cover up the murders?"

"I think so, and the killer didn't do that great of a job." Brody lifted his coffee mug and sipped.

"What do you mean?"

"The car fire was discovered before it had a chance to completely burn the bodies. We were able to get identification of each girl from the autopsies."

"So what's the connection between the four murders?" she asked, wanting to put all the pieces together.

"For one thing, they were all preteen girls. We don't have identification of the first two. The two bodies in the car fire were identified as Sophia Bradford and Amanda Jenkins. They were both thirteen-years-old and from opposite ends of the state. Sophia stole her sister's car, but we don't know yet how Amanda got to Morel."

"How long had the two girls been missing?"

"Sophia was missing for nine months. Amanda for a year and a half," Brody answered, as he ran a hand through his thick hair and sighed.

"Your killer is holding them somewhere, probably in your county," Carly predicted. "Any similarities between the two girls?"

"Both girls were unhappy at school and spent a lot of alone-time on their computers. Sophia's mother said she received a box in the mail she was secretive about. It was a web cam, but her mother didn't know who sent it. They both took their laptops and cell phones when they disappeared."

"It sounds like our guy may be finding and communicating with the girls online," said Carly. "Did you get any pings on the cell phones?"

"We got a hit on Amanda's phone just outside Terre Haute, and then nothing. Same thing happened with Sophia's cell. Once she got outside Gary, she either turned it off or removed the battery."

"Most teenage girls would not think to do this to avoid being tracked by the cell phone's GPS."

"I agree. I think the killer instructed them to do it."

"An online killer?"

Brody nodded his head in agreement and said, "What are your initial thoughts?"

"I need to study all of your evidence before I can give you anything conclusive," said Carly.

"Off the top of your head?"

"My initial thought is sex trafficking. If I'm right, there are a lot more girls involved. Could be twenty or more. It could be the dead girls disobeyed him in some way and were made an example for the others."

Brody rubbed the tense muscles in the back of his neck before responding. "Christ, I hope you're wrong."

"I could very well be wrong. I can't make an analysis until I review your evidence file. Did you bring it with you?"

"Yes, it's out in the car."

"Good, I can start reviewing it on the plane."

"Does that mean you'll take the case?"

"Yes. When do we fly to Indiana?"

"Tomorrow," said Brody as he slid an airplane ticket across the table.

She held the ticket up and asked, "Are you always so sure of yourself, Sheriff Chase?"

"We need your help to track and stop a monster. I couldn't return without you."

They were seated near the front of the airplane, though not in first class, so Brody couldn't stretch his long legs. He sat next to Carly, and was engrossed in a copy of *USA TODAY*. She took the opportunity to check him out. She would have to be blind not to notice how attractive he was. He wore a white polo shirt with his county sheriff insignia, along with faded jeans. The sheriff was at least six feet two inches with the promise of hard, lean muscle under his leather jacket and faded jeans. Gracie was right. He did resemble actor Joe Manganiello with his dark brown eyes, rough edges, and a punch of pure masculinity few men possess. He had this magnetism thing going that made her feel very female, which was such a change from the federal agents she was used to working with.

Brody finished his paper, folded it, and turned to Carly.

"Why haven't you asked me about how much we can pay you?"

"Because I didn't take the case for money."

"Then why did you take it?"

"For several reasons. The first is the case interests me. What kind of a monster targets preteen girls? When it comes to helping you stop this pervert, I'm in. The second reason is that Morel is only forty-five minutes away from my brother and his family, and I hope to visit them. I miss him, and he has a new baby and five-year-old son who I'm dying to spend more time with. So when it comes to the money, I don't care. It's just icing on the cake."

"Your brother has a *new* five-year-old son?" Brody asked, his dark eyebrows raised inquiringly.

"It's a long story, but Blake and Jennifer adopted the most amazing little boy. I met him briefly in January when I flew in to see the new baby, Mylee. We had an instant connection, and I can't wait to see Shawn."

"Sounds great. We don't have any kids in our family yet."

"Do you have any brothers or sisters?"

"I've got two brothers. Cameron is thirty-three and the lead detective on my team. Gabriel is twenty-seven and runs a private investigation company."

"What about your parents?"

"I lost my dad to cancer when I was ten," Brody said. "I don't remember much about him except how much he loved my mom."

"I'm sorry. What about your mom? Does she live in Morel?"

"Mom died seventeen years ago."

"I'm so sorry, Brody.

"Don't be. She was a fantastic mother and excellent sheriff. We were lucky to have had her in our lives," Brody said. "Aren't you going to ask me where you're going to stay while you're in Morel?"

"I assume you have a hotel," said Carly.

"Actually, we have an ancient historic hotel on Main Street, but I wouldn't let you stay there."

"Why not?"

"There are rumors that guests have seen rats as big as cats."

"Ugh. I'm not a big fan of rats or spiders. Where am I going to stay?"

"My family has a cottage on a lake on our property and our housekeeper is getting it ready for you. By the time we arrive, there should be fresh sheets on your bed and food in your refrigerator."

Before Carly had a chance to respond, Brody's cell phone went off and he was deep into conversation. He turned to her as soon as he ended the call.

"That was Cameron. Yesterday, before my flight, we learned about a thirteen-year-old girl reported missing in Indianapolis, which is about an hour from Morel. I want to talk to her mother tomorrow. Do you want to go?"

"Absolutely! By then, I will have made a first pass through the evidence in your file."

By the time they rented a car and finally reached Morel from the airport, Carly was starving, so Brody drove straight to Mollie's Cafe. If there had been another decent restaurant in town, he would have gone there. Anywhere but Mollie's.

As his luck would have it, Mollie was working when they arrived, and made a beeline for them.

"Hi, handsome," she said to Brody. To Carly, she extended her hand, "I'm Mollie. Welcome to my cafe."

"I'm Carly Stone, and thank you."

Mollie led them to a quiet table in a corner of the restaurant, placed their menus on the table, and headed back to the kitchen for their iced teas.

Brody watched Mollie walk away and remembered the time he'd loved her as much as any teenage boy could love. But that was a long time ago and things had changed.

"Are you seeing her?"

"No." He concentrated on the menu in the hope Carly would stop asking personal questions.

"She's an ex?"

"I'd appreciate it, Ms. Stone, if you'd limit your intuitive talents to our case, and not my personal life."

"Sorry, Sheriff Chase, I didn't know you were sensitive about it," Carly murmured.

"Who said I was sensitive about it?" The second the words came out of his mouth, he realized how defensive he sounded and wished he could take them back.

"I'm sorry. Blake tells me I'm too blunt sometimes. I didn't mean to make you uncomfortable."

Brody glanced at Mollie, who was now busy taking care of a customer at the cash register.

"It was a long time ago. Mollie and I were just teenagers," Brody said.

"First love?"

"Yeah. I was the high school jock and she was a hot cheerleader. Pretty stereotypical."

"So what happened?"

"I was nineteen and in training at the police academy when it happened. Mom was the county sheriff back then," Brody began. "One day while I was sitting in a classroom in Indianapolis listening to a DNA expert from Quantico, my mom was getting shot by a drug dealer who didn't want her to open his car's trunk."

"I'm so sorry," Carly whispered.

"She'd just stopped him for a broken tail light. That's all. By the time she got to his driver-side window, it was too late to avoid the gun he had aimed at her heart. One shot and it was over." Brody swallowed hard. A raw and primitive grief overcame him. Clenching his jaw, he picked up his menu again.

Carly watched him carefully. After all this time, his grief was still like a steel weight on his shoulders. Though she said nothing, she knew there was more to the story. Someday she would ask him to finish the story. His body language, the pain in his eyes, told her that he felt somehow responsible for his mother's murder. That was the thing about guilt; you could be a hundred miles away from the event and still blame yourself.

Carly had an up-close-and-personal relationship with guilt. Two years earlier, she'd arrived late to a sex trafficking bust to find the targets had beheaded her partner and best friend. The visual still had the power to fill her eyes with tears.

A slender, delicate thread was beginning to form between Brody and Carly, and she was unsure of how she felt about that. She was here to do a job. That's all. Once the killer was captured, she'd head home to Florida. Carly intended to go home with her heart intact.

Besides, her work required her undivided attention. Carly didn't need a distraction, not even one as tempting as Brody Chase.

Mollie refilled their iced tea glasses and asked to take their orders. Suddenly, Brody's cell phone sounded. He pulled it out of his pocket, looked at the display, and said, "I need to take this."

Carly watched as Brody left the restaurant to take the call outside.

"Have you and Brody been seeing each other long?" Mollie asked.

"Uh, no, I just met him last night," Carly said.

Mollie held up her hand. "Listen, I didn't mean to pry."

"No, no, you don't understand. I'm working for Brody as a consultant."

"I shouldn't have asked. Do you want to wait until Brody returns to order?"

"Yes, thank you." Carly replied.

Brody rushed back to the table, "We've got to go." He gulped down his iced tea and slapped a five dollar bill on the table.

He raced the rental car down the street to the Sheriff's Office where he picked up his sheriff SUV in the parking lot. "What happened?" Carly asked, as she buckled her seat belt.

"Cam said a couple of boys found a human skull," Brody explained as he flipped on the lights and siren and headed toward Indiana State Road 32.

"Where?"

"Outside a small town called Perrysville. The kids found the skull in the woods on a farmer's property. It's the same place we found the car fire and the two murdered girls."

"So we could be talking about a killer preferred dump site?"

Brody nodded. "I don't understand it. I had my deputies along with the CSI techs comb those woods for evidence the day of the car fire. They didn't find anything."

"Anything could have happened in the meantime. The skull could have been covered by leaves and debris, and the boys or the wind could have uncovered it. The important thing is we find the rest of the bones for identification. They could be scattered throughout the woods by animals."

Brody slammed on the brakes to avoid hitting a huge John Deere tractor that pulled onto the road, and Carly slid forward on the seat until the seat belt restrained her.

"You can slow down, Sheriff. The bones aren't going anywhere," Carly said as she reached for her small overnight bag in the back seat.

"What are you doing?"

"I've got a sweatshirt and a pair of Reeboks in here. I can't work the scene in a business blazer." She fished out a gray hooded sweatshirt and the pair of shoes.

"What do you know about working a scene like this?" Brody asked.

"Plenty. I wasn't one of the federal agents officially assigned to the case, but I helped search for the bones after meter reader Roy Kronk found the skull of two-year-old Caylee Anthony in a wooded area in Orlando."

"You're kidding," Brody exclaimed. "You worked on the Casey Anthony case?"

"With the rest of the team, I searched those woods for days for bone fragments. When I wasn't searching in the blistering heat, I was sieving through buckets and buckets of dirt for bones or anything else of potential evidentiary value," Carly said. "So, Sheriff, you can rest assured I know how to work this scene."

Carly tugged her arms out of the blazer sleeves, and threw it in the back seat. She slipped the gray sweatshirt over her head, pulled an elastic band out of her jeans pocket and pulled her long hair back in a ponytail. Then she pulled off her heels, threw them in the back seat, and slipped on her Reeboks.

When they reached the crime scene, a deputy waved the Sheriff's vehicle through so they could turn onto a dirt road and park. Brody and Carly followed yellow crime scene tape and maneuvered through brush and vines until they came to a clearing in the woods. It was the same site where the burning car was found. A couple of canopies had been set up that covered long tables. Several CSI technicians were using screened sieves to sift through dirt and rocks. What looked like a set of ribs and an arm bone lay on the blue tarp covered table next to them. Carly reached into a box of blue latex gloves and slipped on a pair.

Brody headed to the second tent where he saw Cameron and Bryan talking.

"Glad you're here, Brody," said Cameron.

"What's going on?"

"We got a call about three hours ago from Sherry Johnson, Wally's wife and mother of the two boys. It seems the boys were playing in the woods when they found the skull. They took it home to Mom, and she called the police."

"What more have you found?"

Bryan said, "We've got a rib cage and an arm bone. The more bones we find, the better we'll be able to put the skeleton together."

"Do you have any guesses as far as the age and sex?"

"Not yet. We won't be able to determine the sex until or if we find the pelvic bones," Bryan began. "As far as age, judging by the teeth, I'd guess between ages twelve and seventeen. That's just a guess. I'm not saying anything official until Dr. Harris gets here."

"Who's that?" Brody asked, hands on his hips.

"Dr. Ken Harris is a retired forensic anthropologist who lives in West Lafayette. His specialty is assisting in victim identification through skeletal remains. I heard he's one of the best," said Bryan as he brushed a fly away from his face.

"Sounds good," Brody replied. "Cam, who's searching the woods?"

"I pulled in four deputies who were off duty and a couple of CSI technicians. I've also got a trainer and a cadaver dog on the ..."

"Hold on. Who's that?" Bryan asked, pointing toward the first tent.

"Who are you talking about?" Cam responded, as he scanned

the area.

"The woman there in the ponytail. The one with the curves who's holding a sieve. Who is she, and what's she doing in my crime scene?"

"That's our consultant," Brody replied.

"That doesn't look like a 'Carl' to me," said Bryan.

"It seems Sheriff Brennan made a typo in the email he sent to me when I asked for the consultant's name who helped him solve the serial murder case he had last year. Her name is Carly Stone."

It was Cameron's turn to question. "Brody, didn't her name appear on her resume?"

"I didn't read it until last night. Tim Brennan's recommendation was enough for me."

Bryan let out a short laugh and shook his head. "I wish I had been there when you discovered Carl was a raven-haired beauty with those kinds of curves and mile-long legs."

Remembering the first time he saw Carly, swimming nude in her pool, Brody said, "It was a moment I won't soon forget." Although it was a moment he *should* forget. The relationship between Carly and him needed to stay strictly business. Once her work on the case ended, she'd leave for her home in Florida. If there was one thing he didn't need in his life, it was a broken heart.

Bryan poked him in the ribs. "So aren't you going to introduce us?"

Carly shook the sieve gently to reveal a couple of pebbles, but no bone fragments. She looked up to see Brody walking toward her with two other men. One of the men looked a lot like Brody, only a couple of inches shorter and with a stocky build that was all muscle. He had to be one of Brody's brothers. The other man wore a white lab coat and was handsome in a traditional sense, but lacked Brody's confident, sexy swagger.

"Carly, I'd like you to meet my brother, Cameron, and Dr. Bryan Pittman, our county coroner," said Brody.

After shaking hands with each man, Carly said to Bryan, "Do you have experience identifying victims through skeletal remains?"

"Not much," replied Bryan. "That's why I have a retired forensic anthropologist on his way here."

"Good to know," Carly said. "If this area is one of your killer's favorite body dumping sites, there is more to find here than the rest of this body's bones."

"What do you mean?" asked Bryan, frowning thoughtfully.

"Serial killers often prefer a particular area for their body dumps. Ted Bundy favored the Taylor Mountain Forest where he dumped many bodies or body parts, especially heads. He'd toss the head fifty feet from the road, or if he was thinking clearly, he'd bury his victims' heads."

"Not liking the visual," said Cameron with a grimace.

Carly continued. "Gary Ridgeway, the Green River killer, dumped his victims' bodies in wooded areas around the Green River, except for two confirmed and another two suspected victims found in the Portland, Oregon, area."

71

"So what are you saying?"

"I'm saying it's very likely there are more bodies buried in shallow graves in these woods."

"Well, if that's true, the deputies and technicians I have searching the woods will find them."

"Are you saying you already have searchers in the woods?"

"Yes, they've been out there about an hour," Cameron replied.

"You've got to call them back," insisted Carly.

"Why?"

"Because when it comes to finding bone fragments and shallow graves, they can accidentally do more harm than good. They need to be briefed by your forensic anthropologist."

Before Cameron could respond, three young men led by a middle-aged man with a shock of white hair and a trim mustache approached the tent. He focused on Bryan, wearing his white lab coat and said, "I'm Ken Harris, the forensic anthropologist you called."

Bryan made introductions and Dr. Harris introduced the three young men with him as Indiana University interns completing field experiences.

"What have you found so far?" asked Dr. Harris.

Bryan pointed to the table behind him, "We have the skull, a rib cage, and what looks like an arm bone."

"I see," Dr. Harris responded as he fingered the bones. "And it looks like you've already started the sieving process. That's good. Do you have search volunteers?"

"Actually," Cameron said. "we sent a group of deputies and CSI technicians into the woods looking for bone fragments an hour ago."

"That's not good," said Dr. Harris. "They cannot be out there searching until I talk to them about what to look for, and what to do if they find something. These woods are your crime scene. Any site of human remains is a crime scene where the potential for evidence is significant. Untrained searchers can unknowingly destroy valuable evidence."

"I'll call them back," Cameron said as he stepped away.

"I apologize," said Brody. "It's just that we've never experienced anything of this magnitude."

Carly stepped forward. "My name is Carly Stone. I'm a former FBI agent who is working as a consultant for the county. I have reason to think we are working with a serial killer. These woods may be his preferred body dump site. When you brief the searchers, please teach them what to look for and what to do if they should find a shallow grave."

"I agree, Ms. Stone. There may certainly be more to find in the woods than just bone fragments. As soon as the searchers return, I will brief them thoroughly. In addition, my interns, who have already been trained in searching for human remains, will join them in the search."

In record time, Cameron gathered the searchers. Dr. Harris stood before them.

"You are searching for human bone fragments, but you must

keep a sharp eye out for shallow graves. If your killer has dumped one body here, there may be more.

"The wooded area you are searching is a crime scene where the potential for evidence is significant. It is, therefore, critically important that the entire scene, and evidence within it, remain in context. That is, not be moved or tampered with. Respect the entire area you are searching as a crime scene.

"We only have one chance to extract the remains completely and correctly. If you should find anything, do not attempt to remove it yourself. Flag the area and call your supervisor so he can send someone on my team to your site immediately." Dr. Harris paused briefly and drank from his water bottle.

"What are some of the things we should look for?" asked Jason, a deputy in his first year of service.

"You may come upon a large area of disturbance in a search area that may represent where the perpetrator rested or re-adjusted the weight of the body. Alternately, the same disturbance may simply be a result of animal activity. There may be signs of passage leading to a specific area, including human or tire tracks and signs of dragging.

"Ask yourself what is the likely or probable path taken by the perpetrator? Was the body dragged or carried to the scene? Look for evidence of the killer's activities, such as the presence of cigarettes, food wrappers, etc."

"This is my first search for human remains. How will we know if we've found a shallow grave?" asked Tessa, another one of the deputies.

Dr. Harris advised, "Some shallow grave indicators to look for are changes in vegetation, or bare patches in an otherwise plant-filled area.

"You may find a halo of little or no vegetation. Depressions in the soil often indicate a shallow grave. Significant bloating of the body will cause soil to be pushed upwards, and then resettle as the body collapses.

"In older graves, you will find depressions with plant growth."

"Is there anything else they should look for?" asked Cameron.

"Yes," said Dr. Harris. "Look for animal burrowing or signs of digging, especially in relation to ground depressions. Cracking or fissuring of the soil is often present around grave sites.

"In addition, look for maggot trails that leave a wet and dark trail consisting of decompositional fluids. Maggot trails have been seen extending as far as twelve feet from remains. Lastly, look for fly activity."

Cameron took over from there. "Before you go back out, get a couple of bottles of water and some fluorescent yellow flags to mark your findings."

The searchers had only been back in the woods thirty minutes, when a deputy signaled he'd found a shallow grave. An hour later, another was found. By nightfall, they'd found three shallow graves, a leg bone, pelvis bones, and the second arm complete with skeletal fingers. On the arm was a stainless steel identification bracelet. They'd found the skeletal remains of thirteen-year-old Kayla Stuart, who had been missing from Attica, Indiana, for three years. Bryan would use dental records to confirm the identification.

Two of the skeletons found in shallow graves were loaded into the coroner van, along with the bones of the partial skeleton the boys had found. A third skeleton was carefully placed in the CSI van, and both vans headed back to the coroner's facility so Dr. Harris and Dr. Pittman could analyze the skeletal remains for identification.

By the time the deputies had loaded up the tables and canopy tents, a media helicopter was circling overhead.

"Just what we need," said Brody with a sigh. "Once this hits the news, this county is going to be spinning with fear and there's not a damn thing we can do about it."

4 CHAPTER FOUR

Alison tried desperately to adjust her eyes to the dark. Where was she? What was happening? Naked and shivering, she felt the clammy chill of the air on her skin as it settled into her bones. Where were her clothes?

She tried to rub her aching neck where the man had jabbed her with his stun gun, but remembered the silver duct tape he'd used to bind her wrists and ankles. A sticky strip of it covered her mouth. How many times had he used the stun gun on her? Three? Four? Each time she tried to sit up in the backseat of the car, he poked her again, turning her muscles into Jell-O.

A faint stream of light from the only window in the room and the smell of mold and mildew let her know she was in a basement, like the one her grandmother had in her house. The room was filthy, with old, sagging storage boxes, broken televisions, and ancient furniture. A swath of cobwebs was on nearly every surface, and hanging from pipes running along the ceiling beams. The thought of spiders made her skin crawl. How could she be thinking of her fear of spiders when it was very likely her very existence was threatened?

What had the man done with Mrs. Burns? Surely Anthony would report them missing and have the police look for them.

Sounds gushed in from the floor above her, footsteps walking overhead, voices, and a television. A ticking of metal sounded as a gas furnace kicked on, its flickering flame adding more light to the room. It was then Alison realized she was trapped inside a large wire dog crate, the door secured with a padlock. She'd been locked in a cage from which she might never escape.

Alison caught herself glancing uneasily over her shoulder. A young girl curled in a fetal position lay in the dog cage next to her, barely breathing, her face swollen and streaked with dried blood. Alison's scream, muffled by the duct tape, vibrated through and tore her throat. "No, no, no," her brain repeated, as her blood turned to ice.

The light was fading, creating new shadows and dark patches in the trees. One by one the searchers returned to the makeshift camp, calling it a day.

Carly's back, aching from bending over the sieve for hours, throbbed in protest as she straightened and stretched. She glanced at Brody and Cameron, who were giving the searchers instructions for the next day. Brody, his white shirt and jeans coated with a fine layer of dirt, was as filthy as she was. The wind had picked up since they arrived, and a coating of dry grit from the barren field covered her hair, clothes, and skin. Carly craved a long, hot shower and food.

She'd been starving since their plane landed hours ago.

She waited for Brody, and then started the trek across the field to the dirt road leading to their vehicle. A hot shower and clean clothes were calling her name. They'd almost reached the sheriff's SUV when one of Carly's feet got tangled with the tree root of a large oak tree. She slammed to the ground with a whoosh as the air burst from her lungs. She felt Brody lifting her, supporting her with a strong arm wrapped around her waist.

"Are you okay?" he asked, dropping his arm and stepping back to look for injuries.

"I'm fine," she assured him, embarrassment flooding through her as she dusted herself off.

"No, you're not; you've got some scratches on your face." With his hand on her elbow, he led her to his vehicle as she struggled to pluck dead leaves out of her hair. Once there, he opened the back and pulled out a large bottle of Purell hand sanitizer and a first aid kit. He scrubbed his hands with the Purell, and handed the bottle to Carly, who did the same.

"Sheriff, there's no need for first aid. What I need is a hot shower with plenty of soap."

"Nonsense. Your face is covered with dirt. I can't have my consultant getting an infection," he said with a grin.

Brody unrolled some gauze and dampened it with a squirt from his bottle of water. He lifted her chin as he gently cleaned a couple of scratches on her cheekbone with the wet gauze.

Carly's immediate thought was how wonderful it was to look up at a man for a change. She'd been sensitive about her height since a growth spurt in adolescence when she'd shot up to five feet and ten inches. The nickname the mean kids called her stuck, and she was referred to as "Giraffe" throughout her school years. What was it about the cruel teasing one endured in adolescence that shadowed you the rest of your life?

Brody ripped open an alcohol packet and said, "This is going to sting a bit." His large hand cradled her face and held it gently.

"I'm a big girl. I can take it," she replied. Brody's usual no-nonsense facial features softened as he tenderly dabbed the scratch.

It was positively, absolutely the last thing she should be thinking, but Carly had this overwhelming impulse to kiss him, and not on the cheek. The mere touch of his hand sent a warming shiver through her, her body tingling from the contact.

Once he covered her scratch with Neosporin and a Band-Aid, he dropped his hands and closed the first aid kit. She experienced an odd twinge of disappointment. Carly got into the passenger seat and reminded herself how really, really stupid it would be if she got involved with Sheriff Brody Chase. This was a job, and once it ended, so would her contact with him.

Alison jerked out of a restless sleep when she heard creaking from the wooden steps that led into the basement. Someone was coming. Sitting up, she pushed her body to the back of the cage, curling up to hide her nakedness. Trembling, she watched as a light came on when the man yanked on a pull switch. The basement looked even worse in the light. A box filled with ropes, belts, whips, and handcuffs lay in a corner near her cage. Another corner was sectioned off into a small, makeshift room by soiled white sheets. Camera equipment lined a small shelf near the opening.

The man unlocked the padlock and flung open the cage door. With long arms, he reached for her as she edged away from him.

"Come here," he growled. "It will be much worse for you if you don't."

Alison's heart jumped to her throat, and her pulse beat erratically at the threatening tone of his voice. "Please don't hurt me," she tried to say.

Suddenly he lunged, clamping his hand around her leg and pulled her out of the cage. "You will obey me, slave, and call me 'Master.'" She winced when he pulled a sharp knife out of his pocket. He sliced the duct tape that bound her ankles and wrists, then pulled her roughly to her feet.

Her legs numb, Alison stumbled as he led her to a wooden chair. The man ordered her to stand on the chair. Terrified, she obeyed.

"Lift your arms up above your head," he ordered. When she hesitated, he shouted, "Now!"

Alison jumped down and tried to bolt from the basement, but he caught her easily and slapped her so hard across the face that she fell to her knees. She heard whimpering and looked toward the second cage into the hysterical eyes of the other captive who was watching in horror.

Yanking her up by her hair, the man shoved her toward the chair and she climbed on top of it. Stretching her arms toward the ceiling, she felt him secure her wrists to an overhead pipe with a leather strap. As he slid his hands down her naked body, she could feel him trembling with excitement. What was he going to do to her? The question formed a cold, hard knot in her stomach.

Swiftly, without warning, he kicked the chair out from under her, hanging her from the ceiling like a ragdoll with her legs wildly thrashing the air. Minutes that seemed like hours passed as he stood before her, thirstily drinking in each part of her body. Nausea rushed to her throat as the leather restraints pulled painfully on her wrists.

Dragging a magazine out of a box, he found a page, and then splayed the periodical out on the floor. It was a dirty magazine like the ones she'd found in her stepfather's dresser drawer. One of the pages he'd chosen featured a naked woman hanging from a ceiling just as she was.

From the area behind the sheets, she saw him pull out a video camera connected to a tripod that he set up directly in front of her. He turned the camera on.

Moving out of her sight, she heard him searching for something in a box, and then footsteps as he moved back to her. 'Crack!' A fiery burst of pain cut across her back, then another. Alison wanted to scream out in pain, but couldn't. She realized he was using a whip. She thrashed her legs as if she were running in mid-air. 'Crack!' Pain leapt from her back to her stomach. 'Crack!' The whip bit into her flesh again and again, until her body went limp as she silently sobbed against the duct tape.

Alison braced for another slash of the whip but suddenly she heard a loud pounding on the door at the top of the stairs. The man froze. The hammering against the door started again. Cursing, he threw the whip to the floor and ran up the steps, slamming the door behind him.

Once upstairs, he found the kitchen empty and screamed, "Slave!" He and his sister were careful to never use names when slaves were in the house and to keep their faces covered by ski masks.

Erin came into the room, and he shoved her against the wall, so hard it knocked the wall clock down and the glass splintered into a million pieces.

"How many times do I have to tell you never to disturb me when I'm in the basement?" He was so furious he could barely speak.

"Master, there is something you should see," she said quietly as she led him into the living room. Mounted on the wall was a large flat screen television. Erin lifted the remote control and turned up the volume.

"Though the sheriff's department has not confirmed, a number of shallow graves have been discovered on farmland outside of Perrysville. This is the same site where police recently discovered a burning car with the bodies of two murder victims inside," reported the news anchor. A video that was obviously shot from a helicopter scanned a farmer's field that was filled with searchers and CSI technicians working under makeshift tents.

He grabbed the remote from Erin and turned off the television.

"How did they find the graves? Were they searching the woods because you stupidly left the burning car there?"

"The farmer's kids were playing in the woods and found a human skull," she answered. "Then the sheriff's office was called. I am so afraid they will find something that leads them to us."

"They'll find nothing but a shitload of bones," he declared as he began pacing. "Good luck identifying all of them. I'm smarter than Sheriff Brody Chase and his band of idiots."

"Yes, Master," Erin uttered, her eyes glued to the floor.

"Besides, those little bitches deserved what they got. Each one of them disobeyed the Master and discovered the consequence." Still pacing, his anger was accelerating, igniting a white-hot fury.

His sister nodded fearfully like a frenetic bobble head on a dashboard. He sensed her fear, felt a rush of power and relished it. He'd always had a mean streak, just like dear old Dad.

"The local sheriff's office is a joke. The Chase brothers make me want to puke. Do they really think they can find or stop me? Those boy scouts have no clue. None. Do they realize what it takes to manipulate, dominate, and control a slave? No! They don't have the balls to do what I do. They'll never find me. They are not even worthy adversaries. *I'm* the Master."

A vivid image formed in his head. He was aiming his assault rifle, and in the cross-hairs of the scope was Sheriff Brody Chase on his knees in submission, begging for his life. The vision was delicious, and his sex was throbbing like a toothache.

Brody turned onto a paved driveway, pausing at the security gate to punch in his code. He continued driving until a massive redwood and stone house appeared. It looked more like a lodge than a home with huge glass windows and a million tiny lights lining the driveway, entrance, and lawn.

"You live here?" wondered Carly.

"Yes," answered Brody. "My dad was the county coroner before he died. The house took five years to build, but Dad was in no hurry. He oversaw every aspect of the building process. He and Mom had a dream to turn the house into a bed and breakfast or a nature lodge when they finished raising Cam, Gabe and me."

"It's huge."

Brody smiled, "Yes, it is. There are six bedroom suites within the main house and a small guest house in the back. I'll show you the inside of the house tomorrow."

"I'd like that."

"You said in Florida that you liked to run. Cam, Gabe, and I do, too, so we made running trails around the lake and through the woods. The property is three hundred acres of woods, hills, valleys, a fishing lake, and miles of trails with absolute privacy."

"A couple of years ago, I was on surveillance, and my partner asked me what I thought was an ideal vacation," Carly said. "I told him I yearned for a place where I could have absolute privacy: no phones, and no computers—just my thoughts and nature. I think a lot of people yearn for the lodge your dad envisioned."

When Brody drove past the house onto a gravel road, Carly asked, "Where are we going?"

"I told you that there's no hotel for you to stay in, but I have something better."

Soon they approached a smaller house. Like the main house, it was built with redwood and stones with floor-to-ceiling windows. A porch, complete with white rocking chairs, graced the front of the house; another porch was in the back. Brody parked behind the house. By now it was nightfall and the wooded surroundings were difficult to see.

Brody got out of the vehicle and pulled Carly's luggage from the back. She followed him to the back porch and watched as he slipped a key into the lock. He opened the door to a living room with large windows gracing each wall, except for the one where the stone fireplace stood from floor to ceiling. The living space was open and included a living and dining room. An open staircase led to a loft and additional bedrooms upstairs.

At the front of the house was an open kitchen with new white cabinets and dark granite counters.

"Our housekeeper stocked the kitchen so you should be good with food for a week or so. If you don't mind company, I'll make dinner for us tonight."

"Sounds great," Carly exclaimed. "So you cook?"

"Actually, it's Cam's turn to cook, and he has the steaks seasoned and ready for me to toss on the grill. Hope you like steaks."

"Love them."

"Welcome to the Honeymoon Cottage. Dad built this as a wedding present for my mom. They lived here until the main house was built. I was the only son born while they were living here," explained Brody. "My brothers and I have a project every year, and last year's project was to give the cottage a new kitchen and bathrooms."

"I love it, Brody. Thanks for letting me stay here."

Brody picked up her suitcases and led her up the stairs. "There are two bedrooms up here, as well as the loft. Which one would you like to claim?"

"The loft. I want to sleep in the loft with all the windows so I can watch the stars at night."

He grinned and laid her suitcases on the bed in the loft. Then he pointed to a large adjacent bathroom with a shower and a garden tub.

"Our housekeeper stocked the bathroom, too, so you should have everything you need," said Brody. "I'm going to the main house to give you time for a shower and for me to get cleaned up. I'll be back in about twenty minutes with our dinner."

Alison hung from the ceiling; a hot painful strain on her wrists radiated shards of pain to her shoulders. The man had left her like that for what seemed like an eternity. She sobbed quietly, wishing this were a nightmare from which she'd soon awake. Her regrets were many and started with running away from her problems at school and her stepfather. She should have trusted her mother enough to confide in her.

Thoughts of her mother were painful. By now her mom was

fully aware she'd run away. Was she looking for her? Did her mom contact the police?

Earlier Alison heard shouting from the floor above her. But it was quiet now, and the only sound she heard was the drone of a television and the soft breathing of the young girl in the cage behind her.

Suddenly, the upstairs door flew open, and soon the man appeared on the lower stairs wearing a black ski mask like before. Her blood turned to ice and her heart raced. What would he do to her now?

"Oh, I see you're still hanging around," he said with a bitter laugh. Walking around her, he went to the camera and removed the DVD recording of her beating and stuck it in his pocket.

"A guy's gotta have a little entertainment," he said, as he reached for her wrists, loosened the restraints, and let her drop to the floor like a ragdoll. Alison had no feeling in her arms, her legs were rubbery, and her body ached painfully from the beating. She struggled to stand up, but she fell to the floor in a heap.

"Get up!" he shouted, as he jerked her to her feet and pushed her toward the cage. "I had so many plans for you tonight, my slave," he said with disappointment and a chilling smile. "But they'll have to wait. But then, we have time. Don't we? It's not like you're going anywhere."

Alison crawled to the far end of the cage and curled into a ball. He pulled a couple of quilts from a box and tossed one into her cage, and the other into the cage next to hers. On the last step of the stairway, he picked up two plastic sandwich boxes and bottles of water, one of which he set at the front of her cage, locked her in, and then moved to the next. Finally, he slammed the girl's cage door closed, secured the heavy padlock, and looked around the room as if he feared he was forgetting something. Finally satisfied, he headed back up the stairs, closing the door behind him.

The second he was gone, Alison pulled the duct tape from her mouth, took a deep, cleansing breath, and turned to the girl in the cage next to her. "Are you okay?"

Two or three seconds of silence passed and Alison repeated her question. "Are you okay?"

The girl crawled closer to Alison. She was a pretty African-American girl with dark hair and wide eyes the color of chocolate. She might be Alison's age. Finally, she whispered, "Yes, but please talk very quietly. If they hear us, they will put the duct tape back on our mouths and wrists, and beat us."

"They?"

"Yes, there are two of them, always wearing a ski mask to cover their faces. A man and a woman."

Alison shuddered. There were two of them. Where was the woman, and what role did she play? Was the woman as cruel as the man? She wondered why such evil existed.

"What's your name?"

"Jasmine Norris," the girl quietly replied.

"My name is Alison Brown. How long have you been here, Jasmine?"

"Seven days, counting today," Jasmine said with a sigh, her eyes brimming with tears. "Do you think anyone is looking for us?"

There was such sadness in her eyes that Alison had to look away. Jasmine was losing hope, and hope was all they had. "Yes, I'm sure our families have reported us missing, and the police are searching for us. They will find us, Jasmine. We have to believe that."

"You should know something, Alison."

"What's that?"

"He'll rape you while he films it, just like he did me. I lost my virginity to a monster."

Brody returned to the Honeymoon Cottage and carried plastic containers filled with seasoned steaks, vegetables, and salads to the outside living area he and his brothers had built at the side of the house. What was once a cement slab patio was now an outdoor covered space filled with heavy wood furniture and soft cushions, a stone fireplace, and a wrought-iron dining table and chairs. He set the food down on the kitchen counter, washed his hands in the sink, and then fired up the huge stainless steel grill.

With his hands in his pockets, Brody took a deep breath. This was the first evening in months when he was not at work. The twelve-to sixteen-hour days were wearing on him, but what choice did he have until he caught the monster? He was becoming one of those cops who had no life outside the job. He should have headed to the office instead of home, but he needed to clear his head. Hearing the side door open, he turned to see Carly standing in the doorframe. Her thick, black hair, still damp from her shower, hung in long graceful curves over her shoulders, framing her face like a pool of glossy silk. Wearing a red V-neck sweater with tight jeans tucked into boots, she was beautiful with curves in all the right places. Gone was the buttoned-up, conservatively dressed woman hiding her sexuality who met him at the restaurant the previous night.

Carly smiled at him, and a blast of lust hit him as hard as a freight train. He froze, barely remembering his own name, as the blood rushed from his head to the pounding pulse in his crotch.

"Wow, this outside room is amazing. I wish I had something like this at my house in Florida," she said as she skimmed her hand across a chair cushion before she sat down. "What's for dinner?"

Brody cleared his throat to gain his composure. "Thanks to Cam, we've got steaks and vegetables to grill. Mrs. E., our housekeeper, made a couple of salads and one of her chocolate cheesecakes for dessert."

He threw a couple of steaks on the grill and sat near her. She smelled like fresh lilacs and honey, and the scent had the potential of driving him insane.

"I love this house," Carly declared. "I love it so much you may have to evict me once this job is done."

At that moment, the last thing on Brody's mind was to evict her. He wanted to crush his mouth to hers, and carry her upstairs. He wanted to bury himself inside her as deeply as he could, and not come out until he'd gotten his fill.

Brody's cell phone went off. He clenched his jaw and tore

himself away from thoughts and sensations he shouldn't be having toward consultant Carly Stone.

"Sheriff Chase," he answered.

"Brody, this is Cam. I need to talk to you and Ms. Stone about the case. Can I come over?"

"Yeah, sure. Have you eaten?"

"Not yet."

"Well, bring another steak from the fridge and come to the cottage. We can talk at dinner."

He turned to Carly. "Cam is going to join us. He wants to talk about the case. Hope that's okay." That was just like his middle brother to save the day. He had a much better chance of keeping his mind off Carly's sexy body if his brother joined them with all the questions he tended to ask.

"That's fine. By the way, do you have the file with you? I'd like to look at your crime scene photos and evidence later."

"Not tonight, Carly," he responded. "After dinner, you should rest. Tomorrow promises to be as exhausting as today was."

Cameron arrived a short time later, put his steak on the grill, and joined Carly and Brody.

"I didn't get a chance earlier to welcome you to Shawnee County, Ms. Stone."

"Thank you, and please call me Carly," she replied. "And Cameron, I apologize for the way I called you out in front of everyone at the crime site."

"No problem. You have to understand that we've never had a

case of this magnitude in our county. This is a place where people don't lock their doors at night." He paused for a second, watching Brody at the grill. "But I'm not offering an excuse. I should have waited for the forensic anthropologist to arrive to instruct the searchers before I sent them out."

"Still, I'm sorry. My brother says I'm sometimes too blunt. He just may be right about that."

"Let's just move on, Carly. You can't be thin-skinned and work in the jobs we do," said Cameron. "I hope you don't mind if we talk about the case a little."

"No, not at all."

He turned to his brother. "The media is camped like vultures outside the sheriff's office. The evening news was filled with their anchor's best bets on what's going on. Thanks to their damn helicopter, they know we found remains, as well as shallow graves."

"I figured," said Brody.

"I ran into our favorite Commission President, Bradley Lucas," Cameron said with not a little sarcasm. "He's pissed he wasn't contacted when the shallow graves were discovered."

"God, I hate politics. I'll talk to him tomorrow. He'll probably want me to do a press conference." Brody said as he headed for the grill to turn the steaks over. He added some chopped vegetables to the grill, and placed the salads and dessert in the refrigerator to stay chilled.

"Sounds good. I was able to arrange schedules so the same group of trained deputies can search the woods tomorrow. CSI will be back working the sieves for additional bones or fragments, while Bryan and Dr. Harris identify the bodies," Cameron reported, then added, "I got a search warrant from Judge Nancy Carlson in case Wally Johnson has second thoughts about us digging up his property."

"Good idea. His wife called my cell twice this afternoon asking when we'd be finished."

While Brody went to his car for a Coleman cooler filled with drinks, Cameron and Carly went to the kitchen. Cameron pulled dinner plates out of a cabinet and silverware out of a drawer. Handing the silverware to Carly, they began setting the table as they talked. Carly lit the candle inside a lantern in the center of the table, as Cameron set out glasses.

Cameron asked Carly, "I assigned surveillance for the night in case the killer returns to his dump site. Do you think he will?"

"There's a chance he will. If he's anything like Bundy or Ridgeway, he's probably already visited the bodies several times already. It helps them relive the murder and it excites them," Carly answered. "However, he's smart. If he's heard the graves were discovered through the media, he might not."

"Do you really think this asshole is smart?"

"Definitely. Your killer has average to above-average intelligence. He is persuasive enough to lure his victims here, use and kill them, and bury them," Carly responded, as her mind raced. "He's an organized killer. That's evident in the way he meticulously buries his victims to cover up his crimes. It was pure chance the skull was found. It was probably unearthed by a dog or coyote. The shallow graves were dug deep enough so that the remains wouldn't be found for months or years."

Brody returned with the ice chest and set it down. "Carly, what do you want to drink? I've got sodas, beer, and wine coolers."

"A wine cooler sounds incredible," said Carly, as she accepted an icy bottle from him. She watched as he handed a beer to Cameron. She set her bottle on the table and then went to the refrigerator where she saw Brody place the salads earlier. There was a macaroni and potato salad that looked delicious. She set them on the table.

Brody placed a grilled steak on each of their plates, along with some grilled vegetables. Holding Carly's chair as she sat down, he ignored Cameron's grin and unspoken promise to tease him later about his new consultant.

Famished, they dug in, the men shoveling food into their mouths.

"This is the best steak I've had in forever," exclaimed Carly as she forked another chunk from her plate. "The potato salad is to die for."

Brody smiled. "I'll tell Mrs. E. you liked it."

"I'm not sure I understand what you're going to do, Carly. How are you going to help us?" asked Cameron.

"I'm going to give you an analysis of your killer so you can narrow the suspect pool and prioritize your search. Once you have a suspect, I'll give you strategies for interviewing him."

"I guess it's too much to ask for you to just give us his name,"

Cameron teased.

"Sorry. With serial killers, we usually don't know the unsub's identity until he is captured. But I can certainly help you narrow down your suspects so you're not looking into every sicko in your county," offered Carly. "I want to run something past you two that bothers me."

"What is it?" asked Brody.

"I've already told you that I think your killer is organized. He went to a lot of trouble to hide his victims in those shallow graves. What disturbs me is why would this same killer set a car on fire with two of his victims inside in the middle of a farmer's field? It doesn't compute."

"I think he might have a partner."

"It's terrifying to think you might have two monsters at work here, but I agree."

"What do you need from us to get your analysis started?" Brody wanted to know.

"I'll need photographs of the crime scene, the coroner's report for each body, a map of each victim's activities prior to death, your investigative notes, and backgrounds for each of the victims, as well as photographs. I'll need the same for the victims we unearthed today."

"I can get you most of that tomorrow," offered Cameron.

"Cam, I forgot to ask you about that missing girl from Indy," said Brody. "Fill Carly in on the details."

"A missing person report was filed yesterday in Indianapolis.

Her name is Alison Brown. She's a thirteen-year-old, and she's a runaway who's been missing for a couple of days now. She was last seen at her home in Indianapolis."

Carly frowned and asked, "So you're thinking she's the same age as your victims and may have been targeted by our killer? If so, I agree and would like to talk to her parents with you."

Early the next morning, Brody was behind closed doors with Commission President, Bradley Lucas, for at least sixty minutes, while Carly sifted through the files of victims Amanda Jenkins and Sophia Bradford. One entire wall of the conference room where she worked was a whiteboard, so she taped a photo of both girls on the board and began reviewing every element in each victim's file. She wanted to know each victim as well as she possibly could, and made plans to call their families with questions.

Carly compared the two victims, looking at their physical traits, age, school experiences, home life and relationships, habits, demographics, medical history, sexual history, and last activities before their disappearances. She knew from experience that learning about his victims would reveal a lot about the serial killer's preferences, getting them that much closer to stopping him.

Picking up a marker, Carly used it to write notes, as well as her questions, on the whiteboard. Each victim was thirteen-years-old, and both were having problems at school: a victim of bullying, or distancing herself from friends. Neither had a boyfriend. Did the girls' lack of friends and loneliness make them an online target?

Each had recently experienced a major life experience. For Amanda, it was the sudden death of both her parents, and moving in with her grandmother. Sophia was adjusting to her parents' divorce. Neither of the girls had a strong support system at home or at school. Did the lack of a support system make them more likely to visit sites where they could meet and communicate with online friends? Did this make them more susceptible to kind words and attention from a predator?

Both girls spent a lot of time online, and each was careful to take her laptop and cell phone with her. Were the girls advised by the killer to take these items with them to delay the police investigation?

More questions occurred to Carly. Sophia was able to take her sister's car to meet the killer. Amanda didn't have access to a vehicle, so how did she get to Shawnee County? Public transportation? She made a mental note to ask Brody and Cameron.

"Looks like you're making some progress," said Brody as he leaned against the door frame. Moving closer, he scanned the information on the whiteboard. "So what are your thoughts, consultant?"

"Obviously, these two victims are the only two I can use to make assumptions until the remains of the other bodies are identified," Carly began.

"Bryan says it make take weeks."

Carly nodded and continued, "Judging from your identified victims, our killer is targeting lonely preteens, who are having trouble either at home or at school or both. Both girls became secretive about who they were communicating with online."

"So what does that say about our killer?"

"I believe our killer is an online predator who knows exactly what to say to young girls to gain their trust, and he maintains the online relationship until he gets them to the point where they will agree to meet him in person. He's patient enough to develop the relationships and savvy enough to move them offline as soon as he can."

Brody ran his fingers through his hair, and said, "I can't believe these girls are naive enough to believe a stranger."

"Keep in mind, many teens and preteens spend hours online chatting with friends. These friendships can easily turn into what they think are 'relationships.' The girls get caught up in the predator's web when they start believing their online buddy is their boyfriend."

"I'm willing to bet Amanda and Sophie had never had a boyfriend before."

"Exactly," Carly agreed. "That's what our predator is looking for. The loneliness makes the girls easier to seduce, and to believe his lies."

"Sick bastard. I'd like to rip his head off," Brody angrily remarked, his clenched fists in his pockets.

"I think a lengthy prison sentence will make him suffer more. Jailed sexual predators of young girls are not popular with the other prisoners."

Deputy Gail Sawyer entered the conference room with a

message for Brody. "Sir, your press conference is scheduled for eleven. That gives you sixty minutes to prepare."

"Thanks, Deputy," Brody said, turning to Carly.

"Have I told you that press conferences are not on the list of my favorite tasks?"

"I wouldn't miss it," said Carly.

Deputy Sawyer interrupted, "Oh, you're going to want to miss this one. You've got some guests waiting for you in the lobby."

5 CHAPTER FIVE

Carly entered the lobby and decided that her second day in Shawnee County was going to be a good one. Standing in the middle of the lobby was her brother, Blake. In a baby carrier strapped to his broad chest was her cooing, four-month-old niece, Mylee. Blake Stone was six feet five inches tall and two hundred and thirty pounds of hard muscle, which made the baby girl look even tinier than she was.

Next to him, his wife, Jennifer, held the small hand of her five-year-old son, Shawn, who wore a green hoodie, jeans and a multicolored backpack.

He shyly pressed closer to his mother until Carly bent down and opened her arms to him. In an instant, Shawn flew across the room, into her arms, and said, "Good to see you, Aunt Carly."

Picking Shawn up and planting a big kiss on his cheek, Carly headed for her brother and sister-in-law and said, "This is the best surprise ever."

Blake said, "This is Shawn's spring break, and we wanted to

spend some time with you before you got buried in your case. Is there a good place to have lunch around here?"

"Yes. Let's go to Mollie's Cafe. It's a short walk from here," she responded as Shawn wiggled free to stand on his own. "But before we go, there is one thing I have to do."

"What's that?" asked Jennifer.

"I have to hold my favorite niece."

Grinning, Blake said, "She's your only niece." With Jennifer's help, he pulled Mylee out of the carrier and handed her to his sister. Cooing and waving her arms, the baby smiled up at Carly.

Carly held her close, inhaling her sweet baby scent and kissing the top of her head. "Hi, Mylee. Do you remember your Aunt Carly?" In response, the baby squealed and grabbed at Carly's earring.

"That means she remembers you," said Shawn in a matter-of-fact tone.

At the restaurant, Mollie found the group a round table near the front window. Shawn insisted on sitting on the left side of Carly and Blake placed Mylee in a high chair on her right. Mollie then gave each adult a menu, and took their drink orders. A short time later, a young, pretty girl returned with their drinks.

"Hi, my name is Hailey, and I'll be your server today."

Carly looked at the young girl curiously. Hailey looked to be around fourteen years old, with rich, glowing auburn hair with a rebellious lock of purple near her face. Her eyes were a brilliant blue, and a perpetual smile revealed a line of silver braces. Carly asked,

"Your last name wouldn't be Adams, would it?"

Hailey giggled and answered, "Yes. Mollie is my mom. Who else would make her only daughter work at her cafe during spring break?"

"Hi, Hailey, I'm Carly Stone. Glad to meet you."

"Hi. Your black hair rocks. It's so long and shiny. I wanted to do my hair the exact same color, but my mom wouldn't let me."

"Thanks, Hailey." Carly said. "I don't blame your mom, though. Your hair is a beautiful color. Maybe I should get a purple streak like yours," Carly teased.

Hailey's smile widened in approval. "That would look great. I'll be back after you've had some time to look at your menus."

As Blake and Jennifer studied their menus, Carly glanced at the little boy sitting next to her. In January, when Carly met Shawn for the first time, he was one of the skinniest little kids she'd ever seen. He'd just emerged from a living nightmare when both his abusive parents died. After searching for him everywhere in a blizzard, Blake found him hiding in his friend's attic. The little boy was the Stone family's Christmas miracle and soon became a permanent member of the family.

Shawn had gained weight and filled out, looking the picture of health with rosy cheeks, a sprinkling of freckles across his nose, and the sweetest smile she'd ever seen.

She rubbed the top of his head. "You look like you've grown since last I saw you, Shawn."

"Yes, Aunt Carly. I've grown one inch. Dad measures me once

a month and marks it on the wall next to the fridge."

The baby squealed and pounded her tiny hands on the tray of the high chair. Pulling off his backpack, Shawn set it on the table and unzipped it. He pulled out a small book called Pat the Bunny and a pink rattle and handed them to Carly. "Would you please give these to Mylee? I think she is getting bored."

Grinning, Carly handed the items to Mylee who wrapped her chubby fingers around them and giggled. She turned to Shawn. "It looks like you have the four-one-one on your baby sister."

"That's for sure," said Jennifer with a smile. "Shawn has nominated himself Mylee's interpreter until she can talk for herself. It's uncanny sometimes how he knows exactly what she's trying to communicate."

"He also knows her 'reading' habits," Blake added. "The other day at the library, he had twice the number of books he normally checks out. Turns out half were for Mylee."

"She likes Dr. Seuss, too. Her favorite book is Go Car Go. Mom or Dad reads a book to us every night before bed. Someday I will read out loud, too," exclaimed Shawn.

Carly smiled at Shawn and glanced at Blake. She'd never seen her brother happier and was thrilled for him. The thought occurred to her that maybe she should move closer to them so she could be active in the kids' lives as they grew up.

Hailey returned for their food orders. Blake, Jennifer, and Carly decided on the lunch special of breaded tenderloin sandwiches with tossed salad. Shawn ordered a peanut butter and strawberry jelly sandwich with carrot slices. He announced his little sister would have some baby cereal mixed with formula.

Once Hailey left with their orders, Carly asked, "How is the house hunting going? Last time we talked, you said you were looking for a bigger house."

"We've decided to build on," shared Jennifer, as she picked up the rattle Mylee dropped.

A sparkle was in Blake's eyes when he added, "I've always loved Jennifer's Craftsman style house and it's been in the Brennan family for years ..."

"*Our* house," Jennifer insisted.

"*Our* house," Blake agreed. "We found ourselves comparing every house we saw to it, so we decided to add a family room, bathroom, and another bedroom."

"That sounds great," Carly said. "I love your house, too. And the location is perfect. It's close to the elementary school and your parents' home. Speaking of your parents, how are Megan and Tim?"

Jennifer gave Mylee a spoonful of cereal and said, "Dad's still doing the sheriff thing. Mom is fixing up rooms for Shawn and Mylee when they visit. They said to tell you hello."

"What about you, Carly," asked Blake. "Are you still dead-set on leaving the Bureau?"

"Yes. I don't miss the bureaucracy, and I like being my own boss. The consultant jobs are coming in on a regular basis, so money's not an issue. I enjoy being able to help the smaller sheriff operations."

"Tim told me that Sheriff Chase really needs your help. Selfishly, I'm glad you took the job so we can see more of you, at least while you're here."

"How long are you staying?" asked Jennifer, as she mixed more cereal with formula in a small bowl for Mylee.

"It could be a month or six months. It depends on how the case progresses. I'm staying in a cottage on the Sheriff's property. I'd love it if you and the kids could spend the weekend sometime while I am here."

Jennifer's eyes danced as she smiled at Blake, then Carly. "That sounds like a fun getaway!"

"What about you, Jennifer? Do you plan to go back to work?" Carly wanted to know.

"Actually, I am working part-time now at home. I'm doing computer work for my cousin, Frankie Hansen's private investigation business. She's gotten a flood of work from several insurance companies and needs the help."

"That is so great you can work at home with the kids," said Carly. "By the way, I have some news."

"Oh, no," said Blake. "Every time you say that, the so-called news concerns Mom and Dad. What now?"

"You're not going to believe this, but Mom and Dad are dating."

"No way!"

"Way. I think they both got lonely over the holidays. They've been dating since January."

A group of reporters and cameramen from the local media

outlets talked loudly in the reception area, interrupting their conversation.

"The press conference must be over," Carly surmised. She wondered how Brody fared with their questions, and if he had been able to calm the county residents.

Hearing him before seeing him, Alison crouched in the far end of her crate, pulling the quilt around herself to hide her nakedness. He was coming for her, just as Jasmine said he would, and the thought tore at her insides. Panic like she'd never known welled in her throat.

In the next cage, she heard Jasmine crying softly. The man, again wearing the black ski mask, appeared next to Alison's crate, staring at her as he rubbed his obvious erection. She felt impaled by his steady gaze.

Disappearing behind the sheets in the corner of the room, he turned on a bright light that revealed his shadow as he moved the tripod, on which he fastened a camera that he spent a few minutes adjusting to his satisfaction.

Bile rushed to Alison's throat, and she swallowed hard. She may have been a virgin, but she knew what he was going to do to her. Even if Jasmine had not told her the night before, she knew.

Why was he filming her rape? So he could watch it later? Humiliation washed over her in a nauseating wave.

There had to be a way to escape. There had to be a way to end this nightmare, and go home. Her mother must have reported her missing. Where were the police?

The man unlocked the padlock and reached for her. No longer restrained by duct tape, Alison huddled in a corner, kicking and scratching at him, fighting him as he dragged her out of the crate by her ankles.

"You bitch!" He roared as her nails slashed across his jaw. "You'll pay for that."

He slapped Alison across the face so hard she fell back and thought her jaw was broken, the metal braces on her teeth ripping through her lips. Blood gushed down her chin and neck. She hurt so much she could scarcely breathe, but she wouldn't let the pain prevent her from fighting back. Alison lunged at him, sinking her teeth into his leg, and he howled in agony. Clamping down hard, tasting blood and flesh, she refused to let go as he pummeled her with his fists until she loosened her hold. Freeing himself, he kicked her savagely in the side and dragged her behind the sheets. Pulling out handcuffs from his back jeans pocket, he secured her wrists then her ankles to heavy metal eyelets that had been drilled into the floor. Wet blood streamed from her mouth, soaking her hair, choking her when she tried to scream.

He loomed over Alison, tall, dark, and deadly as she struggled against the restraints. Her heart froze as she watched him unzip his pants, and then lowered himself over her. She screamed and kept screaming until darkness filled her eyes and she lost consciousness.

By two o'clock, Carly had said her good-byes to her family and was in the passenger seat of Brody's SUV, headed toward

Indianapolis to interview the family of the missing girl, Alison
Brown.

Brody had taken off his suit jacket and hung it in the back. With
the sleeves of his white shirt rolled up and his tie undone, he drove in
silence, seemingly lost in his thoughts.

"You're awfully quiet, Sheriff," she remarked. "Are you going to
tell me what happened or not?"

Brody glanced at her briefly before turning his attention back on
the road. "It went exactly as I expected, reporters firing questions at
me, hungry for some shocking, gory detail to boost their ratings. I
told them as little as possible and hope that holds them off for a
while."

"Were you able to say anything to calm down your residents?"

"I just told them how hard we're working to catch this killer.
There's not much I can say to dispel their fears when it's pretty
obvious a monster lives and kills amongst them," Brody said, before
changing the subject. "Can you see the briefcase in the backseat?"

"Yes."

"There is a file inside it I want you to see."

Carly unzipped the leather briefcase, and withdrew a manila
folder. "Found it."

"Neal Denison, the Indianapolis detective assigned to the Alison
Brown case, faxed some information he's discovered. I think you'll
find it interesting."

Carly opened the file and reviewed the missing person report on
top. Like the two murdered girls, Amanda and Sophia, Alison was

thirteen-years-old. She pulled out Alison's photo. "Poor girl. She's overweight with glasses and braces on her teeth—which could add up to a miserable school experience. Kids can be so unkind to each other." She reviewed Detective Denison's notes from his interview with Alison's parents, Raymond and Margaret. He hadn't gotten much useful information, and Carly silently vowed to get more. When she got to the last piece of paper, her jaw dropped, and she held it up for Brody.

"Did you see this? The stepfather has a record."

"Yes. Denison didn't discover it until yesterday, after he'd already interviewed the parents. He wants us to bring up Brown's record when we interview the parents. He'll be outside the house waiting in an unmarked car. He has a search warrant."

Carly spotted the unmarked police car as soon as they pulled up in front of the house. Denison was parked less than a block down, in an older model, black Mustang.

Alison Brown's home was a two-level, red brick structure, not unlike the rest of the homes that lined the street in her middle-class neighborhood. The lawn was small and plain with an unkempt hedge that lined the front of the house.

Alison's mother answered the door, and invited them inside. Margaret was a petite woman with dark smudges of exhaustion under her eyes. After Brody did introductions, she expelled a long, tired breath as she led them to the living room where her husband, Raymond, was pouring dark coffee into mugs. Raymond was a thin, wiry man who stiffened when they entered the room. He introduced himself, and indicated for Carly and Brody to sit on the suede brown sofa, while he and Margaret sat in chairs on either side.

Margaret, chewing worriedly on her lower lip, said, "I don't want to seem rude, but I don't understand why investigators from Shawnee County would want to talk to us. Has someone reported seeing our Alison in your county?"

Brody answered, "No, Mrs. Brown. There have been no sightings of Alison." He paused, and then added. "If there is a chance Alison is in Shawnee County, we want to be able to help find her."

Carly glanced at Brody, remembering their decision not to tell the Browns about their Internet predator and the discovery of the bodies. Knowing their child was missing was enough trauma for the parents.

"Thank you for your help," Margaret said, her eyes filling with tears. "I can't believe she's gone." She covered her face with her hands and bent over in her chair, crying so hard her shoulders shook with anguish.

Carly patted Margaret's hand to comfort her. "We know how hard all this must be for you. If you and your husband would please answer some questions, what we learn might help us find your daughter."

Pulling a tissue from her pocket, Margaret dabbed at her eyes. "Ask anything you want."

Brody went first, "Have you noticed any changes in Alison's

behavior lately?"

"Yes, the school called me in and told me Alison has been skipping school. I work nights, and it seems Alison was pretending to leave for school. Later when she thought I was asleep, she'd return to the house and hide in her room."

"Had Alison ever skipped school before?"

"Never. She has always been an excellent student and loved going to school. But she changed. For the past few months, she's been quiet, even secretive. Alison spends a lot of time on her laptop in her bedroom behind closed doors."

Brody then turned to Raymond, "What about you? Have you seen any changes in Alison's behavior?

"No. Nothing," he responded, avoiding Brody's eyes.

"There's something else," Margaret offered. "Alison has been especially clumsy lately. She's had a lot of scratches, bruising, scrapes on her knees, even a black eye within the past few weeks. I'm a nurse. I notice these things. When I asked her about them, she said she'd fallen at school or on the way home."

"Interesting." Brody jotted some notes in his small pad. "Ms. Stone, what are some of your questions?"

Directing her response to Margaret, Carly said, "Would it be possible for me to see Alison's room?"

Alison's mother nodded, and led Carly and Brody up the stairs to her daughter's bedroom with Raymond close behind. Once inside the room, Brody stood near the doorway and watched.

Carly looked around the room, taking in everything, questions

swirling in her mind. The first thing she noticed was that the room
looked too tidy for a preteen girl. The white walls were devoid of any
teen rock star posters or bulletin boards with photos of friends. The
white bedspread with large purple flowers covered Alison's bed. A
matching rug lay perfectly aligned with the bed on the hardwood
floor. Crisp white and purple print curtains hung over the windows.
A few textbooks, notepads and a pencil holder lay on a white writing
desk. A surge protector lay on the floor, but there were no
computers, eReaders, or other devices in the room.

"Have you cleaned this room since your first visit with the
police?"

"No, why do you ask?"

Shrugging her shoulders, Carly didn't answer and asked, "Does
Alison have a computer, ereader or cell phone?"

"Yes, she has a laptop, an eReader, and an iPhone. We noticed
they were missing."

"What else did Alison take with her?"

Margaret opened a closet that was as tidy as the rest of the room,
with shoes lined up on the floor, and a few shirts, pants, and dresses
hanging above them.

"Alison has a small blue rolling suitcase that we can't find. I
think she stuffed it with jeans, shirts, and underwear, along with her
laptop. She was never without her iPhone in her purse."

Carly moved to a four-drawer white dresser and began opening
drawers. Most were nearly empty. When she reached the last
drawer, her eyes riveted on the hardwood floor. Bending down to

her knees, she ran her index finger over the deep scratches in the wood, she said, "This dresser has been moved several times. See these tracks?" Carly pointed out the scratches leading from the dresser to the bedroom door. She glanced inquiringly at Margaret, who was bending down beside her.

"I've never moved it," said Margaret.

"What about you?" Carly asked Raymond, who paled slightly as he shook his head.

Carly stood, helped Margaret to her feet, and then brushed her hands against her pants. "Here's what I think. Alison moved the dresser. The deep scratches indicate she moved it several times. The scratches lead to the door, which tells me she was trying to keep someone out of her bedroom."

Walking over to the door, Carly said, "This door knob has been tampered with from the outside of the door." She directed the remark to Alison's stepfather, who wiped at a bead of sweat on his brow and nervously glanced at his wife. "Raymond, do you know why Alison might have been moving the dresser against this door?"

"No, of course not," he said defensively, nervously glancing at the doorway that Brody now blocked.

Carly looked at Margaret hard, and asked, "Did Raymond tell you he served eight years in prison?"

"What?" she demanded, as she shot a searching look to her husband. "What's she talking about, Raymond?"

"Tell her about it, Raymond." Brody dared. "Tell your wife how you served time for sexual misconduct with a twelve-year-old child."

With clenched fists, Margaret moved closer to him, searching his face. "You bastard, tell me you didn't hurt my Alison. If you did anything to my little girl, I'll kill you. Do you hear me?" she screamed.

Bolting from the room, Raymond slammed into Brody, knocking him to the floor, and raced down the stairs and out the front door. Carly hurtled over Brody's body, and gave full chase. Brody was close behind. By the time they reached the front yard, Denison had Raymond pinned to the ground and was handcuffing him. Margaret pushed past Carly, and threw herself on top of her husband, sobbing and pounding him with her fists.

"Where's Alison? You bastard. What have you done to Alison?"

Brody pulled a hysterical Margaret off her husband, so Denison could pull Raymond to his feet, and hand him over to an Indianapolis deputy, who'd arrived with his patrol car, lights flashing. Once Raymond was secured in the back seat, the deputy whisked him away.

Sobbing, Margaret broke away from Brody and went into the house. Denison introduced himself and said, "Obviously, Mr. Brown didn't like his record thrown in his face."

"Nope, he didn't like it much," Brody agreed. "Did you get your search warrant?"

"Sure did. Want to join me as I search the house?"

Carly nodded quickly and asked, "Did you put computer equipment on the warrant? I'd like to see his online activities."

"Sure did. Let's see what we can find," Denison responded as he headed for the house. "Later, we'll head down to the station. You may ask Mr. Brown anything you like. I know I have some questions for the pervert."

"Detective, one more thing. Did you talk to neighbors on this street?"

"Yeah, all except house number 600. No one was home that day."

Carly looked at Brody. "If it's okay with you, I'd like to talk to some of the neighbors about Alison."

"Go for it. I'll catch up with you as soon as we finish searching the house."

Carly talked to the Brown's neighbors, showing each one Alison's photo. No one had much to say about the young girl. A few neighbors didn't even know who Alison was and were surprised to learn the missing girl lived just a few houses away from them.

Walking to the next house, Carly felt her heart squeeze as she thought of Alison. She was certain Alison was being molested by her stepfather. Based on Margaret's reaction, she was also sure Alison hadn't confided in her mother. Add to that typical teenage angst over her weight, braces, and who knows what else, Alison must have been miserable. The girl was an Internet predator's favorite target—vulnerable and lonely with problems at home, ripe for the flattery and manipulation of a stranger.

Carly reached the small white house at 600 Oak Street. At the end of the street, it sat next to a weed-infested lot littered with trash. Carly knocked on the door several times, and had turned to leave when she heard a voice call her back.

Standing on the porch, was a frail man who looked to be at least one-hundred-years-old.

"Sorry, I can't get to the door as fast as I used to. I'm here now. What do you want?"

Carly inched closer and said, "I'm Carly Stone. I'm working with the Shawnee County Sheriff Department. I'm hoping you'll answer a couple of questions I have."

"Don't mind answering questions, but I do mind standing up to do it. Come up here on the porch, and we'll sit a spell." He sat down on an old aluminum glider and motioned for Carly to sit down on a nearby wooden chair. "My name's Edward Webb. What is it you'd like to ask me?"

Carly pulled Alison's photo out of the file folder she was carrying, and showed it to the old man. "Do you know this girl or have you ever seen her?"

Pulling the photo out of her hand, he held it up, studied it and handed it back to Carly.

"Yes, I've seen her, and it wasn't that long ago. I stood right here on my porch and watched a group of girls beat the crap out of her."

"When was this, Mr. Webb?"

"Last week, I think. Not sure about when I saw her, but I know what I saw. Those girls dragged her through the weeds and broken beer bottles until they reached the dead center of the lot. Then they started kicking and pounding on her with their fists. Poor little thing was screaming her lungs out.

"The girls stopped and ran when they heard me screaming at them. But the girl in your photo wouldn't let me help her. She was beaten up pretty bad and bleeding. I wanted to call the police, but she begged me not to. She ran down the street. I've been wondering about her and whether or not she's okay. Is she?"

"Not exactly," Carly said.

"Hell, if her parents want me to testify against those girls, I'll do it," he promised.

"It's not that, Mr. Webb. She's missing, and we're trying to find her. Thank you for your help."

Carly pulled out her cell phone and called Brody, filling him in on the beating Alison suffered at the hands of a group of girls. He promised to give the information to Denison, who would follow up at the school later.

Through closed circuit television at the police station, Brody and Carly watched Denison question Raymond Brown. Sweating profusely, Brown wiped at his forehead with his shirt sleeve. Each time Denison asked him about Alison, Brown lowered his eyes to the floor and refused to answer. Frustrated, Denison prepared to leave the room.

"Could I have a bottle of water or something?" asked Brown.

Over his shoulder, before leaving the room, Denison said, "I'll see what I can do." Slamming the door behind him, he met with Brody and Carly.

"This asshole is not talking," he remarked with disappointment. "We can't hold him on sexual misconduct until we can find Alison to testify."

"What did you find when you searched the house?" Carly wanted to know, still watching Brown who was now pacing.

"Found some porn magazines hidden in his dresser drawer in the bedroom, and a box of them along with DVDs in the attic. None of it was child porn. The women in the magazines and DVDs were all in their twenties and thirties."

Denison got a can of Coke out of small refrigerator and continued, "Our computer tech says Brown's a frequent customer at a couple of porn sites. They also said he visits several social media sites and a couple of chat rooms for consenting adults on a regular basis."

"Was there any online contact with preteen girls?" asked Carly.

"Nope," said Denison after a gulp of Coke. "Brown's been exchanging racy pictures with a twenty-year-old from Ohio for about six months. He's using a photo of a twenty-something blonde body builder instead of his own. There's a lot of sex-talk, but no mention of getting together in person. We're contacting her today for an interview."

"Brown may not be our killer," Brody remarked to Carly.

"But don't forget he was sent to prison for molesting a child twelve-years-old and Alison is thirteen."

"Right. But wouldn't perverts who prefer preteen girls, also prefer porn that features young girls?"

"Yes, but I still want to talk to him," Carly insisted.

Brody nodded in agreement. "You question him first. I can tell by the way he looks at you that he doesn't like assertive women. You might be able to get him emotional and talking."

As soon as Carly entered the interview room, Raymond Brown rolled his eyes in disgust. "Haven't you asked enough questions at the house?"

Carly shot him a sharp look, sat down and placed a couple of manila folders on the table. "By the way, Raymond, your wife called and told me to tell you a locksmith is changing the locks. You'll find your things on the front lawn."

"This is all your fault," he said through gritted teeth.

"How is it my fault, Raymond? I didn't serve time for molesting a little girl, and then didn't bother to share it with my wife."

"Shut up!" A vein near his right eye bulged as his face grew red.

"Not going to happen. I've got some questions for you," Carly said.

"Denison already asked me questions."

"Inquiring minds want to know, Raymond. I have a very inquiring mind," Carly said sarcastically. "Where is Alison?"

He looked down and said, "I don't know."

"C'mon, you can do better than that."

"I said I don't know."

"Want to know something interesting I learned a long time ago, Raymond?"

He glared at her for a second and said, "Not really."

"I learned that when people are lying, they don't make eye contact. I couldn't help but notice when I asked you about Alison, you looked down. So let's try it again. Where is Alison?"

His dark eyes bore into her. "I *don't* know."

"Sure you do. What happened with Alison, Raymond? Did she threaten to tell her mother you were raping her?"

"What?!" He jumped to his feet.

"Sit down." Carly ordered.

He sat and said, "I never raped her. I swear I never did that. I love Alison."

"Oh, you love Alison? Is that why you were molesting her?"

"It wasn't like that. I loved her. I wanted to be her first, so she'd know what love felt like." A tear threatened to spill from Raymond's left eye.

"So you raped her?"

"No, I did *not*," he insisted. "It didn't get that far. Only touching. I just wanted to hold her and touch her."

"What makes me think Alison didn't like you touching her? Oh, I remember. She was blocking her bedroom door with her dresser."

"I never hurt her. I swear. I wish I knew where she was."

"I think you know exactly where she is, Raymond. Where are you hiding her?" Carly asked, leaning toward him.

He scrubbed his hands over his face. "If I knew where she was, I'd tell you."

Picking up a folder, she opened it and slid a photo of Amanda

Jenkins across the table. "Does this girl look familiar?"

Pulling the photo closer with his index finger, Raymond said, "No. Never seen her before."

Ripping Sophia Bradford's photo out of the file, Carly slapped it on the table, "How about this girl?"

Examining the photo, no sign of recognition appeared in his expression. He shrugged his shoulders and said, "No, why are you showing me these?"

Carly pulled out another photograph, and pushed it toward him. "This was taken after the two girls' bodies were pulled out of a burning car."

"Oh, God," Raymond uttered. He looked as if he might get sick.

"Their names are Amanda Jenkins and Sophia Bradford. They're both thirteen and you met them on the Internet. You played mind games with them and convinced them to meet you in Morel where you raped and murdered them."

"No way! I've never killed anyone," he insisted, as he pounded his fist. "I don't even know where Morel is." Unexpectedly, he leaned across the table, and grabbed Carly's arm. "You're not going to pin these murders on me, bitch!"

The interview room door flew open, and Brody pinned Raymond in his chair. "You're in enough trouble, Brown. Do you really want to add a charge for assaulting an officer?"

Carly retrieved the photos, slipped them back into the file and headed for the door. "I'm finished here, Sheriff."

Once they were back in the conference room, Carly confided, "I don't think he's our guy. He'd never seen Amanda or Sophia until I showed him their photos. I don't think he has Alison."

"I agree, plus, there's nothing to connect Alison to our killer yet," Brody said. Touching her arm, he said, "Are you okay? Let me see your arm."

Carly rolled up her shirt sleeve and said, "See, it's nothing."

Brody lightly rubbed his thumb across her arm. His touch was oddly soft and caressing. Standing so close she could feel the heat from his body, she inhaled his clean, spicy scent. He projected an energy and power that undeniably attracted her.

Denison cleared his throat. Carly hadn't noticed he was even in the room. Embarrassed, she stepped away from Brody.

"I thought you might want to know," Denison began. "We talked to his wife and Brown's alibi checks out. He hasn't left the house since the day Alison disappeared."

6 CHAPTER SIX

Alison regained consciousness and discovered her wrists and ankles still handcuffed to the floor, but, thankfully, her assailant was nowhere in sight. In so much pain she could barely breathe, her mouth and jaw throbbed, and the welts on her back were on fire. Every time she tried to move, sharp slivers of pain cut through her body.

The humiliation of the rape washed over her in a nauseating wave. What had she done to deserve such a savage attack? How could she have been so stupid to run away from home? She'd give anything to be held in her mother's arms. Anything. Tears streamed down her face, burning the back of her throat.

Alison thought she heard Jasmine whisper her name.

"Jasmine?"

"Oh, thank God," she cried. "I was so afraid he'd killed you."

"Everything hurts so badly, I wish he had," Alison said.

"Please don't say that," Jasmine pleaded.

"Talk to me, Jasmine," begged Alison. "Distract me from this pain."

"What do you want me to talk about?"

"Tell me about yourself and how you got here."

"Before I ran away," she began. "I lived in West Lafayette. My daddy is a preacher of the First Baptist Church there. Daddy is a huge man and has a voice like thunder on Sundays. He can be heard for blocks around the church preaching his sermon. My mom is the choir director, and I sing soprano in the choir. At least, I used to."

Hearing the sadness in her voice, Alison said, "Jasmine, if this is too hard to talk about..."

"No, I can do it. I want to talk," she insisted. "I started making online friends last year when I was twelve. At school, I was known as a computer geek. I didn't have very many friends, until kids started contacting me on my Facebook page and Teen Chat. It was great having so many online friends, and I couldn't wait to get home after school to talk to them."

"Your home doesn't sound so bad. Why did you run away?"

"I fell in love with a boy online. I've never had a boyfriend before, and he was the best looking boy I'd ever seen. If he had gone to my school, he would have been the most popular boy there. He said he liked everything about me, even the geek part," Jasmine said. She paused for a second. "We wanted to meet each other in person really bad. He only lived forty-five minutes away from me. We figured we could meet on a Saturday morning, and I'd be back by evening. My parents would never know. So he mailed me a bus ticket, and I told my parents I was staying at my girlfriend's house. But when I arrived in Morel ..."

Just then there were loud voices coming from the floor above them. "Did you hear that?" asked Alison.

"Yes, the Master and woman are fighting again. I hope he doesn't come down here. He's extra mean when he's mad."

The upstairs door opened and then slammed shut with a bang. Heavy footfalls on the basement steps announced they would soon have a visitor.

Alison froze, lying perfectly still as sick fear coiled in the pit of her stomach. Suddenly, he ripped open a section of the sheeting, and appeared menacingly above her, his eyes dark and piercing through the holes of the ski mask.

"No, don't hurt me again," Alison begged, pulling at her restraints.

"Silence, slave," he seethed, as he bent down to her. "When are you going to learn to call me Master?"

In his hand was a brown leather dog collar that he fastened around her neck. He attached a long leash to it, and removed the handcuffs from her wrists and ankles. Roughly pulling her to her feet, he steadied her, and pulled her by the leash toward a small bathroom. "Clean yourself up, slave. You're filthy."

Stepping inside, he turned on the shower, shoved Alison under the hot water and closed the door. The water pelted against her welts and stung. There was caked blood on her stomach and between her legs. As blood-tinged water slipped down the drain, she used shampoo to wash her hair, and then scrubbed her entire body with soap again and again. She wished she could wash what he'd done to her off her body and out of her brain.

After she dried herself off, Alison looked around the room for something she could use to defend herself. But the bathroom was empty save for the dingy bath towel she was using. She spied a frosted rectangle window that was nailed shut. If she stood on the toilet, she could reach the window. It was small, and she wondered if she could squeeze her body through it if she could somehow break the glass. Before she had a chance to try, she heard Jasmine screaming in terror.

Quietly opening the bathroom door a few inches, she could see Jasmine, naked, hanging from the ceiling by her wrists, her legs thrashing the air as Alison's had her first night. Standing behind her, was the Master, holding a leather whip. 'Crack!' The whip cut across Jasmine's back, and she cried out in agony. 'Crack!'

"That's it," he said, with a sick smile. "Suffer, bitch, suffer."

Brody organized a task force dedicated to finding their serial killer. Dr. Bryan Pittman, and Cameron and Gabe Chase would serve on the team, along with Carly. Brody finally hired Gabe as a computer forensic consultant. He was initially charged to report back with the Internet habits of Amanda Jenkins and Sophia Bradford.

Carly sat at the end of a long conference table, finishing the analysis that she'd present to the team that afternoon. She checked and rechecked the evidence, as well as her stack of notes. Her analysis would be critical in order for investigators to narrow down the number of suspects and catch their killer.

Deputy Gail Sawyer appeared in the doorway. "Carly, there's

127

someone here to see you."

Thinking her visitor was her brother, Blake, Carly was delighted. "Thanks, Gail. What a nice surprise."

"I'll bring him back," offered the deputy.

Soon the deputy reappeared with a tall man with short-cropped, blonde hair wearing a navy designer suit, looking like he just stepped out of *GQ* magazine.

Carly approached him, coldly shaking his hand as if they'd never met. "Hello, Agent Isley."

To Gail, Carly said, "Please close the door after you, Deputy. Thank you."

Once Gail left the room, Carly glared at him with burning, reproachful eyes. "What are you doing here, Sam? How did you find me?"

"Which question do you want me to answer first?"

"Let's start with how in the hell did you find me?"

"I'm a federal agent. That's what I do," he said with confidence bordering on cockiness. Humility was never his problem, and his arrogance irked her.

"Whatever. My parents told you, didn't they?" she asked as she shot him a hostile glare.

"Are you questioning my investigative abilities, Carly?" he teased.

"Actually, every time I think of you, I question my *own* abilities in choosing men. Getting involved with my supervisor at the Bureau was one of the dumbest things I've ever done. Getting involved with you was pure idiocy."

"Don't say that, Carly. We meant a lot to each other, and you know it."

Gritting her teeth together tightly, she tried to keep her emotions under control. "Why are you here, Sam? Hopefully, it's not to talk about a past I want to forget."

"I need you back at the Bureau, Carly," he said.

"Go to hell. I gave you my resignation months ago."

"I didn't accept it. I put you on administrative leave. I'm saving your position for you."

His tone infuriated her. "I'm not coming back."

"We have three missing children in Tampa. We suspect a child predator..."

Carly interrupted, "I don't want to hear about your case. I'm not coming back to the agency and I'm certainly never reporting to you again."

"If you won't consider returning to Florida for the job, then come back for me. I miss you, Carly. I need you." He put his hand on her arm but quickly removed it when she jerked away from him.

"You need me? That's a joke." She laughed contemptuously. "Let's do an instant replay of what happened last year."

"Carly..."

"Don't interrupt," she warned. "I finish my profile for Tim Brennan's team earlier than expected, so I fly back to surprise my lover. Once my plane lands, I buy a bottle of champagne, and head to your office. It's after hours, but I know what a hard worker you are and how many late nights you spend at work. Imagine my surprise when I enter your office and find you screwing the new trainee on top of your desk."

"It meant nothing," he insisted.

"It meant everything."

Returning from an early meeting with Bradley Lucas, Brody balanced two lattes in one hand and a box of donuts in the other. "Morning, Deputy Sawyer."

"Good morning, sir," Gail said, glancing up from her computer.

"Is Carly in the conference room?" he asked.

"Yes, sir, but she's not alone."

"Is she meeting with Cam about the case?"

"No, sir. She's in there talking with an FBI agent."

"Oh?" he said curiously.

He headed to the conference room, stopping outside the door. What he heard was a heated conversation inside, and he debated whether or not he should interrupt. Taking the lattes and box of donuts to his office, he returned, knocked on the door, and then entered.

"Good morning," Brody said as he assessed the situation. Red-faced, her hands fisted at her side, Carly stood at the end of the conference room. Standing too close to her was a man who looked annoyed at his presence. Seeing the man in the room with Carly sent a jolt of unexpected jealousy through him as surely as if he'd stuck his finger in an electrical outlet. Where did that come from?

Brody strode to the end of the room, his hand outstretched. "I don't believe we've met. I'm Sheriff Brody Chase. Welcome to Shawnee County."

Shaking his hand, the man said, "I'm Sam Isley."

"My deputy tells me you're with the FBI."

"That's right. I'm with the Criminal Investigation Division in our Tampa office," he responded.

Brody glanced at Carly, noting the tension tightening the delicate features of her face. "I didn't mean to interrupt."

"You didn't interrupt," Carly began. "We've finished our conversation. Agent Isley was just leaving."

"She's right. I have another appointment," said Isley as he moved toward the door. He aimed his final remark to Carly. "Think about what I said." He left closing the door behind him.

"Are you okay?" asked Brody. His brows drew together in a concerned expression.

"I'm fine," she responded. Her voice was low and trembling with anger and something else undefined. Her tough exterior was crumbling. She wasn't fine.

"Do you want to talk about it?"

"No," she said, swallowing hard.

"Not sure I've told you, but I come from a family of great huggers. Would you like a hug?"

"Yes," she said as she fell into his arms, wrapping her arms around his middle.

The hug, meant as a friendly gesture, wasn't the best idea he'd ever had. It wasn't that he didn't want to hold Carly; it was that

Brody wanted it too much. He'd wanted her since the night he saw her swimming in her pool. His face heated in a blush, as if he were fourteen. She smelled like soap, shampoo and woman, and he couldn't remember the last time a woman felt this good in his arms. He was aware of her in every pore of his body — her nearness, the scent of her, the heat of her skin. And if he didn't let her go soon, she'd be very aware of the hard evidence of his arousal.

Brody pulled away and said, "I almost forgot. I brought you a latte and donuts. I'll go get them."

Minutes later, when he returned to the conference room, the first thing he noticed was that Carly had taken off her khaki suit jacket. The snug black tank she wore clung to her figure enticingly. She was amazingly stacked with curves in all the right places. The sight stopped him dead in his tracks as a new blast of arousal hit him like a Mack truck. His dick rock-hard and standing at attention, he shifted the box of donuts to cover himself, placed it along with her latte on the table, and rushed out of the room.

What the hell was wrong with him? Carly Stone was a consultant, nothing more. She was his employee, and the very last woman he should get involved with. Not only would they be a subject of small-town gossip, she was leaving when her job ended.

This is what happens to a man when he takes a moratorium from relationships and one night stands, he thought. How long had it been since he'd been with a woman? Six months? Who was he kidding? It had been at least a year, and one look at Carly Stone had his sexual need hammering at his common sense. What he needed was a cold shower; what he got was a cold drink at the vending machine, and before heading back to his office to distract himself by tackling the stack of work on his desk.

At noon, the serial killer task force was finishing up their lunch in the conference room when Gabriel Chase arrived. Carly couldn't believe how much Brody's younger brother did and didn't resemble him. Gabriel had the same dark hair and eyes, but he looked to be an inch or two shorter than Brody. His jet-black hair curled over his ears and the collar of his shirt. Unlike his serious and equally handsome older brother, Gabe had touches of humor around his mouth and near his eyes. Wearing a crisp white shirt, blue tie, brown leather jacket and jeans, he stood there, devilishly handsome. Carly could see why he was the woman-magnet his brother said he was.

"You must be Gabe," Carly said as she approached him.

"And you must be Carl, the consultant," Gabe returned with a wide smile. "Yeah, I heard about the typo. I would have loved to have seen Brody's face when he discovered you were a Carly and not a Carl."

"You'll have to ask Brody about that," Carly replied. "Good to meet you, Gabe."

Brody joined them. "I see you've met Carly," Brody said as he pulled Gabe into a bear hug. "I haven't seen much of you lately."

"I've got an insurance case, and I've been spending a lot of time doing surveillance in Evansville."

"That explains it," said Brody. "Remember I need to deputize you after the meeting. I don't want to take any chances that a defense attorney could get any computer evidence you find thrown out of court."

"No problem."

"Another thing. Do everything by the book on this one, Gabe. No going outside the box. This case is too important to put the evidence at risk."

"Understood," Gabe said with a nod, adding, "Trust me on this, Brody."

"I am, Gabe," Brody replied. "I've got a boxed lunch on the table for you. We'll get started soon."

Gabe settled down next to Cameron, while Carly sat between Bryan and Brody. She began reviewing her notes. She was an admitted perfectionist when it came to her profiles. It was her contribution to the investigation and she wanted it to make a big difference. More than anything, Carly wanted her profile to be the tool to help Brody and his team stop the killer before more victims were slain.

Brody started the meeting. "First of all, I want to thank each of you for agreeing to join this serial killer task force. You each bring a unique expertise to the table that will help us put the puzzle together and find this bastard. This afternoon, each of you will share what you've learned. Bryan, why don't you start?"

Approaching the end of the conference table, Bryan turned on a laptop connected to an LCD projector. "We've been able to identify the skeletal remains of four of the victims we found in shallow graves through the Missing Persons DNA Database. Unfortunately, the remains of the two victims we found two years ago are still not identified."

Bryan paused, and turned on the projector. The photo of the skeletal remains appeared on the screen. "Each victim was shot execution-style, at point blank range at the back of skull. No bullets were found, but judging from the size of the hole in the skulls, Dr. Harris and I both believe the bullet was a nine millimeter."

Cam interrupted, "It was, Bryan. I have the ATF report, and the bullet from Amanda and Sophia's crime scene is a nine millimeter and could have been shot from a Beretta 92, Sig Sauer Pro, or Glock. This isn't exactly exciting news, since half the damn county, including the county sheriff's team, carry Sig Sauers or Glocks."

Bryan pointed to a photo on the screen. "The young girl you see on the screen is our first victim, Sydney Jackson, who was thirteen-years-old at the time of her death. Sydney lived with her parents in Knightstown in Henry County. She's been missing for two years."

Bryan pushed a button on his laptop and another photo appeared on the screen. "Our next victim is identified as Alyssa Benjamin, fourteen-years-old and last seen at her home in Lebanon in Boone County. She ran away four years ago."

Carly shifted in her seat. It was unsettling to know these beautiful little girls were dead, their lives taken by a monster. She felt such empathy for the parents and loved ones left behind.

Another photo came into view. A preteen with sparkling blue eyes and a shock of red hair appeared on the screen. "This is Kayla

Stuart from Attica in Fountain County. Kayla was thirteen years old when she disappeared three years ago."

Bryan flicked a button on his laptop to reveal another photo on the screen. "The last victim identified is Samantha Grey, age fifteen. She was last seen in Columbia City in Whitley County where she lived. Samantha was reported missing three-and-a-half years ago."

"So counting Amanda Jenkins and Sophia Bradford, we have six identified victims, all murdered in the same manner, and dumped in Shawnee County," said Brody, as he ran his hand through his hair. "Six victims. Damn it to hell."

As he jotted down notes in his tablet, Cameron said, "I'll follow up right away with the detectives in each of these counties assigned to the cases. I'll need any evidence and investigative notes they may have taken when they did their interviews. If I have questions, I'll follow up with each of the parents."

Carly leaned forward. "Cameron, please find out if they were able to find computers or cell phones belonging to the girls."

"Exactly," Gabe agreed. "I'd like to dig around in the victims' hard drives."

"Will do."

"Gabe, I know you haven't had much time, but did you find anything interesting about Amanda and Sophia's Internet use?" asked Brody.

"Actually, I did. They were both very active on their pages on MySpace, YouTube, Pinterest, and Facebook. They visited Craigslist frequently and communicated a lot through Twitter. Amanda and

Sophia participated in chat rooms, but the one they both visited the most is a site called Teen Chat. This chat room appears to be set up for teen girls to meet teen boys and vice versa. Only, I doubt if all the teen males are actually teenagers. The site looks ideal for a predator trolling for young girls."

"Did you find anything else?" asked Cam.

"It's pretty obvious that neither girl had supervision or guidance about her online activities. Both included their names, ages, photos, physical descriptions, and telephone number on the social media sites where they had pages. Providing this kind of personal information is something kids should never do, and it's exactly what online predators look for. Unfortunately, these girls were ripe for the picking."

"Were any of the postings suspicious?" asked Brody.

"Not really. The savvy predators, like our killer, want to move the online relationship off-line as soon as they can. I'm not surprised I didn't find much."

"Why is that?" asked Cameron.

"Internet predators prefer kids who have instant message accounts. Although some of the creeps use email, many predators prefer communicating with their victims through instant messages. They know that while emails are saved automatically and have to be manually deleted, instant messages tend to evaporate once the instant message window is closed."

"Damn it," Brody cursed. "Can we not catch a break?"

"Don't give up yet. There is a hell of a lot of information I can get, but I'm going to need a warrant for their Internet service providers."

"Not a problem," Brody said. "I got one signed from Judge Carlson early this morning. It's on my desk."

"Thanks," Gabe said, as he closed his file. "I'll see what I can find out about our four new victims, too."

"Good job, Gabe," Brody said, and then asked who would like to present next.

Carly straightened in her chair and said, "I volunteer. I want to share my analysis."

"This is my first opportunity to hear a psychological analysis of a killer *before* he's caught," Bryan remarked as he watched her gather her folders. "I'm looking forward to it."

Walking to the front of the room, Carly grinned at him and said, "I'll try not to disappoint you."

With all eyes in the room on her, she began, "I created a PowerPoint program, but if it's okay with you, I'd like to talk to you informally about my findings."

"Sounds good," said Cameron as he put his arms behind his head and rested back against his hands.

"Okay, let's get started. There is a folder in front of each of you with a detailed analysis and comparison of similarities between the victims that you can read later. Let me give you a quick summary before we talk about our killer.

"Considering victims Amanda Jenkins and Sophia Bradford, our killer is targeting lonely, vulnerable preteens, who are having trouble either at home or at school or both."

Walking back to her seat, Carly sipped from her water bottle, and then continued, "I believe our killer is a white male, who may be married, and he's in his twenties or thirties. He's in good enough physical condition to handle two victims without a problem. I say this because he carried their lifeless bodies to the car and put one in the trunk and one in the back seat before setting the car on fire.

"I think he works a five-days-a-week job and he's available on Saturdays. I don't think it's an accident that both Amanda and Sophia ran away on a Saturday."

"Our unsub is an online predator who knows exactly what to say to young girls to gain their trust. He's patient enough to develop the relationships and savvy enough to move them offline as soon as he can, just like Gabe described. He maintains the online relationship until he gets them to the point where they'll agree to meet him in person here in Shawnee County."

"How do you think he is talking them into traveling here to meet him?" Cam asked.

"He's offering them something they want. Some predators use promises of modeling. Others use promises of romance or adventure. Our victims were lonely girls with problems at school and at home. I'm sure he honed in on those things."

"Tell us more about the psychological aspects of our killer," prompted Brody.

"We're dealing with a sadist. When he killed Amanda and Sophia, he had them watch. One had to watch while the other one dies, knowing she'll be next."

"No one should have to die that way," said Bryan.

Carly nodded in agreement. "Our killer looks 'normal'. Later when he's caught, friends and neighbors will be shocked he committed the crimes he's accused of. It is quite possible one or more of you know this killer, since he likes to hang around crime scenes and talk to officers. He's eager to know what we know."

Bryan interrupted, "The CSI techs took a lot of photos at the car fire crime scene. He may have been there and we didn't notice. Cam, I'll get some additional photos to you."

Carly went on, "It is likely he was sexually abused as a child, since research suggests a great majority of sexual criminals have been childhood victims of sexual abuse. He's a big fan of pornography, both women and children, but his *preference* is preadolescent girls. When he is captured, pornography in digital and hard copy formats will be found. Much of the pornography will center on sexual bondage."

Looking at Bryan, Carly added, "The vaginal tearing, abrasions, and scarring you found in the autopsies of Amanda and Sophia suggests our killer is a sexual sadist, as do the dog collar marks around the girls' necks. The collars also suggest sexual bondage, which is a hallmark of the sexual sadist. He's attracted to and sexually excited by the helplessness and vulnerability of the bound victim."

"But isn't he raping them for sexual release?" asked Bryan.

"Sexual sadists get excited by the physical and or psychological pain they can cause a victim. But the *suffering* is the most important thing to them. That's what gets them off. Our killer rapes his victims to achieve gratification, not from the sex, but from his power over them. It is likely he photographs or videotapes his rapes, so that he can relive the attacks later. You will find videotapes or DVDs when you capture him. In addition, he may be collecting souvenirs from each victim."

"What a sick freak," said Gabe with disgust.

"Our killer may be using the girls as sexual slaves. Did you read James Patterson's *Kiss the Girls* or see the movie? In this book, the killer lived out his fantasy by abducting women and using them as sexual slaves. Those who disobeyed were killed. Our killer may have the same fantasy. It is very possible Amanda and Sophia disobeyed or were caught trying to escape."

"Just a guess, but I bet they were trying to get away. Who wouldn't?" asked Gabe.

"Exactly," Carly said. "Our killer is organized; the victims were chosen and stalked online by him. Nothing about his actions is random. He went to great pains to hide his crimes by burying them in shallow graves, which brings me to a problem I have."

"What's that?" asked Brody.

"Putting victims in a car and setting it on fire is not characteristic of this unsub, and not something our careful, organized killer would do. He would have carefully buried them with the others. This suggests to me another unsub is involved." Carly ended her discussion with, "I hope you will use this profile as a tool to focus your investigation so you can apprehend this killer."

"Thanks, Carly. Well done," Brody said.

Cameron spoke up, "I have something to show all of you that backs up Carly's theory that our killer is not working alone. Amanda Jenkins did not have a car, so one of the only ways she could have gotten to Morel was on a bus so I got surveillance tapes from the Greyhound Bus Station."

"Wait a minute," Brody butted in. "Since when does the bus station own surveillance cameras? I've advised Ernie McBride for years to get security, but he always refuses to spend the money."

"I know, but a month ago, after a break in, his son, Terry, had a new security system installed, complete with surveillance cameras." Cameron moved to the laptop and pulled up some footage.

"This footage is from the Saturday Alison Brown ran away. In a second you will see her in a long line waiting to enter the station."

"I see her," Carly exclaimed. "She's the fifth person in line."

"Right. Now watch what happens when she enters the lobby. See the figure in the black hoodie and gray sweatpants approach Alison?"

"Is it a man or a woman?" asked Gabe.

"It's hard to tell in this shot, but you'll see in a little while it's a woman," stated Cameron. "She says something to Alison and they leave together."

"Damn it," said Brody, his frustration increasing. "She's hidden by the hood, and you can't see her face."

"Careful, isn't she?" asked Carly. "See how she looks around as they leave through the door. She's nervous and afraid to be seen or caught."

Brody asked, "Doesn't that door lead to the parking lot? Can we see what kind of car they got in?"

"No," said Cameron. "Unfortunately, the parking lot camera is a fake until Ernie shells out more money to get a real one."

"What about witnesses?" asked Carly.

"I've got two detectives working through a list of passengers who were on Alison's bus from Indianapolis that day."

"Oh, shit," said Brody. "We were right. Alison Brown is here in Shawnee County."

"We've got to find her before it's too late," said Carly.

"Hold everything," Gabe said excitedly. "When was the last time the county did an online predator sting?"

Brody thought for a second, and then looked at Cam, "Has it been two years?"

"At least that," said Cam.

"Let's do another one and see if our killer responds."

"I think it's an excellent idea," added Carly. "When I was in the Bureau, we did a child sex sting in Florida and nabbed fifty child sex predators. It was highly successful."

Bryan asked, "Don't we have to be careful about how we set this thing up? I mean, if the net is too wide, we'll attract perverts from all over the country."

"I agree. So we'll set up this one specific to Indiana."

"How about this for a tag line: Thirteen-Year-Old Girl Seeking

Indiana Boy?" Carly offered.

"Good one," replied Gabe, with a grin. "Obviously, this is not your first rodeo."

"We can set up the sting in a home here in Morel, just like last time," said Cam.

"But this time, our goal is different," Carly began. "We want our guy to suggest she travel to him in Shawnee County."

"Who are we going to get to be our preteen girl? Our female deputies are maxed out," said Brody.

"I volunteer," Carly announced. "Like Gabe said, this is not my first rodeo. I know exactly what to look for and how to draw this guy out."

All four men agreed with her, and a meeting was set up for the next day to discuss details.

After work, Brody led Carly to the employee parking lot, but she didn't see his sheriff SUV anywhere.

"Where are you parked?" she asked.

"I went home after my meeting this morning and changed vehicles. I figure if you're going to drive it, you need to get familiar with it," Brody said with a grin.

Brody led her to a shining, new Jeep Wrangler Sport S. It was cherry red and looked like it had never been driven.

"This is what you want me to drive if I need a vehicle?" She asked with surprise. "Are you sure?"

"Yeah, why?"

"Because this looks like one of those car babies that men keep in their garages and never let anyone touch."

Brody flashed a sexy smile at her, and it was all she could do not to melt at his feet. Carly smiled right back, but the curve of her mouth had nothing to do with humor.

As he handed her the keys, he opened the driver's door for her, and said, "You driving or not?"

Without a word, she jumped into the car and noticed it still had the new-car scent she loved. Draping her long fingers around the leather-wrapped steering wheel, she pressed her foot on the brake and put the key in the ignition to start it.

Getting in the passenger seat, Brody closed his door and draped his arm on the back of her seat. "So what are you waiting for?"

"I have a question."

"What's that?"

"How do you feel about Italian food?"

"Love it. Who doesn't?"

"How about a home-cooked Italian meal at the cottage tonight at seven?"

"Who's cooking?"

"That's very funny," she said as she jabbed him in the side. "I am. It just so happens that my Italian grandmother was a chef and gave me a mouth-watering chicken parmigiana recipe."

"I'd say that's too irresistible an offer to turn down."

Adjusting his mirrored aviator glasses, he focused on Brody Chase and

Carly Stone who entered the sheriff's office parking lot, heading toward a new red Jeep. The grapevine was burning with talk about the consultant the sheriff had hired to create a profile of the killer. Like big-shot former Federal agent, Carly Stone, knew anything about him. Such bullshit. He was bullet-proof. Undoubtedly, she was as stupid as the bitch slaves in his basement. What he wouldn't give to hang Carly Stone from his basement ceiling and beat her raw while she screamed. His dick throbbed at the thought, hot and hard.

Through the scope of his assault rifle, he'd watched her for hours the night before. He'd gained a new appreciation for homes with a multitude of huge, uncovered, glass windows like the cottage on the sheriff's property. He watched as Carly Stone worked in the front room most of the night, reading and re-reading papers and typing notes on her laptop. The bitch didn't have a clue he stood behind a tree in the woods, aiming his assault rifle at her, fighting an urge to blow her away. He'd learned long ago that timing was key. The right time would come to snuff out Carly Stone. Being a patient man, he'd wait until the perfect circumstances arose and then Little Miss Profiler would be history.

The sheriff was now showing Stone his brand-new Jeep and flirting with her like he was a damn teenager. Seriously? Brody Chase was a fucking idiot, and that the man had discovered the graves he'd dug for dead slaves still pissed him off. He felt his temper rise, but he worked to keep it in check. He had to stay in control, because once the demons took over, there was no telling what he would do. Right now, the important thing was to keep watch over the consultant, the sheriff and his brothers. What did they know? How close were they to discovering his identity?

Cameron Chase entered the parking lot and strode toward his unmarked car. He followed Cameron as he turned right on Main Street. When the detective parked outside the Greyhound bus station, he smirked as he noted the security camera cheap-ass Ernie McBride had installed. It was pointed toward the parking lot, and was as fake as a three dollar bill, just like the ones inside. Good luck finding surveillance footage, Detective Chase.

Pulling out of the parking lot, he headed toward the public library so he could use their Wi-Fi to visit Teen Chat. The week before, he'd hooked up online with Amber Patterson, a thirteen-year-old from Nashville, Indiana, who was the wild-child daughter of wealthy parents who spoiled her rotten. Bored at school, failing her classes, and experimenting with sex and drugs, poor Amber was being threatened by her wealthy parents to improve her bad behavior or else. How lucky she'd found him to lend a sympathetic ear to her troubles with her strict parents. A slow, evil smile spread over his face. It wouldn't be long before he could move from empathetic to romantic, and then persuade Amber Patterson to join him in Shawnee County. Game on.

Brody was pushing a shopping cart inside the IGA grocery store, while Carly directed him to the things she needed for her recipe. If he was trying to curtail local gossip about his love life, shopping with Carly was not the way to do it. They were getting so many stares, he started to sympathize with celebrities' battles with the paparazzi. There was no such thing as privacy for public officials in a small town. Why people were so curious about his love life was beyond him.

It was his first time shopping for food with a beautiful woman and he found he liked it — a lot. Carly Stone was certainly not hard to look at, he thought, as he admired her tight, little behind. Every time she reached for something, her typical buttoned-up work shirt rose, giving him a glimpse of her smooth skin beneath. He got so turned on, he made an excuse to find a bottle of wine in another aisle. As soon as he turned the corner, he bumped into Gabe, who was smiling like a Cheshire cat.

"Hey, Gabe," he said.

"I never would have believed it, if I hadn't seen it with my own eyes."

"Believed what?" Brody asked, even though he worried about what Gabe was about to say.

"That you let Carly drive your new Jeep. How many times have Cam and I asked you if we could drive it, and you turned us down flat?"

"This is different. I can just see you and Cam taking it for a joy ride or off-roading or worse, mudding at the Badlands. It's not likely Carly is going to do any of those things. Besides, I promised I'd have a vehicle for her while she was here working."

"Uh-huh," Gabe said with a smirk, clearly not believing him.

"What's that supposed to mean?"

As he turned to head for the check-out line, Gabe said over his shoulder, "I think my big brother has called off his moratorium for relationships and one-night stands."

Rolling his eyes and groaning, Brody turned back to the wine selection wondering what wine goes with Italian food.

"Chianti might be nice," said Carly, as she rested her warm hand on the middle of his back. It was the first time she'd touched him, and his body tingled with awareness. "Was that Gabe I just saw? Do you think he'd want to join us for dinner?"

"No," Brody said a little too quickly. Then he lied. "He has plans."

"Oh, okay. So what sounds good for dessert, cheesecake or tiramisu?"

"You choose. I like them both."

"Tiramisu it is," said Carly, as she led him to the dessert section.

Carly opened the door and Brody entered the cottage wearing a light yellow V-neck sweater that stretched across his powerful chest and faded jeans that fit him like a glove. The man radiated testosterone and she'd been going through some serious withdrawal. She could feel the giveaway heat in her face.

Carrying a bottle of Chianti, Brody handed it to her and looked toward the huge stone fireplace. "Would you like for me to start a fire?"

Carly managed to say, "Yes" and took the wine to the kitchen. Considering every hormone in her body was sizzling, Brody Chase had already ignited one fire. Walking into the kitchen, she laid the wine on the island, and searched for a corkscrew.

Things had changed between them, and she knew the exact moment it had happened. Earlier in the conference room, she stood watching Sam Isley and Brody interact. She'd always thought of her former lover as being bigger than life, but he paled in comparison to Brody Chase. Only an inch or so taller than Sam, Brody seemed to tower over him, looking huge, powerful, and very dangerous. Polite and professional, he handled Sam Isley, but there was no mistaking who was in charge.

But it was the hug that did her in. What started as the kindest gesture she'd experienced in a long time, the action, slow and deliberate, ignited a need deep in her that she fought to extinguish, but it kindled brighter and hotter as she melted against him. Sparks of excitement shot through her, and it was difficult to hide her disappointment when he pulled away. That was the exact moment she knew she had to have Brody Chase. Carly wanted him in her bed, and in her life — the sooner the better.

The rest of the day, she'd let herself fantasize about getting involved with him. Imagining working together during the day, and afterwards making slow, sensual love in every room of the cottage at night.

Brody brushed past her in the kitchen, and used the sink to wash his hands. Turning, he seemed to notice her for the first time, and a flicker of the heat like the one she'd seen in his eyes in the conference room flashed across his expression. He was appraising her with more than mild interest, and Carly felt a burst of pure feminine pleasure. She wanted him to find her desirable. Better yet, she wanted him to find her irresistible.

"The food smells amazing," Brody said as he pulled the corkscrew out of her hand. Opening the Chianti, he poured a glass for Carly and handed it to her. Standing before him in a low-cut, white top embellished with tiny turquoise beads and a long, ruffled denim skirt, she had a curvy body that pushed all of his buttons in a very big way. There were two Carly Stones, he decided. There was the stuffy, buttoned-up former federal agent, and the tantalizingly sexy woman who stood before him. Their gazes locked and a crackle of energy passed between them, an undeniable pull. All he could think about was how much he wanted to press her sweet body against his.

He tried to think of a woman to whom he was ever this attracted, but he couldn't name one — not even Mollie. Carly was the first to come to mind and the thought was unsettling. Clenching his jaw, he gritted his teeth as he fought his feelings. He had no business fantasizing about Carly, no matter how attracted he was to her. With all the available women in the world, why this one?

Pulling the baking pan of chicken parmigiana out of the oven, Carly sprinkled a thick layer of mozzarella on top and then returned the dish to the oven to melt the cheese.

"Ten more minutes," she announced to Brody, who was pulling dinner plates out of a cabinet and silverware out of a drawer and placing them on the kitchen island.

"Lucky for me, your Italian grandmother was a chef," said Brody with a grin. "Were you able to spend much time with her?" Knowing little about her personal life, he realized he wanted to know everything.

"Yes. Blake and I spent a portion of every summer with her. Some of my favorite memories are cooking with my grandmother and Blake in the kitchen of her restaurant."

"You're lucky. Both my grandparents died at an early age, so I don't remember much about them."

From the refrigerator, Carly pulled out fresh lettuce, tomatoes, carrots, and mushrooms for the salad. Brody washed the vegetables at the sink while Carly set out a cutting board on the island. Cutting the vegetables as Carly tore the lettuce into pieces, Brody decided he liked working in the kitchen with her. He savored the warm nearness of her body, and the way she brushed up against him as she worked. Every time he got near her, he felt this buzz of sexual awareness.

The oven timer sounded, and Brody pulled the heavy pan of pasta out of the oven, sliced it into squares, and placed a square on each of their plates along with a scoop of salad with dressing. They retreated to the dining room to have their meal.

Shoveling a mouthful of parmigiana into his mouth, Brody moaned with pleasure. "This is incredible, Carly."

"I had some stiff competition from your steak and salad the other night," she replied with an easy smile that played at the corners of her mouth.

Brody didn't know if the moment was right, or if there would be a right time to ask her, so he plodded ahead, "Do you mind if I ask you a personal question?"

"Since I've already blasted some personal inquiries your way, how can I say no?"

"Who is Sam Isley?"

Carly visibly tensed and a moment of silence passed before she answered. "Sam Isley was my supervisor when I was with the Bureau in Tampa."

"I think he was more than your supervisor. That was obvious by the way he looked at you," Brody replied. Dancing around the topic wasn't happening. He wanted the whole truth, not a portion of it.

"It's not something I'm proud of, but I was involved with Sam. It turned out to be one of my biggest mistakes."

Watching her over the rim of his wine glass, he asked, "Because he was your supervisor?"

"Yes, because he was my supervisor and because he is who he is."

"Why was he here today?"

"Sam wants me to come back to the agency in Tampa ..."

Brody interrupted. "And to him?"

"Yes, but neither is going to happen. I have no desire to return to the bureau and even less to be with Sam Isley. He's a part of my past I want to forget."

"Are you sure about that?" Brody wanted to know, as he started to gather their plates. He waited uneasily for her response.

"More sure than I've ever been about anything."

While Brody was in the kitchen, Carly settled on the sofa in the living room, watching the fire licking the logs in the fireplace. Thinking about Sam Isley was her least favorite activity and talking about him was something she detested. She hated the mix of anger and humiliation that washed over her whenever she thought of her ex-lover. The last thing she wanted to do was spend any more of the evening talking about Sam to Brody.

Moving to the stereo, Carly flipped it on and soon the soulful sound of "Any Love" by Luther Vandross filled the room. Brody soon joined her with the bottle of Chianti and their two wine glasses. Squatting down to feed the fire another chunk of wood, Brody said, "I see you've found Mom's old CDs."

"I love this whole collection. I found CDs from Tina Turner, Aretha Franklin, and Prince. I've been playing them every night after work."

"Really?"

"I'm a big fan of eighties and nineties music. When I was growing up, most kids had mothers who sang them lullabies. My mom sang Aretha Franklin and Tina Turner songs to me."

Pulling the wine glass from Brody's hand, she set it on the table and opened up her arms to him. "Dance with me."

Her fingers curled around his hand, as his arm wound around her waist, supporting her as they swayed sensuously to the music. Holding her gently, he rocked her back and forth as she softly sang along with the song. The warmth and scent of him was so male, so bracing. Relaxing, she sank into his embrace, her head fitting perfectly in the hollow between his shoulder and neck. Pressing her hands against his chest, she felt his heart pounding wildly beneath his hot skin. Tightening her arms around his neck, she pulled him closer, molding his rock hard body to her, and capturing his mouth in a slow kiss that deepened with mind-blowing intensity. A delightful shiver of need ran through her, as she pressed even closer to him.

Kissing her thoroughly and possessively with his entire body, Brody ignited a bone-melting fire that rushed through her veins. She opened her mouth, eager for the taste and feel of his tongue stroking hers. Sealing his mouth over hers, he took full possession of her lips, kissing her, exploring her mouth with his tongue until she was so aroused every hormone in her body sizzled.

As suddenly as the kiss began, it stopped, leaving her trembling with her thoughts spinning. Cradling her face in his hands, Brody closed his eyes, pressing his forehead against hers. Breathing hard, the muscle at the side of his jaw tightened. He kissed the top of her head and rushed out the door.

"Brody?"

Waiting until dark, he positioned himself in a stand of trees outside the cottage, peering through the scope of his assault rifle aimed at Brody Chase and Carly Stone. Their bodies entwined as they kissed, it was a perfect shot. His finger trembled near the trigger. One shot and he could blow them both away. Such frugal use of a bullet and no two people deserved it more than these two. They were causing him some needless anxiety and they'd pay for it.

He'd fantasized many times of the exact way Brody Chase and Carly Stone would meet their end. In his basement, the sheriff would be beaten and bound inside a dog cage, forced to watch as he repeatedly raped and whipped his precious Carly Stone until she bled. He'd make sure she suffered, but the idiot sheriff would suffer much more. Brody would have to watch and he'd be completely powerless to do anything about it. Such a perfect plan. He couldn't wait to put it in motion, but he'd wait until the perfect time.

A sound from his cell phone indicated he'd received a text message. Pushing away from the tree, he headed back toward his car so he could communicate with his brand-new, oversexed, preteen girlfriend, Amber Patterson.

7 CHAPTER SEVEN

Sitting on the main house patio, Brody slammed his fist down on the chair arm and cursed. Then he chugged a second bottle of Coors and cursed again. What the hell was wrong with him? Was he really this afraid of getting involved in something that might be meaningful? What the hell? He was a guy who feared nothing and no one. So what was going on with him?

He was ten when he lost his father, and nineteen-years-old when his mother was killed. Even though his friends were partying and doing all the things that young men did during their twenties, Brody didn't regret a minute he spent taking care of his brothers. His first priority was their welfare. They needed him. Damn it. And any sacrifices he might have made, including a relationship, were worth seeing Cam and Gabe grow into the good men they'd become.

Was it the loss of both parents that had him running from Carly? Perhaps, he thought. He didn't need a shrink to tell him that he had loss issues. People he loved left him. People he loved died.

The screen door opened, and Cameron joined him, sitting down in the rocking chair. "What's up?"

"Nothing," Brody said angrily. "Not a damn thing."

"Just an observance, but it doesn't sound like nothing." Cameron pulled an icy bottle of beer from the cooler next to Brody's chair.

"Drop it, Cam," Brody warned irritably.

"Gabe said you were having dinner with Carly. What happened?"

"Nothing."

"Are you distancing yourself from her like the others?"

"Maybe."

"You kill me, Brody. I know you want her. Hell, a man would have to be blind not to see how much you want Carly Stone."

"Think so?"

"I know so," said Cameron. "Just curious, but when was the last time you did something just for you, Brody? Doesn't it get tiresome carrying the whole damn world on your shoulders? Isn't it time you let go of this martyr thing you got going and really start living? Gabe and I are all grown up. We don't need, nor do we want, your damn sacrifices."

"Don't hold back, Cam," Brody said, his voice laced with sarcasm.

"When's the last time you made love to a woman, Brody? And I don't mean the one night stands you have with women who live in any county but this one."

Wordlessly, Brody took another gulp of beer and stared into the dark night. Like he was going to answer *that* question.

"Consider what *you* want for a change, Brody. Forget what someone else wants or needs. For once in your life, take what *you* want. If you've got a window of opportunity with Carly Stone, then take the chance with her while there is one."

"Thanks, Dr. Phil," Brody said over his shoulder as he headed for his Jeep.

Carly sipped the rest of her Chianti and fought the urge to smash her wine glass in the fireplace. She'd thrown herself at Brody Chase and made a fool of herself. It was a humiliating and deflated feeling, and her cheeks burned in remembrance. How in the hell was she supposed to face him at work?

The cottage was quiet, save for the crackle of burning wood in the fireplace and the soft, sultry sounds of Luther Vandross still playing on the stereo. Turning off the lamps, Carly lit two large candles on the mantle and another on the coffee table, then sat on a thick, soft rug in front of the fireplace, relishing its warmth. There was nothing she could do about the situation now, so why agonize about it? She'd handle it.

Suddenly, Carly heard a vehicle race down the driveway and screech to a stop in front of the cottage.

Brody burst through the front door, spotted her in the dim light and cut the distance between them with long, purposeful strides. Before she knew what was happening, he'd pulled Carly to her feet, his strong arms tightening around her body as he held her. The heat in his eyes startled her as he crushed his mouth down on hers. His mouth all but consumed her in a frantic rush of kisses, each hotter than the last.

Brody kissed her like he'd been waiting his whole life to do it. Pushing her to the wall, he pinned her there with his big hands gripping her wrists above her head. And again his mouth was on hers, urgent, and relentless. He wasn't asking this time. He was taking. And nothing she'd tasted in her entire life had been so delicious, demanding, and satisfying.

Carly moaned with pleasure and struggled to free her wrists from his hands so she could pull him even closer. It was obvious he was in good shape, but now she could get her hands on him. Running her slender fingers over the corded muscles of his back, dipping into the deep valley of his spine, she ached to have him naked, his rock-hard body against her. She tugged at the bottom of his sweater, and he stopped what he was doing to take it off. His impressive chest and abs were illuminated by the golden flicker of the flames in the fireplace, burning as hot as the one inside her.

Ripping off her top, he threw it to the floor, then he unzipped her skirt and shoved it down to her feet. Her body tingled with awareness as he appraised her body with a long, lingering look, taking in her full breasts, small waist, and long, long legs. It was as if he couldn't get enough of looking at her, and in response, wet, sexual heat flooded between her legs.

"You're so damn beautiful, Carly. I've wanted you since the first moment I saw you," Brody whispered in a low, husky voice that made her bones melt. "I've never wanted anyone or anything as much as I want you."

His fingers skimmed up her stomach, sending quivers of anticipation shooting through her body. His warm hand cupped her breast beneath the lace of her bra, his thumb circling slowly, lightly over her nipples, and her breath caught in her throat. Sighing with a pleasure that came from deep within her core, Carly knotted her hands in his hair to pull him closer.

Unhooking her bra, he let it fall to the floor. His firm, wet mouth closed over her nipples, sucking, tonguing, and teasing until she thought she'd go insane with need. Brody's mouth moved up her throat, his tongue hot and wet, until he reclaimed her mouth with intensity like she'd never known. She felt the heat of his hot bare chest as he cupped her bottom, aligning her body with the hard ridge in his jeans. Rocking against him, she began an erotic grind as old as mankind itself.

She struggled with the zipper of his jeans. Wanting him flesh against flesh, man against woman, she had to have him deep inside her. She couldn't wait another minute.

Gently, Brody eased her down onto the rug before the fireplace and quickly stripped off his boots and jeans. Standing before her, he was six foot three inches of hard muscle with amazing biceps, sexy sculpted abdomen, and a hot sexuality that had Carly burning from the inside out for him.

He lowered himself to the floor, bracing himself over her body with his elbows as she adjusted her curves to the hard, flat planes of his body, pressing herself against the thickness of his erection. His body was shockingly hot over hers. Her over-aroused sex rubbed against the length of his penis, in surges of throbbing heat.

Brody sealed his mouth over hers, taking possession of it, and seducing her with hot, deep glides of his tongue. Stroking between her legs, he probed for the bud that throbbed with need. As his magic fingers slid over her sensitive nub, she moaned aloud with desire.

"Now, Brody, please," she cried.

Leaning on one arm, he pulled a foil packet from his jeans pocket, opened it, and made a growling sound in the back of his throat as he covered himself. When he shifted over her, she eagerly arched her hips up to meet him as his steel drove within her. She gasped at the force of it. Finally, she could feel him inside her, and a fire such as she'd never imagined seared her sexual center.

Rocking her hips, Brody pumped and thrust so deep inside, it made her ache until she felt a white heat in her core. It was building and building until she exploded with pleasure. Moments later, Brody made a violent thrust, shuddered and cried out her name. Slowly rolling over, he held her tightly against him until she could feel his heartbeat, and every breath he took.

Winded and breathing heavily, he said, "Just so you know, I don't do one-night stands."

Pressing a kiss against the pulse in his neck, Carly whispered, "What a happy coincidence."

The next day, Carly presented her profile findings at Brody's roll call and briefing before each shift. Deputies and detectives listened attentively, each more eager than the next to catch their killer.

"Are you saying this guy has killed at least six girls?"

"Possibly eight," Carly responded. "Counting Amanda Jenkins and Sophia Bradford, plus the four victims identified through their remains, there are six identified victims and two possibles that are not yet identified."

Stunned, the group of law enforcement officers began conversing with each other. It took Brody several minutes to call them to order.

"Listen, I know you're as upset as I am about someone doing this in our backyard, but we've got to stay focused so we can stop the bastard," Brody said.

Carly continued from where she left off. "Here is a description of who we are looking for." She clicked a key on her laptop, and a list appeared on the screen behind her. "Our killer is a white male in his twenties or thirties who is in good shape physically. He works a five-day week and is off on Saturday, which is the day both Amanda and Sophia arrived in Morel. In addition, he has a female accomplice who was seen on surveillance picking up two of the victims at the Greyhound Bus Station. We have a still photo of her. Our unsub is an online predator who's patient enough to develop trust so he can persuade the girls to join him. He targets preadolescent girls who are having difficulties at school and/or with her parents. Lending them a sympathetic ear, he soon moves into romancing them."

Cameron got Carly's attention and asked, "Please talk a little about the way this guy thinks."

"We're dealing with a sadist, who enjoys sex only when his victim is experiencing intense pain and suffering. A big fan of pornography, he'll have digital and hard copies of it when we find him. There may even be photographs or DVDs he's made when torturing his victims in his home or place of work. Our unsub is into bondage, which is the hallmark of the sexual sadist. He's turned on by the helplessness of the bound victim."

"Are there any other ways we can identify him?" asked a deputy in the back row.

"Unfortunately, no. You're not searching for someone who looks like a monster. His appearance is quite normal, and after you catch him, his friends and neighbors will be shocked he's committed the crimes he's accused of," Carly began. "It's likely one or more of you know this guy already. He likes to hang around crime scenes to talk to officers. He wants to know what we know about him." The last statement caused several officers to frown as they searched their minds for anyone they knew who fit this description.

Brody ended the meeting by providing each officer with a photo of Alison Brown and the female accomplice caught on the surveillance tape. He assigned a house-to-house visit to discover whether any of their residents had seen the missing girl.

Later in the afternoon, Carly, Gabe, Cameron, and Brody gathered in the conference room to make plans for their sexual predator sting. Carly tried not to glance at Brody because every time she did, she remembered every toe-curling, erotic thing he did to her the night before, and her face heated in a blush like a teenager. They'd made love once in the living room on the rug before the fireplace, and twice in her bedroom in the loft. Then in the morning, he'd taken her against the tiled wall in the shower. They couldn't keep their hands off each other. Though her mind should have been on the meeting, she kept thinking of every delicious thing she wanted to do to Brody after work.

"We've run online predator stings before, but this one will be a little different." Brody began. "We have two goals. Our first is to arrest any online predators who travel to our county to have sex with minors. The second is to use the online communication from Carly to catch our serial killer, who will try to lure our 'teen' to Shawnee County."

"Phil Emerson gave us permission to use his spec house on Covered Bridge Road, so all we need is a photo of a preteen girl and an enticing ad for social media," said Cameron.

"Excellent," said Brody, whose cell phone sounded. He pulled it out, looked at the display, and then went to his office to take the call.

Carly slid a photo across the table and said, "Here's our thirteen-year-old girl." In the photo was a pretty dark-eyed preteen wearing her glossy, black hair in a ponytail, with silver braces covering her teeth.

"Cute kid," said Cameron. "Who is it?"

"That's me in my awkward preteen days," said Carly with a grin.

"So now all we have to post is our teen's introduction. Let's go with something like 'Thirteen-Year-Old Girl Seeking Indiana Boy'."

"Where do you want to post the ad?" asked Gabe, poised over his laptop.

"I want to post on the sites you discovered that Amanda and Sophia used: Facebook, MySpace, Craigslist, and Teen Chat, to increase the chances our killer will see it."

Gabe's fingers flew over the keys as he posted the message on the sites. As he prepared to leave, he said to Carly, "I have insurance fraud surveillance to do this afternoon, so call me on my cell if anything interesting happens."

"Absolutely," she assured him.

Cameron joined Gabe at the door, and turned back to say, "I'll be at the bus station. We've found a couple of people who rode on Alison's bus who agreed to meet with us."

Alison spent a sleepless night listening to Jasmine crying and whimpering in her sleep. The Master had beaten the girl so badly that her face, arms, back and legs were covered with angry, bleeding welts and abrasions. When he'd unfastened her wrist restraints, she collapsed to the floor and he had to carry her to the dog crate.

A dim light illuminated the room from the only window, enabling Alison to see Jasmine huddled in a fetal position at the far end of the cage. Still sleeping restlessly, she cried out each time she moved.

With absolute certainty, Alison knew if they could not escape, he would kill them. Her hope that they would be rescued by the police diminished with each passing day.

The door at the top of the stairs opened, and the woman who always wore the red ski mask soon appeared, carrying a tray of food.

Unlocking the padlock on Alison's cage, she set a bowl of oatmeal and a bottle of water inside, and then did the same for Jasmine.

"Jasmine's hurt," Alison said. "She's bleeding. Can't you clean her wounds and put something on them so they don't get infected?"

Pausing for a moment to look at Jasmine, who had still not moved from a fetal position, she shook her head no. In all the times she'd brought them food, she'd never spoken. She appeared to be afraid of the girls identifying her by her voice.

"Please help her," Alison pleaded.

Shaking her head again, the woman went back upstairs.

Alison focused on how they could escape. There were two ways out of the basement, through the door at the top of the stairs, or through the small bathroom window.

If the Master were to allow her to shower alone again, she could try getting out of the bathroom window. But what about Jasmine? Her wounds looked serious. Could she even walk? Alison could escape and bring back help. But what would he do to Jasmine if she left her behind?

By three in the afternoon, using @SweetTeen as a call name, Carly had five respondents to her lonely teen ad. All five wanted to see her photo, which she hadn't initially posted with the first message. Two were actually teenaged boys who responded to her Facebook page and wrote to her using their real names, which she quickly verified.

In Teen Chat, the other three messengers used call names like BigJohn, TeenIdol, EarlH and LoverBoy. Each wanted to know what kind of music she liked, and some of her favorite things to do. Carly sent them her junior high school photo, and answered their questions as a preteen would. According to her profile, she was into Justin Bieber music, *Twilight* movies, and hanging out at the mall. If whoever was behind the four call names were predators, they were taking it slow and trying to create an online relationship, before moving into discussions about romance or sex.

By five o'clock, Brody, Cameron and Gabe were in the conference room with Carly talking about what Gabe was grilling for dinner, when a ding announced a new message for her in Teen Chat. It was @EarlH again. According to his profile, @EarlH was a fifteen-year-old boy who liked Justin Beiber, playing soccer, going to movies, and hanging out at the mall. He'd been contacting Carly all afternoon and had already asked her the standard introductory questions along with requesting her photograph.

@EarlH: Thanks for sending the photo. You're really hot. I bet all the boys tell you that because it's the truth.

@SweetTeen: Thanks for saying that. I don't feel all that hot or pretty.

@EarlH: Well, you are pretty. Hey, I see in your profile that you like Twilight movies, too. Where do you live? Maybe we could meet up this weekend for a movie.

@SweetTeen: My parents won't let me date or do anything else that's fun.

Carly was purposely evasive with her response, wondering how aggressively he would try to get her address, or if he would begin his persuasion process to lure her to Shawnee County, but he didn't bite. Instead he honed in on her dissatisfaction with her parents.

@EarlH: Do they have to know?

@SweetTeen: I guess not.

@EarlH: You could tell them you're with a girlfriend.

@SweetTeen: I'm not sure.

@EarlH: C'mon. We'd have a great time.

@SweetTeen: Well, maybe.

@EarlH: How close do you live to Morel? The theater here in town is having a Twilight movie marathon.

"Bingo!" Gabe called out as he flipped open his laptop. "We've got your call name @EarlH. Now let's see who you really are." It took a couple of moments for him to log on. Then he turned to Carly, "Which site are you on?"

"Teen Chat," she responded.

"Okay," Gabe began. "I'm going to trace the pervert through his IP address, and then I'll go to my Internet Service Provider contact at Teen Chat. Got to tell ya though, this site was not all warm and friendly when I served the warrant. We'll soon find out how cooperative they're going to be."

169

Brody asked, "What do you do if they're not cooperative? Can you still find him?"

"Yes. I can go outside the box, but not without your buy-in," Gabe offered.

"No," said Brody emphatically. "They better be cooperative. I'm sure they wouldn't want to be known as the ISP who protected a serial killer."

After a couple of moments, Brody got impatient, "Find anything?"

A sly smile crossed Gabe's face. "How much info do you want? I've got his real name, address, and place of work."

"Hurray!" Carly cheered, as Brody gave his youngest brother a high-five.

"@EarlH is Earl Haas who lives at 230 Elm Street in Morel. Earl is thirty-seven-years old and works for Ernie McBride as a Greyhound bus driver."

"You're kidding," said Brody excitedly. "At least two of our victims got to Morel by riding on a Greyhound bus. He could be our guy."

"Hold on," said Cameron. "Gabe, get his criminal history."

"Easy. Just a second," Gabe said, his dark eyes shining with excitement as he clicked a couple of keys to enter the database. "My, my, my," he began. "Our Earl was convicted of sexual misconduct with a minor and spent five years in prison. Four years ago, he got an early release for good behavior."

Cameron shot a glance to Brody. "Four years ago? Just so

happens our victim, Alyssa Benjamin, from Lebanon, went missing four years ago around the time Earl Haas was released from prison."

"This could be our killer." A broad grin split his face as Brody jumped to his feet, and said, "I need to get a search warrant for his work locker at the bus station and home. We need access to his computer. Also, I want to search his home for pornography, any iPhones, laptops, or eReaders that can be traced back to any of our victims. Most of all, I want to get into his house in case he's hiding Alison Brown there," Brody said as he rushed out of the room.

Carly typed a message to @EarlH: Got to go. Parents home. Have to do the dishes. Talk to you tomorrow. Can't wait.

The slowly fading light told Alison another day in her living nightmare was ending, and soon it would be difficult to see in the darkness of the basement. She'd spent the day pressed against the end of the cage, worriedly watching Jasmine and calling her name, but she'd received no response. The girl hadn't touched the food the woman brought hours before. In fact, she hadn't stirred at all. Jasmine lay in the same fetal position, and had stopped moving sometime in early afternoon.

The quiet in the room was eerie and unsettling. Alison strained to hear if Jasmine was still breathing. She had no idea if the girl was still alive. It didn't take a rocket scientist to realize Jasmine needed medical care, and time was running out. Alison had to do something. But what could she possibly do to help while locked in a dog crate? The only chance at survival either of them had was Alison's escape through the bathroom window, but when would another opportunity arise? Having no idea where she was, how could she find help in time to save Jasmine?

Brody drove Carly down the lane to the cottage and parked next to Gabe's car. It was Gabe's turn to cook dinner, and he was grilling tilapia and vegetables in the outdoor living area at the side of the cottage.

Turning off the ignition, Brody turned to Carly. "There's something I've wanted to do all day." He leaned forward and in one smooth movement covered her mouth with his own. Kissing her ignited a bone-melting fire that spread through his blood. Feeling her arms tighten around his neck, he knew just kissing this woman was not going to be enough. When Brody spoke again, his voice was a husky whisper. "I can't wait to get you alone later. I have plans for you, Carly Stone." Carly's features softened as a slow, sexy smile eased across her face. Kissing her again for good measure, Brody turned off the ignition and opened the driver's door.

Just as Brody and Carly got out of the vehicle, Cameron pulled up and parked next to them. He took one look at Carly's flushed face and swollen lips, shot a knowing grin at his older brother, and took off for the side yard with the big tub of macaroni salad he was carrying.

Insisting on being called the "Grilling Maestro", Gabe turned out to be as talented a cook as Brody. He declared the dinner a celebration for finding Earl Haas, prime suspect for the serial killings that plagued their county. The brothers were overdue for a celebration.

Cameron handed Carly and Brody tall glasses of ice tea, and asked, "Brody, did you get the search warrants?"

"Absolutely," Brody replied. "Carly and I picked them up before we headed home."

Carrying a platter of grilled tilapia that smelled incredible, Gabe worked his way to the dining table as Carly dashed to the grill to retrieve the grilled potatoes, carrots, leeks and onions.

Hungry after a long day at work, they dived into their food and didn't come up for air for a while. Finally, Cameron said, "I've been thinking about Earl Haas and how this should go down. I've got a couple of ideas."

"Let's hear them," said Brody, before he chugged his ice tea.

"For one thing, I put him under twenty-four-hour surveillance," Cameron began. "He's a registered sex offender. Let's see if there are under-aged girls visiting his house."

"Good thinking."

"I know how badly we all want this guy, but I think we should be patient to see how the surveillance goes and what we discover," Cameron said.

Carly interrupted, "I agree. It gives me more time to communicate with him through Teen Chat. Earl hasn't started sending me signals that he wants to meet for sex yet. But, if his communication today was an example, he's moving faster than a lot of sex predators would move in one day's time."

"Just be careful to let him lead the conversation and make the suggestions, requests and sexual overtures. We don't want some overzealous defense attorney to scream 'entrapment'," Brody advised.

"Right," Carly said. "Tomorrow, I'll tell him I live in Shawnee County and that my parents are going to be out-of-town this weekend."

Excited, Gabe added, "I like it. Talking on the computer may not be enough to arrest and hold him, but if Earl shows up at our sting house, we can charge him with traveling to meet a minor for sex and soliciting a minor for sex."

Brody agreed, "It's a good plan. Once he's arrested, we implement the search warrants at his work and home, targeting his computer and any electronic devices."

"And then we do what I am most looking forward to doing," offered Cameron.

"What's that?" asked Brody.

"We get him in the station and interrogate his perverted, psychotic ass."

Watching from a stand of trees in the wooded area outside the cottage, he peered through the scope of his assault rifle, as his mouth spread into a thin-lipped grin. What were the chances of having all three Chase brothers in his sight at the same time? He'd give anything to be able to hear what they were talking about and was tempted to move closer, but immediately, he dismissed the idea. Taking risks were a turn-on, but he wasn't suicidal. He'd be a fool to think he could take on four armed law enforcement officers at the same time. He'd much rather pick them off one-by-one, savoring each experience. Killing had become orgasmic. The very thought of it made him hot.

Leaning against a tree, he remembered something that had happened the previous year. He'd just finished burying a slave in his favorite body dump in the wooded area on Wally Johnson's farm. His body coated with dirt and sweat, he made his way through the woods with the help of a flashlight. Soon he came upon the dirt lane off a graveled country road where he'd parked his truck, and found a late model, steamed-windowed, Chevy Impala parked next to him. Inside were two teenagers immersed in a make-out session. Just as he'd lifted his gun to take them out, a county sheriff car, with lights blazing, pulled up. Retreating within the woods and hiding behind a huge oak tree, he'd watched as a burly officer lectured the teens. Moments later, both vehicles left, and he thanked his lucky stars the officer did not notice his truck or run the plates.

He was a lucky and smart sonofabitch. Just look how long it'd taken the idiot sheriff to find his shallow graves. It'd been four years since he'd dug his first grave there. If it hadn't been for those kids playing in the woods, they might never have found them. He wondered if the remains they'd taken from his graves had been identified. Not that he cared. He was way too clever and smart for these county sheriff hicks. There was no way they'd find anything to connect him to the victims. That was the beauty of it. He was, indeed, the Master.

Not that his current slaves, Alison and Jasmine, seemed to think of him as their Master. They were disappointments like many of the others. Neither of them had yet to start calling him Master as he demanded when he beat them. Slow-learning bitches.

One of them would have to die soon, anyway, to make room for his new plaything, Amber Patterson, who was itching to hook up with his online persona.

Erin ambled around the old farmhouse. She'd already cleaned and swept each room and fed the slaves in the basement. Jasmine, the African-American slave, didn't look so good. The Master had given her quite a whipping the night before. The other slave, Alison, was pitching a bitch about it. Erin wanted to tell her brother about it right away, but the Master forbade her from calling his cell phone. So she'd wait until he came home. He was an hour late. Where was he, anyway?

Plopping down on the living room sofa, she gazed out the front window. It was nearly dark, but she could still see rows of corn growing in the field across the road from the house. Familiar boredom filled her. She was only twenty-six-years-old. What was she doing wasting away out in the middle of Nowhere, Indiana? Then she remembered what her brother had done for her years earlier, and felt a wave of shame sweep over her for having such ungrateful thoughts.

Erin owed her brother a great deal for rescuing her from a nightmarish existence in Utah where they'd lived with their pathetic mother and violent father, the town drunk. Though her brother had suffered frequent harsh beatings, she was the one that Daddy savagely raped and used as a human punching bag. Her eyes filled with tears, she shuddered as she recalled the attacks which had started when she was only eight-years-old.

Once in junior high school, her teacher pulled her aside to talk to her privately. She asked about the bruises covering Erin's face and arms. Erin did what she was taught to do. What happens at home stays at home. She lied to her teacher, saying she'd gotten the injuries from a nasty fall down their basement stairs. Though her teacher let it go, Erin knew she didn't believe her story. But like the rest of the adults in her young life, she didn't report the abuse.

That last night at home had been like no other. Around midnight, Daddy had come home so drunk he passed her bedroom, going to his own, and collapsing on the bed next to her mother. A short time later, her brother came to her. He was running away and asked Erin if she'd like to join him. Jumping at the chance, she threw some clothes into a duffle bag, crept out of the house, and got into his old Ford Mustang.

Slipping the key into the ignition, her brother paused, turned to her and said, "Erin, do you want me to kill him?" He asked the question as nonchalantly as he would ask what she needed at the grocery store.

Only considering his question for a second, Erin responded, "May I watch?"

Going back into the house, they stopped in the kitchen where her brother withdrew her mother's sharpest butcher knife from the silverware drawer. Turning to Erin, he whispered, "What about Mommy?"

"It would be cruel to let her live. How would she survive? She's depended on the bastard for years," she'd responded. "It's almost like a mercy killing."

On tiptoes, they crept down a small hallway until they reached

177

their parents' room and quietly opened the door. On the bed, illuminated by a wash of light from the nightlight in the adjoining bathroom, their two parents slept, unaware that their time on earth was about to end. Her brother slid next to the bed and his arm shot up in a blur, coming down again and again as the butcher knife sliced into Mommy's chest and neck. In a drunken stupor, her father didn't even stir as their mother's body thrashed about in the throes of death.

As her brother moved to her father's side of the bed, Erin followed him and stood so close she could feel the heat of his body, her heart pumping wildly in her chest. He stood over their father for only a moment and then made a clean sweep with the knife, cutting his throat from ear-to-ear. It was the most gratifying experience of her life, and she'd relived it again and again in her dreams.

Her brother became her hero and Master that night, saving her from a demon who would never hurt her again.

The slam of a car door outside pulled her out of her reverie. The Master was home.

Brody and Carly were cleaning up in the kitchen and were nearly finished when Carly backed him up against the refrigerator.

"Just so you know, I'm not a big fan of waiting," she whispered.

Pressing against him until he could feel the hard nipples of her breasts, Carly pulled him into a hungry kiss that turned into a full contact, wet-tongued, tonsil-probing kiss that made his head reel.

His breathing ragged, Brody lifted his head to gaze down at her, before crushing her mouth with his, spinning her around so that she was now pressed against the refrigerator. A rush of desire clawed and clutched at his insides as Carly tugged at his shirt and worked her hands beneath it, pressing her long fingers into the ropes of muscle in his back. A little purr that sounded in her throat enticed him to draw the kiss out.

Pausing to tame his rapid breathing and heartbeat, he picked her up and carried her to the kitchen table and struggled with the buttons on her shirt as she did the same with his, until they were skin against skin with her long legs wrapped around his hips, his throbbing cock aligned perfectly against her sex. He wasn't sure where he began and she left off. But there was one thing he was absolutely certain of. He wanted her like he'd wanted no other woman. Brody kissed her ribs, her cleavage, each sweet breast, and finally her mouth, kissing her with toe-curling determination as his erection throbbed like a toothache.

Pulling the zipper of her pants, he lowered them to her ankles, threw them to the floor, and then made quick work of his jeans. Carly worked her hands behind her back to unfasten her bra, and Brody rewarded her efforts by drawing on her nipples, sucking, tonguing, and teasing until she threw her head back and moaned aloud with erotic pleasure.

His thoughts fragmented as her hands and lips continued their hungry search of his body. In a raw act of possession, Carly tilted her hips to receive him and took his rock-hard, velvet-like steel into her fingers and led him to her.

An electric shock seared through his body as he entered her. He heard a tiny moan catch in her throat as he grasped her bottom. Her nails digging into his shoulders, Carly arched hungrily up to meet his next thrust, and his next, clinging to him, sinking into his body as the hot tide of passion raged through them both. Thrill after thrill shot through him as he possessed her body. Never had he experienced such intense chemistry before. The sexual tension built and built until the earth fell away, and he went with her to that place of rapture, utterly consumed.

8 CHAPTER EIGHT

In the early morning light, Brody lay next to Carly and watched her as she slept. She'd rocked his world the night before, again and again. Loving her physically had already led to loving her emotionally. Carly had awakened something within him that hadn't been touched in years. The more time he spent with her, the harder it was going to be to let her leave at the end of her job, if that's what she chose to do.

Brushing some silken strands of hair from her eyes, he watched as eyelashes fluttered and a smile spread across her face. She cuddled closer to him and ran a smooth hand down his back.

"Good morning, sleepyhead," he whispered, as he kissed the top of her head. Levering himself up on his elbow, he traced the shape of her face with his finger.

"Good morning, Brody," Carly said with a smile that lit up her face. "May I ask you a question?"

"Like I could stop your inquisitive mind if I wanted to," Brody replied, as he kissed her forehead. "What do you want to know?"

Propped up on her elbow, she asked, "How do you feel about me?"

"Do you mean besides the mind-blowing sex and the fact I can't keep my hands off your unbelievably sexy body?" He asked with a slow, sensual smile, as he snaked a strong arm around her waist to press her against his hard body.

"I'm serious, Brody," she returned.

"Sorry. Talking about my feelings is not my forte," he said as he lay back and stared at the ceiling.

"How do you feel about me?" Carly asked again.

"I think I'm falling in love with you, and it scares the crap out of me. How's that for honesty?" Brody said as he turned on his side and ran his hand down her back to her bottom. "What about you?"

"I'm way past thinking about it. I *know* I'm in love with you," whispered Carly, as she stared into his eyes, as if she were trying to determine what he was thinking. "And it scares the crap out of me, too."

"I guess you'll be making a big decision at the end of the job — go back to Florida or stay here with me in Indiana," Brody said as he rolled on top of her, bracing his weight on his elbows and subtly shifting so the hot, hard ridge of his erection was cradled snugly between her thighs.

"Just so you know," he said in a husky whisper as he looked down into her eyes. "I can be very, very persuasive."

Erin lay quietly in her bed listening to her brother slam cabinet doors, along with pots and pans in the kitchen. He'd never been a morning person and could be especially nasty, so she pretended to sleep until he left the house for work.

The night before she'd told him there might be something wrong with one of the slaves. Flippantly, he replied, "Why don't you tell somebody who cares?" Claiming he was dead-tired, he'd taken a shower and gone straight to bed.

Maybe the girl was better this morning, she thought. Sometimes all it took was a good night's sleep. Daddy had beaten her just as hard, and she'd survived it.

Once she heard the back door slam, signaling her brother had left for work, she got out of bed to make breakfast. Getting into the refrigerator, she pulled out a carton of eggs and a container of bacon. After pouring herself a cup of coffee, she fried up scrambled eggs and bacon and scooped them into two plastic containers and on a plate for herself.

Sitting at the small kitchen table, she ate her breakfast looking out the window and wondering how she'd fill her lonely day. She was tiring of spending her days out in the sticks with no one to talk to. One would think after five years, she'd be used to it.

There were times when she thought about having conversations with the slaves, but then she reconsidered. That would make her as stupid as her brother often told her she was. People were often identified as committing crimes by their voices alone, her brother had warned her. So she kept her mouth shut and stayed away from the slaves. Besides, she didn't want to have another little incident like the one that resulted in her shooting two of them.

Erin wanted a job — any job that would get her out of the house and off the farm. Her brother, the Master, vehemently disagreed. He said he could support his little sister and didn't want her to have to work, but Erin reasoned he didn't trust her to have friends at work she might confide in. Friends could find out things they shouldn't know and contact the police. Then she and her brother would find themselves spending the rest of their lives in prison or on the wrong side of a needle.

Finishing her breakfast, she laid the dirty dishes in the sink, picked up the plastic containers of eggs and bacon, and opened the basement door. Once downstairs, she noticed Alison was awake and watching her as she huddled beneath a quilt at the far end of her crate. The other girl lay in the same position as she'd seen her the day before.

Unlocking Alison's padlock, she opened the door and slipped her stun gun out of her pocket. Erin used it to point to the small bathroom at the end of the room. The girl knew the drill, nodded, and crawled out of the crate. Erin followed Alison to the bathroom and stood in the door while the girl did her business. Once Alison finished washing her hands at the sink, she hesitated, as if she were considering her next move. Erin shoved the stun gun at her and Alison went reluctantly but quietly back to her cage. Pushing the plastic container of eggs and bacon across the floor of Alison's crate, she locked the padlock and headed toward the next cage.

The slave named Jasmine, curled up in a fetal position, and hadn't moved an inch since the day before. Slipping the stun gun back into her pocket, she unlocked the padlock, opened the door, and poked at the girl with her finger. Jasmine didn't respond. Deciding to investigate further, Erin pulled Jasmine to her by her ankles. Once Jasmine's body was close enough, she tried to find a pulse. Not only was there no pulse, but the girl's body was ice cold. The girl was dead!

Erin backed out of the dog crate and scrambled up the stairs until she reached the kitchen. Where was her cell phone? She had to call her brother. She raced to her bedroom to get her cell out of her purse when she heard a loud pounding on the side door.

Slipping into the kitchen, she peeked out the window to see a Shawnee County Sheriff patrol car parked in the driveway. Her blood turned to ice. Did the cops know what they'd done, what they were doing? Breathing in shallow, quick gasps, panic sliced through her like a knife. Oh, God. They know. They know.

Glancing toward the back door, she wondered if she should run for it. There was a handgun in a kitchen drawer. Using the element of surprise, should she kill the deputy? Erin cursed her brother for not being there when she needed him. He would know what to do. Damn it. The deputy pounded on the door a second time, the sound echoing through the empty house. She froze for a moment, collected herself, and went to the kitchen for the handgun. Slipping it into the pocket of her sweatpants, she walked to the door and opened it.

Tall and slender, a deputy who looked young enough to still be in high school, stood before her, with one hand resting on the gun in his holster.

"Good morning. I'm Deputy Jeffrey Walker with the Shawnee County Sheriff's Office," he began. "We're trying to find a missing girl and could use your help."

"Missing girl?" Erin managed to get out, and then crossed her arms tightly across her breasts praying he wouldn't notice how badly her hands were shaking.

"Yes, we're looking for Alison Brown," he said, as he pulled a photograph out of his file and handed it to her. "She's thirteen-years-old and missing from Indianapolis. We have reason to believe she's in this area."

Erin's heart froze as she looked down at the photograph in her hand. Why yes, she'd seen Alison Brown, about five minutes earlier in a dog cage in her basement. Sweat dotted her brow as she handed the photo back to the deputy.

"No, I can't say I've seen her," she said, as she fought the urge to shoot him, or turn and bolt.

Forcing the photo back into her hand, the deputy said, "Take a better look. You may have seen the girl in town somewhere while you were shopping for groceries, or eating in a restaurant."

Feeling the deputy's eyes on her, Erin looked down at the photo again. Sure enough, it was the slave called Alison, grinning from ear-to-ear in what looked like a school photo. Of course, since the girl had arrived at the farmhouse, there had been few reasons to grin. "No, I'm sure I haven't seen her, but if I do, I'll call you right away."

Erin started to close the door, but the deputy stopped her.

"If I could keep you another minute or so," the deputy said. "I have another photo I'd like you to see." Once he inserted Alison's photo back into his file, he withdrew another one and handed it to her. "This picture is a little hard to make out because we took it from a surveillance videotape from a camera at the Greyhound Bus Station."

Glancing down at the photograph in her hand, Erin couldn't believe what she was seeing. Though it was a little blurred and grainy, it was definitely her in the photo at the Greyhound Bus Station the day she picked up Alison Brown. Luckily, the hood on Erin's sweatshirt blocked a direct view of her face. Distinctly remembering her brother telling her the security cameras in the bus station were fake, she cursed him. Who's stupid now, big brother?

As casually as she could manage, she said, "No, I haven't seen this woman either. Who is she?"

"We're looking for her in connection to Alison Brown's disappearance," he replied.

A new wave of apprehension swept over her in response to his steady, suspicious gaze. Her hands started shaking anew, and she clenched one hand so hard her nails cut into the palm.

"I wish I could help. Like I said, I'll call if I see either of them," Erin said, now holding onto the handle of the gun in her pocket.

"We'd appreciate it," offered the deputy, as he shoved the photo back into his file. Turning, he strode back to his patrol car, and got inside.

Relieved, Erin closed the door and leaned against it as she choked back a cry, but her relief was short-lived as she peered out the kitchen window. In his vehicle, the deputy was writing something down as he periodically glanced back at the house. What the hell was he doing? Now he was talking to someone on his cell phone. Was he calling for backup? Would the house soon be surrounded by armed deputies? Was he calling for a search warrant? What a career-making move that would be with one dead girl and the one he's looking for caged in the basement. Erin was torn between watching the deputy in her driveway and racing to her bedroom to get her cell phone to call her brother.

Suddenly, she heard the roar of the patrol car's engine as the vehicle started and backed out of the driveway. When she was sure the deputy was gone, she sprinted to the bathroom, huddled over the toilet, and vomited.

Finished shaving, Earl Haas stood back to admire himself in his bathroom mirror. Okay, so he wasn't fifteen, but he still had a lot to offer a thirteen- year-old girl. At five feet eleven inches tall, he was slender without an ounce of fat on his body, and still attractive enough to get a second glance from the women who rode on his bus. Too bad, a woman wasn't what got him off. He liked his sex partners young, nubile, vulnerable, and inexperienced. Earl was just the guy to show them the ropes in the bedroom.

Retrieving a bottle of beer out of his refrigerator in the kitchen, Earl went to the computer on his desk in the living room. He could think of no better thing to do on his day off than to sweet-talk little honeys in the comfort of his living room. First, he'd scour his usual sites like Facebook, MySpace and Teen Chat for girls who posted personal profiles that included their names, physical descriptions, telephone numbers, and best of all, photographs. One would think, in this day and age, that this kind of information would be harder for him to find. Luckily for him, there were still lonely-as-hell preteen girls out there who provided it all with abandon. Just asking for it.

Currently, he had three such girls on the line. One girl was getting close to agreeing to meet up with him for sex; another had just emailed a couple of nude photos of herself that had sent him flying to the bathroom to masturbate.

Little did the girl know the photos put her in his complete control, just where he wanted her. She'd have sex with him or he'd threaten to post those naked photos all over the Internet. The last girl he'd successfully seduced met with him in Indianapolis, and he'd had some of the best sex of his life in the back seat of his car parked behind a closed O'Charley's restaurant. He was getting hard just thinking about it. He'd gotten tired of the girl, however, after the third hook up when she wouldn't quit crying for him to stop, blubbering the whole time. Returning her naked photos, he told her to keep her mouth shut about the hookups because he still had some negatives, not that she even knew his real name. He wasn't stupid, and he sure wasn't about to spend any more time in prison for screwing a little preteen bitch who had it coming to her.

The third girl was a thirteen-year-old knock-out with long, silky black hair and dark eyes he'd found on TeenChat. @SweetTeen was a new contact for him, and the girl had a lot of potential. Immediately attracted to her, he could visualize her begging him for more in his bed, and he'd be more than happy to give it to her.

Online today, he'd try again to persuade her to join him for a *Twilight* movie festival at a local theater. Such a festival didn't exist, but she wouldn't know that until she'd arrived in Morel. Maybe he'd send her a webcam so she could take some photos of herself. He'd sure like to see this little beauty without her clothes.

As usual for lunch time, Mollie's cafe was bustling with downtown retailers, employees from the Sheriff's Office, and anyone else who wanted a quick and tasty meal. Perhaps she was imagining it, but it seemed to Carly that Mollie made a beeline for their group as soon as she saw Cameron standing near the cash register. He and Mollie teased each other and chatted all the way to the table she'd saved for them, which made Carly even more curious. She'd been told early on that Mollie didn't take reservations.

Once they were all sitting with menus in front them, Mollie flashed a big smile at Cameron, Brody, and Gabe, but simply nodded at Carly. What was she? Chopped liver? In the scheme of things, Carly thought, the gorgeous men at her table oozed testosterone, so what hot-blooded female would behave any differently?

Just as she considered her options on the menu, a light tap on her shoulder made her turn to see Mollie's fourteen-year-old daughter, Hailey, standing with a girl who looked about the same age.

The girl had heavily moussed, spiked and dyed blue-black hair and a small silver ring piercing the edge of her upper lip.

"Hi, girlfriend," Carly said to Hailey. "How are you?"

Blushing, Hailey pointed to the girl beside her. "Carly, I'd like you to meet my best friend, Christy Hilton."

"It's nice to meet you," Christy said before she turned to Hailey. "Is she the FBI agent you were telling me about?"

Hailey poked Christy in the ribs and whispered, "Yes."

"Wow, that is so cool," Christy said to Carly. "I want to be an FBI agent when I grow up. Can I see your gun?"

Hailey gasped and said, "Christy, you're embarrassing me."

"No, it's okay," Carly said as she pushed back her navy blazer for a moment to reveal her Glock in its holster.

The girls stared in awe, inspiring Cameron to say, "Why haven't you girls ever asked to see *my* gun?"

"Oh, you're just a local detective, Mr. Chase," Hailey replied.

"Thanks," said Cameron, pretending to be insulted.

"Are you coming over again tonight to see Mom?" asked Hailey and all eyes focused on Cameron.

Cameron cleared his throat and said, "Hailey, I'll bet you're here to take our drink orders. I'll have a Coke."

Hailey took the rest of their drink orders and headed back to the kitchen, her friend in tow.

Gabe, who was sitting next to Cameron, pointedly held out his hand. "I believe you owe me five bucks."

Digging in his back pocket for the money, Cameron slapped a

five dollar bill in Gabe's hand.

"Do I dare ask what the bet was about?" asked Brody as he tried to smother a smile.

"No," Cameron insisted.

Hailey returned to the table with their drinks, along with Mollie who quickly took their orders.

After a gulp of his sweet tea, Gabe said, "I had some time to look at the Internet habits of the four girls found in the shallow graves. It seems all four had profiles on MySpace, Facebook, and Teen Chat. They also frequented Craigslist on a regular basis."

"Just like Amanda and Sophia," Carly said with a sigh. "I'm curious, Gabe. How much personal information did they give in their profiles?"

"All four girls included their ages, physical descriptions, and phone numbers. Two of them posted multiple photographs, some of which were pretty suggestive."

Brody shook his head and commented, "An online predator's wish come true."

"Unfortunately," Gabe agreed.

Brody asked Cameron, "What did you find out when you interviewed the passengers on Alison Brown's bus?"

"Alison must be a quiet, low-key girl because out of the eleven passengers I interviewed, only one remembered her and that's because she sat next to her the entire trip."

"Really?" asked Carly leaning forward in her chair.

"Yes. Mrs. Henderson traveled on the bus to be in Morel for

the birth of her first grandchild. She said she and Alison talked during the trip, but only if Mrs. Henderson initiated the conversation. She said for most of the trip, Alison read a young adult romance on her laptop. Mrs. Henderson couldn't remember the title. She said at one point, Alison asked her questions about Morel, and what it would be like to live here."

"Alison's questions about Morel are telling," said Carly. "It makes me think our killer romanced Alison. She wanted to know about Morel because she planned to live here with him."

"That's a hell of an important decision to make based on an online suitor," exclaimed Brody.

"I know, but consider that teens and preteens spend hours and hours chatting with online friends. Most of them are having problems at school or at home and get caught up with these online friends who appear to completely understand what they are going through. Before long, the online relationships turn into romances, and the kids get involved with something dangerous when the online buddy turns into their boyfriend or girlfriend."

In a small booth at the other end of the restaurant, the Master ate his lunch and watched the sheriff's group with interest. It pissed him off that once again, he was too far from them to hear what they were saying, and he desperately needed information about where they were on their serial killer case. None of the cops he hung out with knew a thing. They said the sheriff was keeping most of the investigation on a need-to-know basis.

Draining the rest of his tea from his glass, he shook it to make the ice rattle to get the waitress's attention. Not noticing, the waitress headed back toward the kitchen, but soon a young girl appeared with a refill.

"Thank you very much," he said in a smooth, sexy drawl as he scanned her from head-to-toe, appreciating her seductive young body and wholesome good looks. Eyeing her name tag, he remarked, "Hailey is a pretty name for a pretty girl."

Blushing, Hailey said, "Thank you. Is there anything else I can bring you?"

Looking at his watch, he said, "I have time for dessert. What do you recommend?"

Hailey named off a variety of pies and cakes available.

With his best seductive smile aimed at her, he asked, "Which one is your favorite, Hailey?"

"I really like the chocolate brownie cheesecake that Mom makes," Hailey said with a wide grin that revealed a line of silver braces.

"Then that's what I'll have."

As he watched Hailey walk away, he imagined her naked and hanging by her wrists from the pipe on his basement ceiling and became aroused.

Suddenly, his cell phone chimed announcing a new text so he fished it out of his pocket to look at the display. His damn sister, Erin, had sent him another text. It was the third one in an hour's time. What the hell was wrong with her this time? Erin was getting on his last nerve. She came up with something new to freak out about nearly every day. He'd told her a thousand times not to bother him at work. He called home.

"What?" He growled.

"A deputy came to the house looking for one of the slaves in the basement. He's got a photograph of Alison."

"So what? Unless you took him on a tour of the basement, he's got nothing on either of us."

"There's more," she said, nearly hysterical.

"Spill it," he said impatiently, wishing he were home so he could slap Erin.

"The deputy had a photo of me at the bus station the day I picked up Alison. It's grainy and I had the hood on my sweatshirt pulled up, but it was definitely me."

"What? That's impossible. The surveillance cameras at the bus station are fake."

"Bullshit!" Erin screamed.

Furious, he disconnected the call and tried to calm himself. He'd known about the house-to-house search for Alison Brown, but knew they didn't have search warrants, so he'd dismissed it in his mind as unimportant, so he hadn't given his idiot sister a heads up. The two cops he'd talked to about the search hadn't mentioned any photo taken at the bus station. Damn it. When did that cheap-ass Ernie McBride get real surveillance cameras installed? He should have kept better track of the situation. If he had, he would have known. He couldn't afford these kinds of mistakes. Now the cops had a photo of his sister with Alison Brown. The smart thing for him to do was to kill them both. And when was he anything but smart?

Lying with half of her body inside the dog cage and the other on the outside, Jasmine was dead, her face a frozen mask of pain. Alison wept and cursed the monster who had ended such a sweet girl's life. She'd never hated anyone, not even the bullies who'd made her life miserable at school. But she now hated the Master, and if she had the chance she'd kill him herself. A shimmering wave of pulsing fury clouded everything as she wished the worst for him.

"Jasmine, I am so sorry this happened to you," Alison whispered as she crawled to the end of the cage closest to the girl's body.

Leaning against the cage, Alison closed her eyes. The Master would kill her soon. She'd witnessed him killing Jasmine and her knowledge would be too dangerous for him to let her live. Her blood turned to ice, and she held back the urge to scream.

Sun streamed through the small bathroom window, and a flicker of light cast off something metallic that caught Alison's attention. Lying next to Jasmine's foot was a set of keys. In her haste, the woman must have dropped the keys to the padlocks securing the cages. Shoving her hand through a slat, she discovered she could only push her right hand as far as her index finger knuckle — not far enough to touch the keys. She tried again, this time with her left hand, but no luck. Using both hands, she pulled on the heavy gauge wire in an effort to widen the gap, but it wouldn't budge. Somehow she had to get to the keys before the woman upstairs realized they were gone.

In the opposite end of the crate, Alison noticed the plastic container that held her breakfast. Peeling it open, she removed the lid. Using it, she might be able to reach the keys and pull them toward her.

Sliding the plastic lid through a slat, she wanted to cheer out loud when it touched the end of a key. Although she was unsuccessful with her first attempts, eventually Alison was able to use the lid to pull the keys close to her crate until she was able to grasp them.

Moving to the other end of the crate, Alison held the padlock between two fingers as she worked the key with her other hand. In minutes that seemed like hours, the padlock finally opened, and she pushed out of the crate. Leaning against the crate to steady her legs, Alison remembered the washer and dryer were housed in a small room under the staircase. As fast as her wobbly legs would carry her, she headed for the room. Inside there were clean clothes stacked on top of the dryer, and Alison found a pair of black sweats along with a sweatshirt. She quickly slipped these on and searched the room for a pair of shoes. Finding no shoes, she grabbed a thick pair of men's socks and raced to the bathroom.

Pulling on the socks, she noticed the dingy towel she'd used for her shower was draped over the rod. Alison grabbed it and wound it around her right hand. She then stepped on top of the toilet and punched at the glass in the window several times to no avail. She whacked at the window one more time and the sound of the glass startled her so much she nearly fell off the toilet. Gaining her composure, Alison shook the slivers of glass from the towel and tried to pry the larger slivers out of the window frame. Pulling out most of the larger pieces of glass, she folded the towel and placed it across the lower section of the window frame.

Boosting herself up, she pushed her head and shoulder through the opening. Bracing her hands against the outside wall, she was able to twist the rest of her body through the window and drop to the ground.

Looking to her right, she saw a driveway that led to a small garage, then wound around the property to a red barn. To her left, was a wooded area that seemed to stretch forever. Deciding to take her chances in the woods where she'd at least have some cover, she rushed to the thicket of trees. Alison ran until her lungs burned and her legs ached, fearing if she hesitated for a second, she could be discovered. Sharp pains at her mid-section caused her to stop and lift her sweatshirt to see a long, jagged cut near her belly-button that was bleeding profusely. Alison must have cut herself without realizing it as she shoved through the window.

Pressing against the cut with one hand to stop the bleeding, Alison pushed on, ignoring the briars that caught at her sweats. The only sounds in the quiet woods were her ragged breathing and the crunch of branches and leaves beneath her feet.

Carly opened her laptop in the sheriff's conference room and couldn't believe her eyes. She had over twenty additional respondents to her ad. Spending the next hour hurriedly responding to each one, she went back through her messages looking for anything from Earl Haas. She was not disappointed.

@EarlH: Hi. How is your day going?

@SweetTeen: Great, since I'm hearing from you.

@EarlH: Are you going with me to the *Twilight* movie marathon?

@SweetTeen: I can't go this weekend. My parents are

leaving on Friday to go out of town and I have to stay home alone watching the house.

@EarlH: No kidding. Why don't I bring a six-pack and come over to keep you company?

@SweetTeen: I don't know.

@EarlH: Sure you do. You can't convince me you haven't had a boyfriend over before.

@SweetTeen: Of course, I've had boyfriends.

@EarlH: Sex?

@SweetTeen: Maybe.

@EarlH: Baby, I want to do things to you your old boyfriends never thought of.

@SweetTeen: Really?

@EarlH: Invite me over this Friday night and find out.

@SweetTeen: See you at eight o'clock at my house at 654 Covered Bridge Road in Morel on Friday.

@EarlH: Can't wait to see you.

The Master skidded to a stop in his driveway and sat in the car for a couple of minutes to calm down. Still royally pissed from Erin's call, he waited until pixels of red faded from his eyes. His anger could be a scary thing, even to himself.

Erin was in the kitchen waiting for him when he entered the house.

"The Master is home," he called out, jokingly.

His sister's face was a twisted mask of fear and anxiety. "We're in a lot of trouble. I think the cops are closing in on us," she said as she brushed a tear from her cheek. "They've got my photograph with that slave they're looking for. How long do you think it will take for them to figure everything out?"

"Shut up, Erin," he warned in a low voice.

"Not this time, Master," she spat.

Erin saw only a blur as he raised his hand and struck her across the mouth, knocking her into a kitchen cabinet.

"I knew about the search, and I should have warned you. They didn't have a search warrant, so I dismissed it as being unimportant. They're on a fishing trip. They've got nothing, Erin. Nothing. Can your pea-brain understand that?"

Wiping the blood from her mouth, she said, "What I understand is that they have a photograph of me, but you said the surveillance cameras were fake."

"Gee, Erin," he said sarcastically. "Don't you think the deputy who was standing a foot away from you would have recognized you if the photo hadn't been so grainy?"

Getting some ice from the refrigerator, she filled a plastic sandwich bag, wrapped a dishcloth around it, and pressed it against her lips. "I don't know," she said.

"Well, I do, and he didn't, so stop freaking out. I'm sick of the drama."

"Speaking of drama, I wished you'd checked on the slave last night when I asked you to."

"Why?"

"Because she's dead," Erin replied.

"Are you sure she's dead, or is she sleeping off the beating I gave her?"

"Check for yourself," she said, pointing toward the basement door.

With his sister close behind, he descended the basement steps until he reached the bottom. The first thing he saw was Jasmine's body lying across the opening of her crate. The second thing he saw was the open door of Alison's cage. Where was she?

Furiously, he spun around to face his sister. "Where the fuck is the other slave?"

Her mouth opened in surprise, Erin looked around the room and stammered, "I don't know. She was here at breakfast time in her cage."

"Where are your keys?" he asked, with ice cold fury on his face. He strode to the bathroom, noting the broken window, and then returned to his sister.

"I asked you a question. Where are your fucking keys?" he roared.

Patting both pockets of her sweats, Erin panicked. Her keys were gone.

The Master pulled his gun out of his pocket and shot her point-blank between the eyes. The force of the blast slammed her body against the wall, and then she slid to the floor. One brain-shattering shot and her life was over. Bye-bye, Sis.

Racing up the stairs, he shot out the back door into the yard and tried to figure out which way Alison may have run. Thinking she may be hiding in the barn, he sprinted down the driveway. Taking out his gun, he entered the dark barn and searched every crevice for the girl, but she was not there. Sweating and out of breath, he wiped his forehead with the back of his sleeve, went to the garage and searched it, but Alison was not there either.

Walking to the basement window, he stood before it and thought of what he would do if he'd escaped. He would probably have avoided the driveway, the barn, and the flat fields beside it. There were too many opportunities to spot him. He would have headed for the woods, and he'd bet his last dollar that was the direction Alison went. Grabbing a flashlight from his car, he entered the woods to search for the girl to end her life before she could ruin his.

9 CHAPTER NINE

At six o'clock, Brody, Carly, Cameron, and Gabe arrived at the decoy house on Covered Bridge Road in a white unmarked van. The house was a new, red-brick two story on a cul-de-sac lot in an upscale community. Brody opened the garage door and pulled the van inside to hide it.

Once inside, Gabe installed temporary wiring for a digital camera to record the events, as well as a closed-circuit television. Watching the television on the kitchen bar, they could see anyone approaching the driveway, the front yard, or the front door. The house was staged to lure buyers with designer furniture, so Carly set about turning on lamps on both floors to make it look like someone was home. Cameron had talked to the neighbors days before, and most of them had chosen to go away for the weekend, with the exception of seventy-six-year-old Clarence Jackson, who planned to set his telescope up to watch the action. Three of the neighbors offered their garages to hide deputies in patrol cars who would take each perp to the county jail after he'd been arrested and read his rights.

An estimated twenty-one men were set to arrive that night to have sex with a thirteen-year-old girl — including Earl Haas. Several of the men had asked Carly if she was a law enforcement officer, and they'd believed her when she said she wasn't. A couple of men said openly they thought it was a sting, but were coming anyway, which told Carly a lot about the power their sexual urges had on these predators. They were risking their freedom for the possibility of sex with an underage girl.

Brody asked, "Gabe, do you have the list of party-goers for tonight?

Gabe nodded as he pulled a folder out of his briefcase and handed a stack of papers to his brother.

Brody smiled and said, "Good job. You've got their call names along with their real names and addresses.

"Don't forget the small photographs," offered Gabe with a grin. "I'll pull the list up on my laptop, so we can document anything they bring into the house that can be used as evidence."

"I'll help with that," offered Carly.

Looking at Cameron, she asked, "Anything new on Earl Haas?"

"The surveillance team watching Earl reported the house had been quiet with no signs of underage girls visiting."

Though the news was a relief to Carly, she wondered if Earl had Alison Brown hidden somewhere in the home. Was she still alive? If Earl Haas was the killer, she prayed he had not already murdered Alison and dumped her body somewhere in Shawnee County.

Cameron came in carrying sodas and bottles of water that he

placed in the refrigerator, followed by Brody holding an armful of snacks. It was going to be a long night, but they wouldn't go hungry. Over their shirts, Brody, Carly, Cameron, and Gabe wore black bullet-proof vests with white letters spelling S-H-E-R-I-F-F on the back. They were taking no chances, in case any of these men were armed.

Setting up her laptop in the kitchen, Carly logged onto her Internet account and visited each site her ad was posted on. There were a few new respondents, but no messages from the men who were coming to the house that night. Gabe joined her at the bar and opened his laptop, planning to do some work before the men started arriving.

Brody opened the refrigerator and handed Carly, Cameron, and Gabe bottles of water. The group was filled with anticipation and adrenalin. They might end their night with the capture of a serial killer. At the very least, they'd arrest sexual predators and prevent them from victimizing more young girls. Carly felt good about the operation. Going after predators who prowl the Internet for victims helped keep real children from being abused. She was all for that.

Around seven-thirty, Carly noticed movement on the closed-circuit television, and motioned for Brody. "Our first party-goer is here."

Brody and Cameron rushed to the front door, waiting for the doorbell to ring. From the back patio, Gabe circled around to the side of the house for backup. The doorbell rang and the men sprang into action. Brody flung open the door, and Cameron grabbed the arm of a short, wiry-built man in his late twenties as Gabe rushed up behind him.

Brody shouted, "Shawnee County Sheriff! Stop!"

The second the man heard the word "sheriff" he stopped in his tracks and began sobbing hysterically, tears spurting out of his eyes and streaming down his cheeks.

"Don't do this," he cried as he struggled to free himself. Cameron pressed him against the foyer wall and secured his wrists with handcuffs.

Skimming down Gabe's list, Carly identified the man as Aaron, who used the call name @AHOTGUY.

"His name is Aaron Walls," announced Carly. "He's twenty-nine years old, a full-time grad student at Purdue, and a part-time karate instructor for the After-School Program at Shawnee County Parks and Recreation. He drove here from West Lafayette."

Then with Cameron holding one arm and Brody grasping the other, Gabe asked, "So what did you bring to the party, Aaron?" Pointing at Aaron's jeans pockets, he asked, "Any needles or anything sharp in your pockets?"

Still wailing and begging them to let him go home, Aaron shook his head emphatically.

Gabe pulled items out of Aaron's pockets, announcing each one as he handed them to Carly for evidence bags. "Ten condoms stuffed in his wallet. Oh, what's this?" He asked as he pulled out a small plastic bag filled with marijuana.

Cameron pulled out his cell phone to call the deputy parked in a garage around the corner to come get their first arrest.

They'd barely gotten Aaron in the back of the patrol car and re-entered the house, when Carly, watching an image on the television, announced, "Get back in position, we have another one. He just pulled into the driveway. Wait a second. He's going back to the car. He got out a bag and is now walking to the front door."

The doorbell sounded, Brody whipped the door open, and Cameron tackled the forty-something man on the front porch. Gabe took the bag from his hands, and Cameron shoved the man against the wall to handcuff him.

"What's your name?" asked Brody as he patted him down, searching for weapons.

"Go to hell. I'm not giving you my name. I haven't done anything wrong," he said angrily.

Cameron pulled the man's wallet from his pocket, and flipped it open to see his driver's license. "This is Clay Dylan, age forty-six. Wait a minute." Turning the man around so he could see his face, Cameron glanced at him and said, "This sonofabitch is Hailey's English teacher at the junior high school. She was just talking about him the other night when I helped her with the essay he assigned."

Opening the paper bag Dylan retrieved from his car, Gabe looked inside and said, "English Teacher Mr. Dylan came to party. Look what we have here." In the paper bag were three adult toys, a pair of handcuffs, and a box of candy-flavored condoms. He handed the items to Carly, who recorded them on Gabe's laptop, and put them into evidence bags.

"You haven't done anything wrong, Mr. Dylan? Did you really just say that?" asked Brody incredulously. "Coming here to use those items on a thirteen-year-old girl isn't wrong? You make me sick."

By nine o'clock, they'd arrested fifteen predators, seven of whom were registered sex offenders. The majority of the men had contacted Carly through Craigslist, but three of them she met on Teen Chat.

Earl Haas had not arrived and Carly was getting worried. Their meet-up time was eight o'clock and he was an hour late. A ding sounding from her laptop drew her attention. It was a message from Earl. He was running late and would be there within ten minutes or so.

"Earl Haas is on his way," she announced to the others. "Are the search warrants ready to implement once we get him in custody?"

"Yes!" Brody and Cameron said simultaneously.

Turning her attention to the television, it was only a few minutes before a man came into Carly's view. On the sidewalk in front of the house, he walked slowly past as he eyeballed the house. Carly sized him up. He looked to be around five feet and ten inches or so, with a slender build which fit Earl's description, but she couldn't be sure it was him. As he continued walking, he disappeared in the darkness. Moments later, he re-appeared in the decoy house driveway. "He's here," said Carly excitedly. Focusing her attention on the television image as the man neared the front door, she announced, "It's Earl Haas!"

Not even waiting for the doorbell, Brody dived out the front door and knocked Earl Haas to the ground. Somehow, Earl slipped out of Brody's grasp and sprinted down the street with Cameron and Gabe on his heels. Once he was close enough to Haas, Cameron tackled him and pinned him to the ground while he fastened handcuffs on his wrists.

"Was that one of your old football moves?" Gabe teased, as he dragged Haas to his feet.

"Yup, and I'm happy to find it still works," Cameron returned, as he grinned with amusement.

Back at the house, Cameron pressed Earl against the wall while Brody patted him down for weapons.

"Listen," Earl began, "I don't know what's going on, but all I did was come to this house to ask for directions. I got lost."

"You're not lost, Earl," said Carly. "You're exactly where you planned to be, at the house where you thought you'd have sex with a thirteen-year-old girl."

The Master continued his search for his slave named Alison. The sun had gone down an hour or so ago and the dark of night in the thicket of trees made the landscape barely visible. The girl could be hiding behind a tree, and he wouldn't even see her, unless she made a sound.

The woods were dangerous at night, even with a flashlight. The landscape seemed determined to stop him. Overhanging limbs crossed his path, seen at the last second. Rock outcroppings, ravines, or tree stumps were undetectable, too hidden to avoid. He'd already twisted his ankle after catching a root, falling to the ground hard, ripping his pants. Driven by an unrelenting fury, he ventured forward, determined to capture the girl.

Things were unraveling, and the threat to his power and control was unacceptable. It wasn't in his plan to kill his sister, but what choice did he have? She'd become a liability, and liabilities were too dangerous to allow to exist. And then there was the dead slave. Though not his first victim, Jasmine was the first to die as a result of one of his beatings. His anger was getting more difficult to control, and he was making mistakes that could get him caught.

Thinking back to the restaurant earlier, a visual of the Chase brothers, along with their bitch profiler, appeared in his mind. What a fun lunch they seemed to be having — joking, laughing and planning his demise. He'd make them pay for crossing the Master. One by one, he'd make them pay, especially the asshole sheriff and his little profiling girlfriend. He'd spend more time focusing on a plan to abduct, torture, and kill Carly Stone, with Brody Chase watching helplessly, before he got snuffed out, too.

The crack of a snapping twig stopped him in his tracks. He was not alone. Aiming the flashlight in the direction of the sound, he strained to see. Suddenly, a huge antlered deer rammed into him in his haste to escape a predator, knocking the Master backward to the ground with a painful thud. Lying there for a moment, trying to catch his breath, the Master struggled to his feet, crying out as a sharp pain exploded in the middle of his back.

"Damn you, Alison Brown. You bitch!" he roared. "If you can hear me, know that I will find you and kill you, if it's the last thing I do!"

Heading back toward the house, he vowed to return to his search for Alison in the morning light. The little bitch was going down before she had a chance to run her mouth. He wasn't concerned about her identifying Erin or him because they both wore ski masks. The chance she could lead the cops back to his house was a real concern, however, so he had to find her.

Limping and rubbing his back, he snaked his way through the undergrowth until he could see his house in the distance. There'd be no rest for him tonight. He had two bodies to bury in a new place the cops would never find.

Carly and Brody entered the interview room where Earl Haas was waiting at a table, after spending the night in a jail cell. Brody leaned against the wall behind Earl's chair, and then introduced Carly as the officer who would conduct the interview. Carly sat down directly across the table from Earl, placing her folders on the table.

"I hear you like little girls, Earl," Carly said.

"Baby, with a looker like you, I could change my mind," Earl offered as he stared at her suggestively.

Brody kicked the back of Earl's chair to get his attention, and said, "Show a little respect."

Carly glanced at Brody with surprise. They hadn't discussed playing bad cop, good cop, but she was game.

Earl swung around to glare at Brody, the heavy chain attached to his ankles, clanging against the metal table leg.

"As you know, Earl, last night we implemented a search warrant on your house and workplace. At your house, we made some interesting discoveries. You've been a busy and bad boy," said Carly. "We found over a hundred nude photographs of underage girls." Retrieving a thick stack of pages from her file and placing them on the table, she added, "These are transcripts of conversations with you and underage girls you found on the Internet, some of them as young as eleven or twelve-years-old."

"Oh, shit," Earl mumbled as he scrubbed his hands over his face.

"Believe me when I say we already have our detectives searching for these girls, and they will interview each and every one of them. I, for one, can't wait to hear what they have to say."

Shaking his head, Earl sat back in his chair and stared at his hands in his lap.

"We already had you for traveling to meet a minor for sex and soliciting a minor for sex, charges that will send a registered sex offender like you away for a long, long time. But with this new evidence, that long time may stretch into infinity."

"What do you want from me?"

"The truth."

Carly pulled out a stack of photographs that gained Earl's attention. She then slowly slapped each one down in a horizontal row before him, as if she were setting up for a Solitaire card game. With each photo, she paused to say the victim's name, ending with the last photograph, which was Amanda Jenkins.

Staring down at the photos, Earl stammered, "What the..."

"Shut up until you're asked a question, Haas." Brody growled, delivering another kick to the back of the suspect's chair.

"Contrary to what the sheriff thinks of you, Earl," Carly began. "I think you're a very smart guy. It takes a high degree of intelligence to do what you've been doing for years without suspicion."

"Doesn't take that much smarts to be smarter than the county cops," Earl said as he sneered at her.

Carly nodded, as if in agreement. "Yes, you're certainly smarter than us law enforcement types, who had no idea who you were and what you were doing."

"What are you talking about?" Earl asked pointing at the photos. "Who are these girls?"

"Oh, c'mon, Earl. Don't be shy on my account," Carly said. "I know you're dying to take credit. I mean, you're the man."

Earl shrugged his shoulders. "I've got no clue what you're talking about, Lady. I repeat, who are these girls?"

"Let me introduce you to them again, just to refresh your memory," Carly said, as she tapped the first photo with a long fingernail. "Meet Sydney Jackson. She was thirteen when she disappeared three years ago. Before that, she lived with her parents in Knightstown."

"So?" Earl muttered.

"Keep quiet, Earl, until you're asked a question," snarled Brody, behind him.

Moving to the next photograph, Carly said, "You remember Alysa Benjamin, right? She was fourteen-years-old when she ran away to be with you four years ago."

Saying nothing, Earl visibly gritted his teeth and scowled at her.

Carly described each victim. When she got to Amanda Jenkins, she said, "Earl, you must remember Amanda."

Earl picked up Amanda's photograph to get a closer look. "Okay, this one *does* look familiar. I might have seen her online, but I don't know her personally."

"Sure you do, Earl. A year-and-a-half ago, you transported Amanda to Morel in the Greyhound bus you drive," Carly said. "And once you had her here, you kept her against her will. You raped and tortured her, then shot her point blank in the back of her head. Then you put her, along with Sophia Bradford, in a car you set on fire to hide your crimes."

Earl jumped to his feet and screamed, "That's fucking bullshit. What the hell is going on here?"

Brody pushed off the wall to intervene, but Carly held up her hand to him to signal for him to stop.

In a hard, cold voice, Carly said, "Sit down, and don't raise your voice to me again."

Earl slunk down in his seat, shooting Carly a decidedly nasty grin.

"Oh, I almost forgot. I have one more photo to show you," said Carly, as she pulled it out of her folder. "This is Alison Brown. She's missing and before you leave this room, you're going to tell me where she is."

"Listen," Earl begged. "Alison Brown rode my bus from Indianapolis. I remember her. I also remember that Amanda girl riding on my bus, but I swear to God, I don't know who these other girls are. I swear."

Alison continued to make her way through the woods, stopping periodically to check the long, jagged cut near her belly button, which continued to bleed despite her efforts to stop the bleeding. Her socks, now torn and covered by twigs and burrs, provided little protection for her feet.

Resting a while, Alison sat down and leaned against the trunk of a huge tree. Though it was only fifty degrees or so, she swiped at her sweaty face, and tugged at the sweatshirt sticking to her midsection. Although she felt as if every muscle in her body was crying out for relief, she refused to stop. She couldn't stop until she found help. Exhaustion was creeping in, along with a sense of weakness. If only she could stem the bleeding.

The forest was a scary place at night, filled with sounds of creaking tree trunks, hooting of owls, the cries of prey caught in the jaws of predators, and calls of coyotes and wild dogs. She shuddered to think what a pack of wild animals might do to her. Alison was a city girl who had never camped or ventured out much after dark. Without a flashlight or a full moon to guide her, there were times when she groped blindly in the dark using her outstretched arms to guide her.

Shoving the terror of an animal attack to the back of her mind wasn't difficult. All she had to do was to think of what the Master would do to her if he caught her. That couldn't happen. She'd get help, and once she could talk to the police, she'd do everything in her power to lead them to the Master and the woman who helped him.

Bracing against the tree, she pulled herself to her feet. It was time to move on. Pressing her hand against her tummy, she hiked for an hour or so before stopping again. Aching and hurting so much she could barely breathe, she leaned against a tree, not trusting she could get up again if she sat down.

Thinking of the last time she saw Jasmine alive, swinging near the ceiling by the wrists as the Master whipped her small body bloody, Alison bit back a sob rattling in her chest. If only she could have done something...

She froze as she heard the sounds of branches snapping and dried leaves crunching. Someone was moving toward her, and there was little time to hide. Diving behind a wide tree, she pulled the black hood of her sweatshirt over her head, curled her body into a ball, and prayed whoever or whatever was approaching would not find her.

Crackling of undergrowth continued until it stopped abruptly, very close to where she was hiding. Holding her breath, she froze, willing herself not to move and give away her location. Something warm and heavy bumped against her, and Alison turned her head to look straight into the eyes of the biggest German Shepherd she'd ever seen. Sitting on his haunches, the dog licked her face and began happily panting as if she were a long-lost friend.

Hesitantly, she touched the dog's soft fur. He didn't bite her, so she stroked his back as he inched closer.

"Who are you, and where do you live?" Alison asked, wishing dogs could talk. "I know you're not Lassie or one of those super-smart rescue dogs, but do you think you could lead me to your house?"

The large dog inched still closer until he was almost on her lap, seemingly delighted that she was now rubbing and scratching his ears. Feeling his neck for a collar, she was pleased to find he was wearing one, complete with metal tags. The dog was in good shape, and obviously had a home, which she prayed was nearby. She didn't know how much longer she could continue walking.

Pulling herself back on her feet, Alison moved in the direction from which the dog had come. He bounded ahead of her as if he thought they were playing a game. Barely keeping up, Alison struggled to keep the dog in her sight.

Soon she saw the beam of an outside light. Moving closer she saw a farmhouse and nearly cried out with joy. Alison was so tired and weak, the short distance to the house seemed miles away to her. Feeling dizzy, faint, and nauseated, Alison could barely put one foot in front of the other. She was nearing a structure that turned out to be a large dog house. In front of it, the German Shepherd stood, wagging his tail. She leaned on it for a second, to gather strength to move forward. Sweating profusely, she began to feel a cold chill throughout her body as her legs weakened so badly she could barely stand. Dropping to her knees, Alison crawled into the dog house, seconds before losing consciousness.

Moments before, Cameron pulled Carly and Brody out of Earl Haas' interview. They sat in the conference room discussing the case.

"I don't think he's our killer," said Cameron, as he rubbed his head.

"Why not?" Brody asked. "The bastard looks good for it to me."

"I don't know," said Carly. "If he was our killer, why would he admit to knowing Amanda and Alison, but not the others?"

"He's got an alibi for most of the early murders. Right out of prison, he worked on a construction crew for a new classroom building at Purdue. We found witnesses who place him at work every day, including the weekends," Cameron stated. "After he dropped off Amanda and Alison, Haas hooked up with two separate underage girls. We've talked to both of them, and they've agreed to testify against him."

"What did the girls have to say about him?" asked Carly.

"They both said he begged them to send him naked pictures of themselves. He wouldn't let up about it. Earl even sent one of them a new web cam," Cameron began. "Then once they sent the photos, he told them if they didn't have sex with him, he'd post the pictures on the Internet and deliver copies to their parents."

"What a sick freak," Brody exclaimed, shaking his head in disgust.

"Totally agree with you on that one," Cameron said. "One of them was only eleven when she had sex with him in the back of a car on four separate occasions."

"Earl is a registered sex offender. Add these new charges to the ones he earned from the sex predator sting, and this guy's going away for a long time."

"Earl Haas rotting in a jail cell sounds like the best deal I've heard in forever," said Carly.

Hal and Bettye Locke had run their farm for nearly thirty years, having purchased it just before their wedding. His wife, Bettye, loved their farm probably as much as she loved Hal. Him and Lucky, the German Shepherd they'd rescued from the dog pound three years ago. That's why Hal was wandering around on his property at a God-forsaken four in the morning looking for Lucky, who every morning but this one, practically tore down the screen door to get to his breakfast. If anything happened to that dog ... Well, Hal didn't even want to think about that.

He'd searched the barn, shed, garden, and front yard. Hal was headed toward the doghouse the dog never liked or stayed in, when he noticed a long, furry gray tail, along with a set of human feet sticking out of the dog house. What in the hell was going on?

Reaching the dog house, he pulled out his flashlight and bent down to get a better look. What looked like a young girl was curled into a fetal position, with Lucky's body wrapped around her, like he was trying to keep her warm, and it looked like Lucky had no intention of moving. Tapping the girl's ankle, Hal heard a soft moan, but she didn't stir. Repositioning himself to look from a different angle, he aimed the flashlight directly at the girl and saw there was blood all over her, Lucky, and the floor of the dog house. Hal's heart froze and his knees started to shake as he pulled his cell phone out of his pocket.

"Bettye, call nine-one-one and tell them to get an ambulance out here as quick as they can! There's a girl out here in Lucky's doghouse, and she's bleeding all over the place!"

It was Carly's turn to make coffee, and she planned to surprise Brody with some of the crazy-delicious Italian blend coffee Blake had given her for Christmas. Pouring the dark brew into two mugs on a tray, she added the sugar bowl and a tiny pitcher of cream next to two chocolate croissants.

Climbing the stairs, she could hear the shower running, along with Brody singing some song she'd never heard before. Judging by his singing voice, the Sheriff should not give up his day job. Grinning from ear to ear, she set the tray down on the bedside table and knocked on the bathroom door.

"Come in," Brody called out.

"How did you know it was me?" Carly teased. "Do you invite just anyone who knocks into your bathroom while you're taking a shower?"

Instead of answering, Brody reached out of the shower, grabbed the belt of her terry-cloth robe, and pulled her inside as she squealed.

"I'm sorry," Brody began. "What was that you were saying? I couldn't hear you."

"Brody Chase, you're getting my hair wet and we're going to be late for work if I have to dry it all over again." Pushing against his chest, she only inspired him to tighten his arms around her waist and kiss her soundly.

Just then Brody's cell phone sounded from the bathroom counter.

"You better get that," Carly said. "It could be the lottery department calling or something."

"Yeah, sure," Brody said, laughing as he wrapped a towel around himself and reached for his cell phone.

"Sheriff Chase," he answered without looking at the display. He was too busy watching Carly drop her robe and pat her skin and hair dry with a towel.

"Sheriff, this is Natalie Jones. I'm a nurse in the Emergency Room at Morel Hospital. We've got a girl in the E.R. who looks a lot like the one in the photo your deputies are flashing around."

"Do you mean the picture of our missing girl, Alison Brown?" Brody asked.

"Yes, that's her name. I remembered her face, but not her name," the nurse began. "The reason I'm calling is that I believe she's just been brought in by an ambulance to the E.R. I'm sure this girl is the one in the photo."

"I'll be right there!" Brody disconnected the call and reached for his uniform hanging on the back of the bathroom door.

"Carly, Alison Brown may be in the E.R. at Morel Hospital. Forget your wet hair and grab your clothes. We need to get down there."

With sirens blaring and lights flashing, Brody pressed the accelerator pedal to the floor as he raced past any vehicles on the state road going less than eighty. He'd prayed for the day they'd find Alison Brown, and that day had come. After a near miss at a stop light, Carly gently touched his arm.

"Honey, slow down. We don't want an accident to prevent us

from seeing Alison," she said, her voice gentle and soft.

"I'm sorry." He slowed his vehicle and reached for Carly's hand. What was he thinking? He had Carly in the car. What would he do if anything happened to her? "Do me a favor and call Cameron on his cell. Tell him to meet us at the E.R."

Fishing for her cell phone in her purse, Carly found it and punched in Cameron's number and left a message on his voice mail when he didn't pick up.

Reaching the hospital, Brody parked and helped Carly out of the vehicle. Hand in hand, they raced across the parking lot, flying through the E.R. automatic doors. They asked the first nurse they saw about Alison.

Overhearing them, a nurse rushed from the nurse's station to greet them.

"I'm Natalie Jones. I'm the one who called," she said. "After we talked, they rushed Alison into the operating room. She has a deep, six-inch gash in her midsection and lost a lot of blood. They've got to sew up that gash and stop the bleeding, or we could lose her."

"What are her chances?" asked Carly.

"Not great. She's lost a lot of blood. I'll send the surgeon out to talk to you as soon as he's finished.

"Okay," Carly replied. "Where should we wait?"

"Let me show you where we have a small waiting area for parents. You can wait there," she said, as she led them down the hall to an area near the operating room.

Brody was too anxious to sit, so he stationed himself at the end of the room, gazing out a long window. Carly joined him, lightly touching the middle of his back.

"She'll make it, Brody. She has to."

Drawing in a deep breath and squeezing Carly's shoulder, Brody said, "Do you realize that girl in the operating room may not even be Alison Brown? All we have is the word of a nurse who didn't even have Alison's photo in front of her when she called."

"That means we get DNA and fingerprints as fast as we can," Carly replied.

Cameron rushed into the room and joined them at the window. "Is it true? Is Alison Brown here?"

"We think so," said Brody, "but we won't know for sure until we can get DNA and fingerprints."

"Where is she?"

"In surgery. The nurse said she'd lost a lot of blood because she has a deep cut near her abdomen."

"If she's that injured, how did she get to the hospital?" Cameron asked.

A large man wearing a plaid flannel shirt with denim overalls waved his arm. He was sitting in a corner near a television by himself. "My name's Hal Locke. I found the girl early this morning sleeping with my German Shepherd, inside his doghouse."

"Doghouse? How long had she been there?" asked Cameron.

"Judging from the amount of blood on her, the doghouse and my dog, Lucky, I'd say all night. It's just a guess, but I'd say she was so weak by the time she reached my farm that she collapsed in the doghouse and Lucky took care of her until I found them."

"How?" Carly asked.

"It dipped below the forties last night, and my German Shepherd wrapped his body around hers to keep her warm; otherwise, she might have died from exposure," Hal said. "We still might lose her from blood loss. I'm sticking around to see if they need blood, and if mine matches."

"Hal, why don't you help me get some coffee for everyone? I want to talk to you about exactly where your farm is, and the routes Alison Brown may have taken to reach it."

Once Cameron and Hal left the room, Carly said, "You know what Cameron's thinking, right?"

"That our killer lives in the vicinity of Hal's farm? Yes. I hope the hell he does," Brody slipped his cell phone out of his pocket. "I'm calling for a crime scene tech to get over here. We need to know if that girl is Alison Brown as soon as she gets out of surgery. After that I'm calling Bryan. He's got DNA samples from a hairbrush that Alison's mother gave him."

"Oh my God. Alison's mother has to know," cried Carly.

"We can't contact her until we know for sure the girl is Alison."

A man in blue scrubs entered the waiting area, noticed Brody's badge, and strode over to them.

"I'm Dr. Nathan Ford."

"Thanks for seeking us out," said Brody. "How is Alison?"

"We were able to clean out the wound, stop the bleeding, and stitch it up. She received a couple of blood transfusions in surgery, and will get more in recovery. Her feet were a mess, covered with small cuts and abrasions. She was wearing only socks when she was found." The doctor paused for a second and then said, "That's not all. Someone did a number on the back of her legs, arms, back, and buttocks. It looks like the kind of injury you would receive if you were struck by a whip multiple times. We went ahead and did a rape kit while she was under."

"Is she going to make it?" asked Carly.

Shrugging his shoulders, he said, "She's lost a lot of blood. Right now, I can't predict if she'll make it or not. Honestly, the odds are against anyone who's lost this much blood. We'll have to wait and see."

"Can we see her?" Brody asked.

"Only one or two people at a time and only for ten minutes or so," the doctor called over his shoulder as he walked out of the room. "I'll send the nurse for you."

In the recovery room, Brody and Carly sat in chairs on either side of the girl's bed. Carly had never seen a victim who looked so small and broken. Gently brushing a strand of the girl's hair out of her eyes, Carly scanned her body for injuries. It seemed that every inch of her young skin was bruised, cut, or scraped. On the back of each of her arms, long, angry abrasions were in various stages of healing. Deep purple bruising circled each wrist. They hadn't conducted DNA testing or fingerprinting, but Carly was convinced the girl in the bed was indeed Alison Brown.

Sitting back down in her chair, a tear slipped from Carly's eyes and spilled down her cheek as she held Alison's hand. Across from her, Brody looked as if he were gritting his teeth together tightly, trying to keep his emotions in control.

Natalie Jones came into the room and whispered to Brody, "Your brother says he needs to talk to you."

"I'll be right there." Pausing to kiss Carly on the forehead, Brody headed for the waiting area to talk to Cameron.

As soon as he arrived, Cameron asked, "Is it Alison?"

"I think so."

"A crime scene tech should be here any time to get her fingerprints and take a DNA sample," said Cameron. "If we get confirmation, I'll send a deputy for Alison's mother in Indianapolis."

"Thanks, Cam."

"There's another thing. I've sent deputies out to Hal's farm to determine how Alison got there. I also put a call into Lane and Frankie Hansen to see if one of them could bring their search-and-rescue dog, Hunter, to trace her route. We're close, Brody. We'll catch the bastard."

"The killer will try to get to Alison. He'll fear she'll talk. I want a deputy outside her door twenty four hours a day, seven days a week to protect her."

"Will do." Cameron paused, and then asked, "Can I see her?"

"Sure. Go now while I make some calls. Carly's in there with her."

Cameron crept into Alison's room and sat in the chair Brody had vacated. Glancing at Carly, he realized she was holding the girl's hand. Finally in the same room with the preteen he'd searched for, he hadn't bargained for her to look so small and helpless in the hospital bed. There were monitors and machines surrounding Alison's bed, and bags of blood hung from metal rods, pumping the lifesaving liquid into her veins.

His heart squeezed. Alison was the same age as Hailey Adams, but had experienced things he hoped Hailey never would.

10 CHAPTER TEN

Twenty-four hours later, Brody and Carly were summoned to the office of Dr. Nathan Ford, the physician assigned to Alison Brown's care. As the doctor was attending to an emergency, they waited quietly in visitor chairs across from his desk.

"I have a bad feeling about Dr. Ford wanting to see us," said Carly. "Something's happened with Alison, and I'm sensing it's not good."

Brody, who was reading a message on his phone, turned to her. "I hope you're not right on this one, Carly. We need Alison to lead us to the killer." Turning back to the message, he said, "Just got a text from hospital security, which says the entire hospital staff has been alerted to look for anyone suspicious entering or exiting the hospital. In addition, they've stepped up security at the entrance and all exits. Cam assigned deputies to guard Alison's room, and the first shift started yesterday."

"I can take a shift," offered Carly.

"Thanks, it's kind of you to offer, but we have enough deputies to cover. Besides, you sat with the girl until one this morning."

Before Carly could respond, Dr. Ford entered the room, greeted them, then sat behind his desk. He had a troubled expression which made Carly's pulse quicken.

"I'm afraid that Alison has slipped into a coma," he stated somberly.

"What does that mean?" Carly asked. She'd never known anyone who had been in a coma. The comatose stories she'd seen on the news rarely had a happy ending.

Scrubbing his hands tiredly over his face, the doctor said, "A coma may develop as a result of the body's response to injury, to allow the body to heal the most immediate injuries before waking. She lost a lot of blood, and she's experienced the kind of trauma that occurs in most people's worst nightmares."

Brody leaned forward. "Will she wake up?"

"It can be very difficult to predict recovery when a person is in a coma. Every person is different. She could wake up in a day or two. Or worst-case scenario, she may never regain consciousness."

"What can you do for her?" asked Carly.

"Her condition is critical, and I'm moving her to the intensive care unit. Once her condition stabilizes, we'll do some imaging tests, such as a CAT scan, MRI, etc. to see if there is any abnormal brain functioning. We'll also hook her up to an EEG to continue to monitor brain waves and identify any seizures that might occur."

"When will she be moved?" Brody wanted to know. "I want the armed deputy guarding her room to stay with her in case the killer tries to get to her."

"We're moving her immediately, and I've notified the hospital staff to alert your office if anyone should ask for her room number. Have you located her parents?" asked Dr. Ford.

"We can't do that until we positively identify the girl as Alison Brown. We're waiting for the DNA and fingerprinting results. If the girl is identified as Alison Brown, we'll immediately notify her mother and a deputy will be sent to Indianapolis to bring her to this hospital. I am putting the girl in protective custody. We have reason to believe the man who did this to Alison is the serial killer we've been searching for."

In his office, Cameron typed an update to text to Brody, the most important being that the fingerprint analysis revealed the girl in Morel Hospital was identified as Alison Brown. Cameron had already contacted Alison's mother, Margaret, and sent a deputy to pick her up at her home and transport her to the hospital. He'd worked with the Victim Advocates group to find a safe place for Margaret to stay while her daughter was hospitalized. Once Alison was released, the sheriff's office would put both into protective custody.

He'd assigned ten deputies the day before to search a twenty-mile radius from Hal Locke's farm to try to determine where the killer lived. They discovered two state highways and a half-dozen county roads within the search range, along with five farms, in addition to Hal's, and twenty houses in the Country Way community.

Lane Hansen, along with his search-and-rescue dog, Hunter, arrived
at the Locke farm in the afternoon to try to determine the route
Alison took after she escaped. After familiarizing Hunter with
Alison's scent, the two searched a wooded area nearby, but Hunter
lost the girl's scent about midway. They hadn't made the progress
Cameron had hoped for, and to say he was disappointed was an
understatement.

Just as he clicked the button to text his report to Brody, Deputy
Sawyer entered his office.

"Why aren't you answering your phone?" Gail demanded, her
hands on her hips, making no effort to hide her annoyance.

Pulling his cell phone out of his desk drawer, Cameron realized
he'd accidentally left it on vibrate and hadn't heard any calls.

"Who's trying to reach me?"

"A lady who says she's the director of the Morel Public Library."

"Oh, that's Diana Tan. She's probably trying to reach me to let
me know the two true crime books I reserved are in," Cameron said.

"Maybe it's just me, but it didn't sound like that kind of call,"
said Gail, who limped back to her desk.

While Cameron looked up the phone number for the library, he
thought about Diana Tan. He'd known her since grade school, and
dated her off and on through high school. Very pretty and petite,
Diana had dark, exotic eyes and most of the guys on the football
team were hot for her. But there'd been no sparks between the two
of them, no chemical attraction. Certainly not like the magnetic pull
he had for Mollie Adams, his best friend since kindergarten.

The phone rang a couple of times until she picked up.

"Hi, Diana. This is Cameron Chase. Are the new Ann Rule and Kathryn Casey true crime books I reserved in?"

"Not yet, Cam. That's not why I called. I need to meet with you right away. I just learned about something I need to tell you." Diana's words came out in a rush, making Cameron realize the normally laid back woman was troubled about something.

"Are you okay? You sound like this is serious."

"It is. I have to talk to you in person. When can you be here?"

Retrieving his car keys from of his pocket, Cameron said, "I'll be there in five minutes."

Cameron had always loved the public library that was so old it had been declared a historic building. As a child, his mom had declared Saturday the family's library day, and he remembered spending hours reading his favorite books in an overstuffed chair by the warmth of the brick fireplace.

Entering the building, Cameron noticed a dozen people or more browsing the stacks. As he searched for Diana's office, he passed a filled computer lab where the only sound he heard was the tapping of fingers on keyboards.

Reaching her office, he tapped on the door and the library director immediately appeared.

Diana thanked him for coming and introduced him to Lisa Mitton, who served as the head librarian. Diana closed her office door for privacy as he joined Lisa at a small, round conference table near Diana's desk.

Nervously biting her lip, Diana said, "Lisa supervises a team of five full-time librarians and three part-timers. She's brought something to my attention that I want her to share with you, Cameron."

"About a month ago, I noticed one of my librarians, Daniel Suggs, was spending a lot of time in the computer lab. This isn't all that unusual because it's part of Daniel's job description to help users with the computers. So at first, I wasn't concerned." said Lisa.

"Go on," Cameron prompted.

"I began to notice Daniel spending his work breaks, including lunch, at a computer in the lab. When I asked him about it, he explained he was taking an online course, so I let it go until yesterday. I was getting a cart out of the back room that adjoins the computer lab. As I was rolling the cart through the lab, I noticed Daniel at a computer."

"Excuse me for interrupting, Lisa. Does Daniel use one particular computer in your lab, or all of them at any given time?" asked Cameron as his mind questioned Daniel's need for so much computer time. He'd arrested many men for child pornography and sensed this is where the discussion was going.

"Just one. He uses the last computer in the last row of the lab."

"Thanks. Keep going."

"I could clearly see the computer's screen, and what I saw made me sick. He was pulling up photos of children in various stages of undress in suggestive poses. Some of the kids looked as young as three or four."

"What did you do?"

"I was so shocked I didn't know what to do, so I came to Diana."

"You did the right thing. Glad you called me, Diana," said Cameron as he punched in a number on his cell phone. "I'm calling my brother, Gabriel, who is a forensic computer consultant for the sheriff's office."

"Hi, Gabe. I've got a computer-related issue at the public library and could use your help. Can you come over? Great. See you then." Cameron said and disconnected. To the two women, he said, "Gabe will be here in a few minutes."

Frowning thoughtfully, Diana asked, "What are you going to do?"

"Since the computer in question belongs to the library and can be used by anyone, the first thing I'm going to do is to ask your permission to analyze the data on the computer Daniel uses."

"You've got it," Diana said. Anger narrowed her eyes, stiffening her jaw.

"Do you know if Daniel has a personal computer?"

"Yes," said Lisa. "He has a Dell laptop he brings to work once in a while."

"Depending on what he's uploaded on the work computer, we may get a warrant to search his home, along with his personal computer. Where is Daniel now?"

"This is his day off," Lisa stated. "He'll be back at work

tomorrow."

"Gabe will want to take the computer with him. Let's go get it ready."

In the hallway, outside Alison's hospital room, were bouquets of flowers, small stuffed animals, and colorful balloons. Clutching a soft, pink teddy bear, Carly entered the girl's room.

"Where did all of this come from?" Carly asked the nurse, who was taking Alison's pulse.

"The hospital staff. Several stuffed animals are from the Sheriff's office. Alison has touched a lot of hearts."

Carly nodded with understanding, for the young girl had impacted her heart, too. She knew better than to get so personally involved with a victim, but the small, angelic-looking girl in the hospital bed had already won her heart as well as Carly's fierce determination to keep her safe.

"How is she?"

"The same. We're watching her closely and praying for a miracle."

"So are we," said Carly, as she sat by Alison's side. She gently pulled the girl's hand into her own and waited for the nurse to leave. Alison's face looked so innocent and younger than her thirteen years, as she lay on the pillows the nurse had just fluffed.

"Hello, Alison," Carly said softly. "My name is Carly Stone, and I'm really glad to meet you. You don't have to be afraid anymore, sweetie. We'll protect you from whoever did this to you. I promise.

Oh, I almost forgot. This is for you." Placing the teddy bear in the crook of Alison's arm, she added, "I know you probably think you're too old for this, but there is something comforting when you hold a teddy bear in your arms. When you wake, maybe you could name it. It can be your good luck bear. Heaven knows, you're overdue for some good luck."

A knock at the door drew Carly's attention. She turned to see Alison's mother, Margaret, enter the room. Tears flooding down her face, Margaret went to the other side of the bed and pulled her daughter into her arms and sobbed. The deputy who drove her to the hospital stood awkwardly in a corner to give them privacy. Carly moved into the hallway and waited.

"I never thought I'd see you again, Baby. I love you so much, Alison. I am never going to stop telling you that. It's okay you're sleeping now. Your mommy understands. The coma is going to give your body time to heal, and then you're coming back to me. I can't make it without my little girl. You have to come back to me, Alison."

The next day, Gabe scheduled a meeting to brief the others on what he'd found on Daniel Suggs' library computer.

Tired after a sleepless night, Brody found it hard to hide his annoyance. "Okay, Gabe. This better be good. I'm wondering why you invited Carly and me to a meeting to discuss a librarian's porn collection."

"The full analysis of Daniel Suggs' computer will take days or weeks, but I wanted you to know about the initial results. I have some information you'll find interesting."

"What did you find?" asked Cameron.

"The guy has over one thousand images of children on the computer he uses at the library."

"Damn pervert," Brody said angrily.

"That's not all. He was communicating with Amanda Jenkins on Facebook for over a month before she disappeared. Here is a printout of their conversations through emails."

Accepting the stack of papers, Carly straightened in her seat. "Amanda Jenkins? Was he connected to any of the others?"

"Like I said, I'm not through with the analysis. But I thought you might want to get that search warrant for his home and computer."

"Cam, create a search warrant and get it to Judge Carlson for her signature, then arrest him and bring him in for a little talk," said Brody who then turned to Gabe. "Call me the second your full analysis is completed."

With Brody and Cameron, Carly stood at the observation window and stared at the man sitting in the interview room. Daniel Suggs sat at a metal table, obviously nervous and wiping the beaded sweat from his brow with the back of his sleeve. He was five feet six inches tall and weighed about one-hundred-and-twenty pounds. He had pale skin, with blonde shaggy hair, and large blue eyes.

"I don't think this guy looks physically able to carry the victims' dead bodie, or dig shallow graves. Truthfully, he's so pale and scrawny he looks anorexic," Carly remarked. Was there a chance this guy was their killer?

"You'd be surprised what a smaller man can do with a rush of adrenalin," Brody replied.

Cameron agreed and added, "We have deputies about his size. Believe me, they can handle themselves quite well."

"Let's interview him before he wets himself," Brody said. "Cameron, do you want to join Carly and take a shot at him?"

"Absolutely," Cameron said with a smile, as he followed Carly into the interview room.

As soon as they sat at the table, Daniel Suggs began trembling.

"Hello, Daniel. My name is Carly Stone. Detective Chase and I would like to talk to you about a couple of things."

"What things? Am I in trouble?"

Clearly, Daniel Suggs was freaking out. Cameron answered his question. "I'd say you're in a hell of a lot of trouble, especially if you're not truthful with us. You can start off by telling us why you have over a thousand photos of little kids in various stages of undress on your work computer."

"Oh, shit," Daniel said as he leaned on the table, covering his face with his hands. Still trembling, he started to sob so hard he got the hiccups.

They waited until he calmed down, and then Cameron said, "You're facing a long prison sentence if you get convicted of possessing child pornography."

"Oh, no," Daniel wailed. "This can't be happening. I didn't do anything to those kids. I was just looking. I swear."

"You can tell that to the judge at your hearing. Right now, it is to your benefit that you answer a couple of questions."

"What about?"

Carly held up a photograph of Amanda Jenkins, watching Daniel's reaction as he looked at it. He colored fiercely, stains of scarlet appearing on his cheeks.

"It's Amanda," Daniel admitted.

Placing the photo on the table before him, Carly asked, "How do you know her?"

"She's a Facebook friend."

"That's all?"

"No, Amanda and I moved our conversations off Facebook and communicated through email."

"What about?"

"We talked about school and her difficulties with her parents."

"But that's not all," Carly said. "And don't lie to us because we have the transcript of all your email conversations."

"Oh, shit," he said again, this time with a heavy sigh as he rubbed his hands over his face. "Well, if you already know, why are you asking me questions?"

Cameron leaned forward, focusing all his attention on Daniel Suggs. "Because we want to hear it from you. Tell us about your relationship with Amanda."

"We became close and wanted to meet in person. She lived in Terre Haute, so I sent her a bus ticket to Morel."

"How long ago was this?"

"I don't know, maybe seven or eight months ago."

"Keep going."

"Things didn't go well once she arrived and discovered how old I was. She got pissed that I'd posted a photo of myself when I was fourteen and lied to her about my age. Amanda wanted to get back on the bus to go home, but there were no more buses going to Terre Haute until the next day, so we went to my house."

"How many times did you have sex with her?" asked Carly.

"Sex? I didn't have sex with her. I swear. We went to my house, ordered a pizza, and just talked. Amanda was very unhappy. She'd lost her parents in a car accident and missed them terribly. She hated living with her grandmother and hadn't made any friends in her new school."

Cameron broke in, "That's a pretty story, Daniel. But considering what we know about your obsession with sex, I don't believe that's all that happened."

Weeping again, Daniel cried, "I swear I'm telling the truth. I didn't touch her. I slept on the sofa that night and took her to the bus station the next day. Check at the bus station, maybe someone remembers me buying the ticket."

Cameron slammed his fist on the metal table and Suggs nearly jumped out of his chair. "You know Amanda is dead, don't you Daniel? I think you know how she got that way. What happened? Did she threaten to call the cops on you?"

Visibly shaken, Daniel bawled, "No. You have to believe me. I didn't kill her. I would never have hurt her, not in a million years."

Carly slipped another photograph out of her file and held it up for Daniel. "Remember Jasmine Norris? She's missing. Coincidentally, you communicated with Jasmine online, too. I don't like coincidences. We've got two missing girls, one of them is dead, and guess what? They both talked with Daniel Suggs online. What are the chances?"

Daniel gulped as more tears streamed down his face. "Yes, I knew Jasmine. We talked online, but we never met in person. I didn't even have a chance to ask her, because she met another guy online and told me she was in love with him."

"What guy?" demanded Cameron.

"I don't know. Jasmine didn't give me his name when she dropped me."

Hearing a knock on the other side of the one-way mirror, Carly said, "We need to leave now."

"Please, could you bring me a bottle of water when you come back?" Daniel pleaded.

"Sure," Cameron called over his shoulder as he closed the door.

They joined Brody, who had been watching the interview from the observation glass. "What do you think?"

Cameron replied, "I'll work the next five years for free if that guy killed anyone."

"I agree," added Carly. "He openly admitted communicating with both girls. I even believe his account of what happened with Amanda when she came to meet him. I think he has an obsession with child pornography and may have even molested some children. But is he our serial killer? I don't think so."

It was mid-afternoon, so Brody was surprised to see Deputy Jim Ryder standing in his office. He'd known the deputy for five years and had only seen him in the office in the early morning hours when Ryder was in his cubicle, checking his emails before his shift. But this early? Never.

"What's up?"

"I've got Shelly Tyler in the interview room."

With raised eyebrows, Brody asked, "Shelly Tyler? Isn't she the waitress at the Donut Place? What did she do? Burn your Krispy Kreme?"

"That's funny, Sheriff. That may cost you a couple of your favorite chocolate-filled doughnuts next time I bring in a box," Ryder shot back with a grin. "She's pissed off at her husband, Ron, and claims he has a meth lab at the house."

"No shit?"

"Yeah, she says she can prove it."

"Did you run her background so I can review it before I talk to her?"

"Yes, sir," Ryder said, as he slid the report across Brody's desk. Heading out, he called over his shoulder, "I'm going back on patrol if you need me."

Brody skimmed the report. Shelly Shipman Tyler was twenty-seven- years-old, the same age as his brother, Gabe. After graduation from Morel High School, she married Ron Tyler, thirty-nine, and moved to his farm off state road fifty-five. As far as criminal history, Shelly had one drunk and disorderly when she was twenty, but nothing since. She'd worked at the Donut Place as a waitress for the past six years.

Ron Tyler's background told a different story. He'd been in and out of jail since his early teens and had a variety of charges ranging from petty theft to aggravated assault and battery. If he was running a meth lab, Ron Tyler was entering Class A felony land, with a possible twenty to fifty years in prison.

Brody sighed with relief when he noticed Ron and Shelly Tyler did not have children. At their last meth bust, deputies discovered two children, ages two and four, hiding in a closet. They were poster kids for the malnourished, improperly clothed, and neglected. Both kids had tested positive for having methamphetamine in their bodies because of their exposure to the second-hand smoke lavishly provided by their parents — two people who should have protected their children instead of condemning them to a life of chronic health problems.

Over the past few years, the number of clandestine meth labs was on the rise in Shawnee County. Meth labs were a scourge that meant trouble for law enforcement as well as first responders who have to deal with hazardous materials, corrosives, flammables, and great amounts of trash and debris at the scene. If not handled properly, injuries and deaths could occur.

Brody pulled a file folder out of his desk and slipped Shelly's background information inside. Before he went into the interview room, he slipped into what looked like a small observation room situated next to the interview room and glanced through the one-way glass at Shelly Tyler.

The department recorded all interviews and stored the recordings on DVDs, so Brody flipped on the television and the recording equipment, slipped in a fresh DVD, then stood at the one-way glass to get a good look at Shelly Tyler before he went in. She had to be the most emaciated woman he'd ever seen, just skin and bones, with reddened sores all over her face and arms. With short, spiked hair, dyed a flaming red, she looked like she'd just escaped from a burning building.

Her body was in constant movement, as she alternated between picking at her skin and pulling at strands of her hair. He'd bet anything this woman was a meth-head. At this moment, her anger at her husband was outweighing her need for the drug, but Brody knew that as time went on, her need for meth would supersede all else. If he wanted information, he needed to move fast.

In the interview room, he placed his folder on the table, sat down and looked at Shelly. "Would you like a cup of coffee, water or anything else?"

"Not now," she replied. "You're one of the Chase brothers, aren't you?

"Yes, do I know you?"

"Probably not. You're older than your two brothers, and we didn't exactly run in the same high school circles," she began. "Your brother, Gabe, was in a couple of my classes. I used to be hot for him big time, but don't think he ever noticed me."

Brody nodded and changed the subject, "Deputy Ryder said you have something to tell me."

Shelly crossed her arms tightly across her breasts, as if that were the only thing she could do to still the constant, jerky movement of her hands. "My sonofabitch husband, Ron, has a meth lab and has been cooking for more than five years."

"If that's true, why haven't you reported this before?" asked Brody.

Fidgeting in her chair, she responded, "Guess I was afraid."

"Afraid of Ron, or afraid to lose your supply?"

"Fuck you," Shelly spat, as she glared at him.

"How'd you get those burn marks on your lips, Shelly?" Brody pressed on.

"Hot coffee," she returned, with her eyes glued to the table.

"Hot coffee? Did hot coffee cause those track marks on your arms too?"

Shoving the sleeves of her green sweater down to her wrists, she looked at the floor.

"You're looking very thin, Shelly. How much do you weigh?"

"Not your business, but around ninety pounds. I've been on the Jenny Crank diet," she answered and then laughed bitterly. "Yeah, I'm a user. So fucking what? I'm handing you a meth lab on a silver platter. You interested or not?"

"You may know about a meth lab, or you may not. How do I

know you're not spinning a story just to get back at your husband?" It wasn't that Brody thought she was lying, but he knew unless she had some kind of evidence to back up her story, he couldn't move on it.

Shelly picked up an old brown leather purse from the floor and dug around in it until she found an envelope. Plucking out a photograph, she slammed it on the table in front of Brody and said, "What does that look like to you, Sherlock?"

He picked up the photo of what looked like an ordinary kitchen. Except in this kitchen, a row of Coleman camping fuel cans filled a shelf of an open cabinet. Large open boxes of coffee filters, small plastic bags, and lithium batteries lined the wall under a window. There was also a supply of drain cleaner, paint thinner, and rock salt.

On the kitchen counter were dozens of packages of Sudafed and other types of cold medicines next to a coffee grinder and a blender. This section of the counter appeared to be coated with white powder.

"How's he getting all the decongestants?" asked Brody. If Ron was cooking meth, he'd need a steady supply of decongestants with pseudoephedrine. It was a precursor ingredient, and it wasn't sold over the counter. You had to ask a pharmacist for it, and he or she recorded your name and address.

"There's a group of us who go to different pharmacies at least twice a month."

Brody nodded. This information would be easy to verify. The state's pharmacies recorded in a database any purchases of decongestants with pseudoephedrine.

"I'm going to need names."

Shelly shifted in her chair. Obviously, she had not expected to be asked for names. "Are you trying to get me killed?"

"They wouldn't have to know the names came from you."

Shelly nodded, considered this offer, but said nothing. She slid another photo to him. This one was a shot of a messy living room. On the coffee table was a dozen small plastic bags filled with powder or crystal meth, short straws, a small mirror with a razor blade, a couple of burned spoons, rubber tubing, a glass pipe, and three syringes.

Brody stared hard at Shelly for a moment and said, "So why are you here, Shelly? Sounds like you've had close to five years to report Ron's meth lab. Why now? And don't even think about lying to me."

Tears glittering in her eyes, she said, "He's dumping me." She pulled a tissue out of her purse to blow her nose. "The bastard is leaving me for a thirteen-year-old girl."

An alarm going off in his head, Brody straightened in his seat. "How do you know this?"

"He left his laptop open when he left the house yesterday. I heard a beep and looked at the screen and saw he'd gotten a message from @HotBloomieTeen. I opened it. The email was from this girl in Bloomington. I think Ron asked this girl for her photo." Shelly pulled out a folded piece of paper that she spread out on the table to show to him.

Brody stared at the paper. The girl in the photo looked too

young to even be interested in boys, and here she was sending a naked photo of herself to a man old enough to be her father. It looked like the photo had been taken by a web cam. Posing with a seductive pout, she had one finger in her mouth, and with her other hand was inserting two fingers into her vagina. Bile rushed to Brody's throat; he felt nauseous. Her underdeveloped breasts were a sign that she was more child than even a teenager.

"How do you know Ron is leaving you for her?"

"It was pretty clear in their emails. They're making arrangements to meet," said Shelly, as she dabbed at the stream of tears running from her eyes.

"Do you know where?"

"Ron's trying hard to get her to come to Morel."

Brody just stared at her. He thought about the dead girls, Amanda and Sophia, from opposite ends of the state and how they ended up in Shawnee County. Could the girls have met Ron Tyler online? Could they have been lured here by Ron Tyler?

"Wait here, I'll be right back," Brody said abruptly, as he jumped to his feet. He left the interview room and headed for the sheriff's conference room, where he knew Carly Stone was working. Without knocking, he shoved open the door and rushed in.

Hurriedly, he filled Carly in on what he'd learned from Shelly about the meth lab. "You might want to talk to her."

"What does a meth lab have to do with our two victims?" Carly asked, clearly confused.

"The reason why she's reporting the lab is because she thinks her

thirty-nine-year-old husband is planning to dump her for this girl."
Brody handed Carly the folded, printed photo.

"You have got to be kidding. This kid looks like she's barely eleven."

"Exactly. According to Shelly, she lives in Bloomington, and her husband is persuading the girl to come visit him in Morel." Brody paused for a second.

"So you're wondering if our victims were lured here by Ron Tyler?" Carly said.

Brody nodded and asked, "Do you want to talk to her?"

"I thought you'd never ask," Carly said with a grin.

Brody led Carly back to the interview room, introduced the two women and left them alone. He went to Cameron's office and said, "You might want to listen to this interview."

On the way to the interview room, Brody filled his brother in on what he'd learned. Soon the two men were in the small conference room next to the interview room, standing at the glass wall, watching and listening.

Shelly sat back in her chair, sizing Carly up. "Who are you and why do I need to talk to you? I've given Sheriff Chase more than enough information about my husband's meth lab."

"As he told you, my name is Carly Stone. I'm a consultant on a project with the Sheriff," she said, quietly adding, "I'm sorry this happened to you."

"What have you got to be sorry about?" Shelly squirmed in her chair and smirked.

"You're not the only one who's had a man she trusted cheat on her with another woman," Carly said softly.

At this, Shelly simply nodded and looked down at her hands which now were clenched fists. A tear slipped out of one eye and skimmed down her cheek.

Carly paused for a moment and said, "What I'm interested in is your husband's communication with this young lady." She pushed the printout of the girl's photo across the table to Shelly.

Shelly's face reddened with anger. Leaning forward, she said, "I wouldn't say she's a lady. The words 'teen slut' come to mind."

Carly ignored the remark and continued, "What's the girl's name?"

"If I knew the bitch's name, I'd be in Bloomington kicking her ass for screwing with my husband and breaking up my marriage."

"How did your husband meet her online? Is he active on Facebook, MySpace, or chat rooms?"

"A chat room was mentioned in one of the emails, but I don't recall the name."

"How are they communicating? Email? Chat? Texts? Instant messages?"

Shelly sighed and said, "Just found the emails."

"How many emails did you find?"

"Just a couple. I was printing the photo when Ron came into the house, and I didn't want him to catch me with his laptop. It's off limits." Shelly paused, then angrily added, "Now I know why."

Carly looked down at the folded paper. "This photo and email were sent last month. Were any of the emails you saw dated more recently?"

"No. Jesus. Aren't you listening? I only saw a couple of them." Frustrated and visibly shaking now, Shelly got up and began to pace.

"Do you think your husband is using instant messaging to communicate with this girl?" Carly asked. Experience had taught her that Internet predators prefer children who have instant message accounts. Although some use email, many prefer communicating with their victims through instant messages. Predators know that while emails are saved automatically and have to be manually deleted, instant messages tend to evaporate once the instant message window is closed. If Ron Tyler had switched from email to instant messaging, it would not bode well for collecting evidence.

"How the hell would I know? I only saw the email."

Realizing she wouldn't get much more useful information from Shelly, Carly asked, "Did Sheriff Chase give you his business card?"

Shelly rummaged through her purse, found the card and handed it to Carly.

Carly wrote on the back of it, "Here is my cell phone number. Would you please call me if you think of anything else that might be helpful?"

"Why in the hell do you want to know more about my cheatin' husband's on-the-side romance?"

"What your husband is doing has nothing to do with romance. He's a sex predator." Carly tapped her finger on the folded photo. "This little girl is his victim, *not* his love interest. I need your help and cooperation to stop him from ruining her life or worse."

Shelly just stared at Carly as if confused.

Carly handed her the business card. "You have my number; call it if you have more information about the girl. I'll get Sheriff Chase for you."

Carly left the room and nearly slammed into Brody in the hallway.

"We need a search warrant for his laptop, cell phone, tablet, and whatever else he has."

"Slow down, Carly. I can put those things in the search warrant, but we need to do the meth lab investigation first. I'll list the laptop, phone, and other electronic communication devices in the search warrant. We'll get those things during the bust."

"Okay, then what's next?"

Cameron joined them and answered, "We need to start the meth lab investigation from scratch. The best way to do that is to go undercover and try to buy drugs from the house. I'll need Shelly's help."

"I agree," said Brody. "See if she'll introduce you to Ron."

Brody and Carly moved to the two-way glass window and watched Shelly, who was now wiping sweat from her brow with the back of her shaking hand.

"Do you think she's withdrawing?" asked Carly.

"Maybe. She sure doesn't look good."

Cameron entered the interview room with a can of Coke for

Shelly. He handed it to her and returned to his chair across from her. She popped open the can, lifted it, and took a long drink.

"I'm Detective Chase," he said.

"I know who you are, Cameron," she stated. "We went to the same high school."

"That so?"

"I won't hold it against you that you don't remember me."

"Sorry, but that was a long time ago," Cameron said.

"Listen, I've told your brother and that consultant all I know. I need to go," said Shelly.

"Sorry, Shelly, there's this other thing I need to discuss with you."

"What's that?"

"I need your help."

"I've already helped," she returned.

"Right. But in order to make this bust work, I'll need to go undercover so you can introduce me to Ron as a buyer."

Shelly flew to her feet, knocking her chair over in the process, shaking with rage. "Are you fucking nuts?" She asked incredulously. "No way. There is *no* way Ron is going to believe your Boy Scout ass is a buyer. He'll see you as a cop a mile away. Do you have any idea what he'd do to me if I brought a cop home?"

"This wouldn't be my first time to go undercover, Shelly."

"Get your little brother to do it. I saw Gabe at the Donut Place last week. He's got an edge to him that you don't have. With his long hair and tattoos, there's more of a chance Ron would believe he was a buyer."

"I'm not sure I can get Gabe..."

"Then you can forget this little undercover drama. There's too much risk for me. You don't know how violent Ron can be."

Cameron left the room, closing the door behind him. He quickly found Brody with Carly in the small observation room.

"Did you hear what she said?"

"I heard her and the answer is no. Besides the fact his expertise is in computer forensics, Gabe's not in law enforcement," Brody said.

"Does that matter?" asked Carly. "I've known a lot of informants who were not in law enforcement. Besides, didn't you tell me he graduated from the academy? He just decided to open his private investigation company instead. He's trained. Why can't he do it?"

"Because he has an overprotective older brother who's the county sheriff," said Cameron. He watched as Brody walked away.

"Brody, where are you going?" Carly called after him.

"To my office to call Gabe."

11 CHAPTER ELEVEN

Four law enforcement officers in the area who were certified to process meth labs were sitting around the conference table the next day when Carly entered the room: Brody and Cameron Chase, Deputy Jim Ryder, and Carly's brother, Blake Stone, who was on loan from Sheriff Tim Brennan. Though not certified to process meth labs, Gabe was in attendance, too. Brody had deputized him for the undercover stint, and Gabe wanted to see the thing through.

An unshaven Gabe Chase dressed in torn jeans and a leather vest had successfully purchased three grams of crystal meth from Ron Tyler the day before. Because he was wired, the entire purchase conversation was recorded. In addition, he'd observed a couple of rolled-up dollar bills, a glass pipe, a broken mirror, razor blades, syringes and small bags of white crystals on a coffee table in the front room. Gabe warned them of a modified propane tank in back of the house. He reported that the brass fitting on top of the tank had a bluish-green tint, and was probably filled with anhydrous ammonia, a farm fertilizer used in making methamphetamine. The chemical was highly poisonous, corrosive and explosive.

Ron had even given Gabe a tour of the meth lab he'd created in the kitchen. Shelly had been telling the truth. Ron was not cooking this week because he had plenty of supply. It was the ideal time for the bust.

Fire Chief Wayne Lansky was in attendance, too. Since production of meth carries a strong risk of fire or explosion, his specially-trained hazmat team would follow the sheriff's undercover van.

Carly filled her mug up with hot coffee, squeezed her brother's shoulder, and sat down next to him as Brody opened the meeting.

"You've all been briefed on the operation." Brody began. "Today, we'll discuss the specifics on how the bust will go down." He turned on a projector that flashed a house plan on the screen. "This is a sketch Gabe made of the layout of the house."

Brody picked up a laser pointer from the table and continued, "Detective Chase and Deputy Ryder will enter the house from the front. Once inside, there is a combination living and dining room. The place is a mess, so watch where you walk. There are two openings in this room. The one to your right leads to a kitchen that runs the width of the back of the house. This is where Ron has the meth lab. The doorway to your left leads to a long hallway where the bedrooms are located. Your target is the bedroom where Ron and Shelly sleep. It is the one to your left, just past a small bathroom, as you move to the front of the house."

Brody turned the group's attention to the back of the house on the drawing. "Detective Stone and I will cover the back of the house, including the long kitchen area where the meth lab is housed. Ron told Gabe that he wasn't cooking this week because he has plenty of supply, but we cannot be absolutely certain whether the lab is actively 'cooking', until we get there. So proceed with caution. The simple act of turning on an electrical switch may cause an explosion."

With all eyes on the screen, he continued, "Cameron and Ryder will use the battering ram to breach the front door and communicate with the rest of us as they clear each room."

"The bust will occur at four o'clock tomorrow morning, when it's more likely that Ron and Shelly will be sleeping. Make it look as if we are arresting Shelly, too, so Ron won't identify her as a snitch. She's still terrified Ron or one of his biker friends will off her. As part of her plea agreement and cooperation, Shelly will be taken to a rehab in Indianapolis and registered under an assumed name. Once released, she has an airline ticket to fly to Nevada, where she'll live with her parents and hopefully start her life over."

"And Ron?" asked Carly.

"As the meth cook and distributor, Ron Tyler is looking at hard time. Shelly let us know he has an arsenal of weapons in the bedroom, so be on high alert. Move so quickly that Ron Tyler won't have time to arm himself," Brody said. "Don't shoot unless a life is in danger and you have no choice. We need Ron to pay for the misery of all the lives impacted by the drug he makes. We also want him alive to answer questions related to our murdered girls."

Next, Brody passed out copies of the search warrant. "Once Ron is secured and out of the house, these are the things we're looking for. Take special care with Ron's laptop, cell phone, and any other electronic communication devices you seize. The data on these items is critical to another case we are working."

It was still dark when the group gathered around a white van parked behind the sheriff department building the next morning. They reviewed their plan as they sipped from travel mugs filled with hot coffee. Brody briefed and cautioned them one more time about dangers to avoid.

After he finished talking to the team, Brody pulled Carly aside. "I still don't think it's a good idea that you go along. A lot of things could go wrong. You could get hurt, or worse."

"So could you," she insisted.

"I'll be wearing protective gear."

"You're being overprotective. I'll be safe in the van with Gabe and the surveillance equipment," Carly began. "Besides I'm a trained federal agent, this is not my first time in the field."

If he thought she was going to stay behind while he, her brother and the others put themselves at risk, he was gravely mistaken.

Carly regretted that Tim Brennan had loaned her brother, Blake for this operation. She'd regretted it more after listening to Blake talk to Jennifer on the phone the night before at the Chase main house, where he was staying. Carly could tell he was talking her off the ledge. Damn it. Not only was he her only brother, but he also had a wife, a baby and a young son who needed him. She didn't want to think about what any of them would do if anything happened to him on this op. It was one thing to place herself in danger on the job, it was quite another to think about the brother she adored doing it.

Carly was also agonizing over Brody's involvement. She'd fallen in love with him and didn't want to think about his not being in her life. It was ridiculous for her to feel like this. She loved law enforcement as much as Brody, and knew danger came with the territory. If she were going to stay with him, she had to get used to Brody facing danger, just as he would have to accept her work.

"It *is* your first meth bust," Brody returned, his hands placed belligerently on his hips.

"True. But like I said, I'll stay in the van unless it looks like you need help," Carly added with a slight smile of defiance.

"We *won't* need your help. Stay the hell out of the house until it's cleared and ventilated," Brody returned, exasperated. "Sweet Jesus, Carly. You don't know enough about meth labs to realize how dangerous this situation is. Even short exposure to the high concentration of chemical vapors that may exist in Tyler's meth lab can cause severe health problems, even result in death."

"Once again, Sheriff Chase, let me remind you that I'm a trained federal agent, not a Girl Scout. I already told you I'd stay in the van. I need to be at this scene. I want to be there to see what's on Ron Tyler's laptop and cell phone. The information might help us solve the murders," she answered in a rush of words.

Brody shot her a don't-push-me glare, and then called out to the others, "Suit up and load up. Let's shut this mother down."

Carly watched as the men slipped on yellow Tychem® coveralls. Blake had explained to her that the protective suits came with all the bells and whistles to protect them from dangerous chemical vapors. The coveralls were sealed with taped seams, a zipper front hiding a double storm flap, and they were respirator-fit with a drawstring hood. They each threw on a heavy entry bulletproof vest.

Brody pulled out an air tank for himself and passed the rest out to the team. Each man slipped on an air tank, pulled on his mask, and tested the tank to ensure all the valves were closed. The team members checked the air meter gauges on their chests to make sure they were working and there weren't any leaks. When satisfied with the tests, each person disconnected the air regulator in the front of his mask.

Brody motioned for Carly to get into the van, and the others followed, sitting on benches in the back. She rode shotgun in the passenger seat and Gabe drove. If they were seen, it would look like a husband-wife team off to work. There was a large magnetic sign on the side of the van that read "The Cleaning Crew" with a fake phone number beneath. Following close behind was the Fire Department's hazmat team truck and three patrol cars.

Soon the air in the van was saturated with adrenaline and testosterone. Carly glanced back at the team and prayed the suits would protect the men from the broad range of dangerous chemicals that might confront them in Ron Tyler's meth lab. Apprehension tied a knot inside her and she took a couple cleansing breaths to calm herself.

The sky was still dark with white clouds drifting across a half-moon. There was a chance of rain, but it was predicted to occur later in the afternoon. Once they turned onto state road fifty-five, Gabe gave the team in back an alert that they were six to seven minutes from the Tyler farm. Soon he pulled the van to the side of the road. Carly watched as Brody, Blake, Ryder, and Cameron tested the air meters that take samples of the air to determine whether it was safe to breathe inside the house. A series of beeps sounded throughout the van.

Gabe headed down the highway until he reached a dirt lane leading to a farmhouse. Numerous "No Trespassing" and "Beware of Dogs" signs were nailed onto trees and fence posts at the entrance — Ron Tyler's makeshift security system.

Gabe eased the vehicle to a stop on the highway. They could see the Tyler house sitting about a quarter mile off the road. The property was lined with thick woods on either side of the house and at the property line in the back. The only farming Ron Tyler did was evident by a small barn next to a pen of goats.

Carly rolled down her window. In a light breeze, goat manure, damp earth, and the pine trees emanated from the place. Wafting in the air closer to the house was a sickening chemical odor mix that smelled like cat urine and fingernail polish remover.

Gabe pulled into the lane, turned off the headlights and slowly drove toward the house, guided by a pole-mounted security light that shone across the property. The house was a small one-story white structure in disrepair.

Trash littered the yard, and the house windows were covered with either curtains or aluminum foil. Not exactly home-sweet-home, HGTV-worthy. Seeing no lights shining from any of the windows, Carly hoped Shelly and Ron Tyler were sound asleep inside.

Gabe stopped the van about twenty feet or so from the house. He reached up to turn off all the interior lights of the vehicle, then slipped out to open the back of the van.

Brody used his cell phone to call an the three deputies in the woods covering surveillance of the east, west, and back of the house to alert them that his team was entering the property.

Gathering the team around him, Brody spoke through the voice amplifier on his mask, "Remember, do *not* shoot inside the house unless you have no choice. Secure Ron and Shelly, handcuff them, and hand them over to a deputy who will be waiting outside," whispered Brody, as he slipped on his earpiece. Cameron and the others did the same. "Before you enter the house, put on your respirators and don't take them off. Wait for my signal to enter the house."

Brody watched as Cameron crept toward the front of the house, followed close behind by Deputy Ryder. He and Blake headed toward the back.

In a crouching position, Cameron and Ryder slipped across the front yard, if it could be called that. It was overgrown with weeds and littered with paper, cigarette wrappers, butts, and empty plastic soda bottles. Apparently, curb appeal was not a concept that had visited the Tyler home, Cameron thought.

A board creaked loudly as Cameron climbed the steps of the front porch, and his heart jumped in his chest as he came to an abrupt stop. Pausing for a couple of seconds, he listened for sounds inside the house. Hearing nothing, he ventured forward and grasped the door knob of the front door. Twisting it, he couldn't believe their luck when the door opened easily. One thing for sure, Ron Tyler's security system sucked, and Cameron couldn't be happier. He set the battering ram on the porch.

"Brody, the front door is unlocked. We're going in," Cameron whispered into the tiny microphone connected to his earpiece.

"Okay. We'll cover the back door," Brody responded.

"Shawnee County Sheriff! Search Warrant!" Cameron shouted.

Guns drawn, Cameron and Ryder stepped into the combination living room and dining room area. Cameron scanned the room. Just as he expected, the room was a mess with snack food packages, plastic soda bottles, and drug paraphernalia littering the area.

"Front rooms, clear," he announced.

Cameron was moving toward the hallway that led to the bedrooms when Ryder slipped on a plastic baggie and would have crashed to the floor if Cameron had not caught the heavy deputy. They froze, listening for sounds and movement in the house. Hearing nothing, they continued.

Once in the hallway, Cameron indicated for Ryder to check the guest bedroom. He waited until Ryder appeared and gave a signal the room was clear.

Continuing into the hallway, Cameron approached the bathroom. The door was open and he peered inside. "Bathroom, clear."

At the end of the hall, he saw a closed door. It had to be Ron and Shelly Tyler's bedroom. With his ear pressed against the door, he listened. No movement inside. Everything was quiet. He tried the doorknob and discovered the room was locked.

Just as Cameron lifted his boot to kick the door in, it flew open, and Ron Tyler shot out like a rocket, knocking him to the floor and flying by Ryder.

"Shawnee County Sheriff! Stop!"

In slow motion, Cameron watched Ryder lift his Glock to aim at Ron Tyler. "No!" he shouted. "Don't shoot!"

Jumping to his feet, Cameron shouted through his voice amplifier, "Brody, Ron's heading toward the back."

The most piercing scream he'd ever heard came from the bedroom. Shelly Tyler was sitting up in bed, naked, screaming her head off like a victim in a slasher movie.

"Shut the fuck up, Shelly," Cameron growled, and then turned to the officer behind him. "Ryder, take care of her."

Cameron got to the kitchen in time to see Ron Tyler hurl himself through a sliding glass door onto a cement slab in back. Instantly, Brody tackled him and pinned him face-down in the broken glass as Blake Stone handcuffed his hands behind his back.

From the van, Carly watched as Ryder pulled a hysterical, seemingly terrified Shelly Tyler from the house. She'd known about the bust and was giving an academy award-winning performance that she undoubtedly hoped her husband would hear about. Ryder handed her to a burly deputy who read her rights and secured her in the back of his patrol car. As soon as he turned the car around in the yard, the deputy flipped on his lights and sped off.

Ryder moved back into the house, just as Blake led a struggling and bloody Ron Tyler from the backyard. Cameron appeared on the front porch as a second deputy took control of Tyler, read him his rights, and described the search warrant for the house.

"You bastards!" Tyler screamed, and then spit on the warrant in Cameron's hand. "Who told? Who told?"

"Get him in the car," Cameron told the deputy. "Stop by the hospital and get him some medical care for his cuts. Then take him to the jail."

Brody was nowhere in sight. A deputy stretched crime scene tape as a fireman in a chemical protective suit placed a huge exhaust fan at the opened front door. The rest of the hazmat team was inside the house opening windows, getting ready for ventilating the house and removing the equipment. Where was Brody?

Three deputies dressed in camouflage and carrying assault rifles came in from the woods and stood talking by the hazmat truck. Cameron and the rest of the officers gathered there too. Where was

Brody?

Alarmed, Carly reached for the door handle and felt Gabe gripping her arm.

"Don't even think about it. Do you really think my brother didn't brief me?" Gabe asked.

"Let go of me," Carly demanded.

"Not a chance," he returned. "What's so damned important you think you need from that house anyway? You heard Brody read the search warrant yesterday. Someone will get Tyler's laptop and phone. Sit tight until the hazmat team ventilates the house."

Carly jerked her arm out of his grasp and asked, "Where's Brody? Why isn't he out here with the others? Something's wrong."

His brows drawn together in a worried expression, Gabe studied the group in front of the house. "I don't see Brody either. He should be out here."

Gabe opened his door, jumped out, and met Carly on the other side of the van. "Are you armed?"

"Yes," she said as she opened her jacket to reveal her Glock.

"You take the right side of the house and I'll take the left. This may be nothing, or my big brother may be in trouble."

Pressed against the side of the house, Carly crept toward the backyard. Soon she heard Brody's voice, "Let's stay calm. No need to get upset."

Quickly peeking around the corner of the house, she saw a tall, beanpole-thin white male holding a gun aimed at Brody's chest. The man's facial muscles were twitching, and he was trembling so badly the gun shook in his hand. He was high as a kite. Where the hell did this guy come from? The house was supposed to be cleared. She prayed the group of officers was still talking near the hazmat truck. The last thing they needed was for one of them to stumble out onto the patio and panic this meth-head. Pressing back against the house, Carly slid her weapon out of her holster and looked again, this time to scan the surroundings.

The backyard looked like a county dump. A tall hill of empty plastic gallon jugs was haphazardly stacked near the house next to a mountain of stuffed black garbage bags, and empty camping fuel cans.

The propane tank filled with anhydrous ammonia was where Gabe described it, approximately five feet from the back door — and two feet from where Brody was standing. A wave of apprehension swept through her. If a shot were fired and hit that tank, they'd all die — if not from the explosion, from breathing a chemical so toxic it liquefies the lungs. One breath would be your last.

Carly listened to Brody trying to talk the guy down. "Hey, I know how you feel. You're just a guest in Ron's house. You probably had no idea Ron was cooking meth."

"Yeah, that's right. That's right." The man's words were slurred, and he continued to tremble as he rapidly nodded his head in agreement.

Carly stole another look. The meth head hadn't put down the gun. It was still held in position aimed at Brody's chest.

"So you can lay down the gun," Brody said softly to him. "No one can blame you for anything."

"Are you trying to trick me, man? I'm not stupid. I'm the one with the power now. I've got the gun," he said, waving the gun ominously toward Brody, and inching closer.

"Yes, I can see that," Brody began. "I think you're a smart man. You're too smart to shoot a cop and spend the rest of your life rotting in a prison cell."

When the man didn't respond, Carly peered around the corner. He was trembling so badly now, he looked like a dog shaking his fur after a bath. She saw Gabe at the other end of the house. Carly wanted to wave him back. She was closer to the two than he. If Gabe approached and the man saw him, he might panic and start shooting and if he hit the propane tank, it would be over for all of them.

"Hey, can I join the party?" Carly asked as she slid around the corner, her Glock aimed and ready to fire. If she had to, she'd kill him outright. She'd do anything to prevent an explosion — anything to save Brody's life.

Gaping at her in disbelief, the man swung his gun right and left between Brody and Carly. He was panicking. Panic was not good. Panic could get them killed.

From behind him, Gabe approached and said, "I heard there was a party back here. I'm not one who can resist a good party."

The second the man twisted around to look at Gabe, Brody crashed into him, dropping him onto the cement patio like a rag doll.

They thrashed about as Brody struggled to get the gun. Bang! The gun went off, the bullet rushing so close to Carly she heard a whoosh as it passed her ear. Grabbing the skeletal arm holding the gun, Brody bashed it against the cement again and again until it was slick with blood, until the man loosened his hand and dropped the gun. Rolling him face-down, Brody pressed his knee against his back, secured, and handcuffed his wrists. The man was crying now, his nose bleeding profusely, as his body violently convulsed.

"You sonofabitch," Brody snarled as he pulled his prisoner to his feet. "You are so fucking arrested."

Cameron rushed outside. "What the hell is going on?"

"I think this freak was hiding when you did the initial sweep of the house," Brody said. "He rushed me after you took Ron Tyler to the front."

"He had to have been in the back bedroom that Ryder said he cleared," said Cameron. "Ryder also aimed his gun to shoot Ron Tyler in the house. I had to stop him."

"Seriously? After I distinctly gave an order to not shoot in the house?"

"Afraid so."

"He's suspended without pay or fired. You choose, Cameron."

The Master would no longer have to concern himself about finding Alison Brown. Her whereabouts were splashed all over the home page of the local newspaper's online issue. Pounding his fist on the table, he cursed aloud as he read the article. It seemed the girl made it to a house, and a farmer rushed her to the hospital. Since the police weren't knocking at his door, it was obvious the girl had been unable to talk.

The Master would take care of the do-gooder farmer later. No one disrupted his plans without suffering the consequences. In the meantime, his focus would be on Alison Brown and how he could get to her in the hospital to snuff out her life. Thinking about how to kill her filled him with delicious thoughts of how he could make her suffer. His preference would be for the girl to experience a long, tortuous death where she begged him to end it. But the need for expediency would limit him to slicing her throat, injecting her with poison, shooting her with a gun equipped with a silencer, or simply pressing a pillow onto her face until she suffocated. No matter the method, he was up to the task and honestly, was looking forward to it.

He'd already driven past Morel Hospital early that morning before the sun rose. There were four Shawnee County Sheriff patrol cars in the parking lot. No doubt hospital security had been alerted, and all the entrances and exits safeguarded. At least, that's what they thought. Having faced bigger risks and succeeding, he had no doubt he'd gain entry, unsuspected, and carry out his plan. After all, the authorities still had no idea what he looked like. Since he'd always worn a ski mask, even their star witness could not describe his appearance.

What a wonderful stroke of luck the girl was in a coma. There was no chance of the slave bitch telling what she knew while in that state of unconsciousness. He planned to make sure she never woke up, no matter what he had to do.

A mother of a migraine made his head hurt so bad he could scarcely breathe. He'd gotten little sleep thanks to multiple, vivid dreams about his sister, Erin, entering his bedroom with a butcher knife in her hand. Each time, he couldn't *determine if Erin was actually in his room — poised over his bed with the knife raised above her head, ready to slash down at him — until he jerked himself awake, shooting from deep sleep to wakefulness in a second's time. His body slicked with nervous sweat, his heart threatening to pound out of his chest, he'd pull himself up until he could quell the panic and return to sleep, until the nightmare repeated itself.*

It was his day off and he had a lot of work to do. Today he'd remove the dog crates and any signs of bondage equipment in the basement. He also planned to scrub the entire area with bleach, and set up a living area with old furniture. Even if the stupid police were lucky enough to find him, and searched his house, they'd find no forensic evidence. With no witnesses, that made for a circumstantial case against him that even a lowly public defender could fight and win.

But before he did anything, he'd troll Facebook, MySpace and Teen Chat to see if his new preteen interests were online. As soon as Alison was dead, things would cool off, and he'd be able to bring on a couple of new slaves. He got an erection just thinking about what he'd do to them.

While Brody supervised the processing of Ron Tyler at the jail, Cameron was suspending Deputy Jim Ryder without pay for a month, for his poor performance at the meth bust.

Gabe and Carly sat in the sheriff's conference room with Ron's laptop. The first thing Gabe needed to determine was whether Ron Tyler had profiles on Facebook, MySpace, and TeenChat.

"Ron had accounts on all three social media sites," Gabe said as he adjusted his laptop's angle so that Carly could see the display.

"Ron's been a busy boy, mixing up batches of meth in his

kitchen and casting his net for underage girls, while deluding his wife at the same time," Carly replied, her tone edged with sarcasm.

"It looks like Ron met his Bloomington love interest on Facebook. There is a short conversation before he moves her to email. We'll find out more there," Gabe said.

"Looking forward to it," Carly returned, sipping from her coffee mug.

"He sporadically checked Craigslist, but not the personal ads."

"I find that a little odd, but maybe Craigslist was not his principle hunting place."

"I think he just lurked on the TeenChat site," Gabe said. "There is no record of any conversations."

"Interesting. Let's look at his emails," Carly suggested.

Next, Gabe got into Ron's email account to search for conversations he may have had with underage girls, specifically their victims. He found a month-long communication back and forth with @HotBloomieTeen that started out innocent enough, but turned to a lot of talk about sex and exchanging of suggestive photos between the two of them. Shelly was right, her husband was making plans for the preteen to meet him in Morel.

In the emails, Gabe went back a year, then two years, then three, but found no communications with anyone other than Ron's family and friends. Many messages were written in some kind of strange code and were undoubtedly about his drug making and availability.

On Ron's hard drive, Gabe found hundreds of pornographic photographs of children.

"Got him," Carly declared. "Pile the child porn charges on top of his attempts to entice a child into sexual activity and transmitting obscene material to a minor, not to mention the meth charges, and Mr. Tyler is going away for a long, long time."

"Not so fast," warned Gabe, intently staring at his laptop display.

"What's wrong?"

"This is odd. The kiddie porn photos were uploaded between four-thirty and six o'clock this morning. We were still at Ron Tyler's house at that time. We'd arrested Ron, cleared the house, and were ventilating it by then. Ron couldn't have uploaded these images."

Carly rubbed her temples as she absorbed this stunning news. "Are you saying what I think you're saying?"

"Carly, someone in the house uploaded those photos to frame Ron."

"But the only people in the house were members of the sheriff's team and the hazmat guys."

"Exactly. Brody is not going to want to hear this news."

Suddenly, Carly's cell phone sounded. Pulling it out of her pocket, she answered, "Carly Stone."

"Carly, this is Margaret, Alison's mother. She's awake. Alison is awake. We got our miracle. Please come as soon as you can. She wants to talk."

Volunteering to take Carly to the hospital, Gabe raced through the streets, and arrived in record time. Dashing through the lobby, they took the elevator up to the third floor to ICU and ran to

Alison's room.

Propped up with pillows, Alison sat in her bed as her mother held a plastic cup of water she was sipping through a straw. A nurse, checked her intravenous tubing, finished up, and left the room.

Carly moved to the chair at Alison's side, while Gabe leaned against a far wall. Holding Alison's hand, she said, "Alison, I am so glad to see you awake. I'm Carly Stone, and I'm a consultant for the sheriff's office."

"Mom said you brought this teddy bear for me," Alison said. Carly noticed for the first time that the girl was holding the stuffed animal.

"Yes, I did. I was hoping it could become your good luck bear."

"Good idea. I'll have to think of a name for him," said Alison, as a grin threatened the corners of her mouth. "Thank you, Ms. Stone."

"I want to be your friend, Alison, so call me Carly."

"Thank you for the bear, Carly."

"Alison, I want to find the man who did this to you. Do you feel like talking to me about him? Anything you remember, no matter how unimportant it may seem, may help us capture him so he can never do this to another girl."

Alison's eyes filled with tears, and she grasped her mother's hand and tightened her grip on Carly's.

"It's okay, honey," said Margaret. "We're here to protect you. Tell Carly what you remember."

"The Master killed. I saw him," Alison blurted out, as tears flooded down her cheeks.

"The Master?" asked Carly.

"He made us call him the Master," cried Alison. "He killed Jasmine. I saw him."

"Are you talking about Jasmine Norris?" asked Carly, remembering the missing girl from West Lafayette.

Alison nodded and then continued, "He let me take a shower. When I came out, he was beating her with a whip. Jasmine was in so much pain. When the woman brought our breakfast, she pulled Jasmine out of the dog crate and she was dead."

Dog crate? Carly was sickened. The killer kept the young girls in dog crates. "Woman? So there are two of them? A man and a woman?" Carly wondered. When Alison nodded her head in the affirmative, she asked, "What do they look like?"

Alison looked sadly at her mother, then looked back at Carly. "I don't know. They always wore ski masks."

"So you never saw either of them without the masks?"

"Wait a minute. I did see the woman's face when she picked me up at the bus station. She wasn't wearing any makeup and I remember thinking that a little mascara on her eyelashes and lip gloss on her mouth would make her look better. Her eyes were brown and so was her hair. I don't know how old she was, maybe in her twenties."

"Okay, that's good. If I brought in a sketch artist, do you think you could help him or her draw the woman's picture?"

"I could try."

"Alison, a farmer found you and called nine-one-one."

"There was a dog. Where is the dog?" Alison wanted to know.

"The dog's name is Lucky, and he belongs to the farmer," Carly said. "Do you remember how you got to the farmer's house?"

"Yes, I remember. When the woman realized Jasmine was dead, she ran upstairs. She didn't know she'd dropped the keys to the padlocks near our cages. I was able to get the keys and opened the padlock to my crate. I found some of the woman's sweats, put them on, and then punched out the glass of the bathroom window. I crawled out, ran into the woods, and realized some time later that I had cut myself and was bleeding. But I kept going. I was afraid to stop. The dog found me, and I followed the dog to the farm. I don't remember anything after that."

"You're doing really well, Alison. Just a few more questions. Tell me about the man's house. It sounds like you entered the woods directly from his yard. Is that correct?"

"Yes."

"Tell me what you saw in his yard before you went into the woods."

Alison paused, as if visualizing, and then said, "To my right was a driveway leading to a small garage. From the garage, the drive went to a red barn with a flat field next to it and in front. I remember thinking there were too many chances to see me if I went that way. So I ran for the woods."

Suddenly Usher's "O.M.G." pierced the quiet room as Gabe's cell phone sounded. Alison appeared to notice the man at the back of the room for the first time. Gabe fished his cell out of his pocket, apologized for the disruption and headed toward the door to answer his call.

"Anthony!" Alison screamed.

Confused, Gabe stopped and looked at the young girl who was now sobbing hysterically.

"I'm so sorry about the phone," he began, but Alison interrupted.

"You're Anthony!" she repeated accusingly, as she pointed at him.

Edging closer to the bed, Gabe said, "No, my name is Gabe Chase."

Wiping her eyes, Alison demanded, "Come closer so I can see you better." Once he moved nearer, she added, "You look just like Anthony, except you're older."

"Who is Anthony?" Gabe and Carly asked simultaneously.

"Anthony said he was in love with me. He's the reason I came to Morel."

12 CHAPTER TWELVE

With her heart in her throat, Carly asked, "Did you communicate with Anthony online, Alison?"

"Yes, we met on Teen Chat, but once we'd gotten close, he asked that we use instant messaging."

"So Gabe here looks a lot like Anthony?"

"They could be twins except Gabe is older. Anthony is sixteen. I wish I had my iPhone, I'd show you his photo."

"Carly, I need to get to my laptop back at the sheriff's office," Gabe interrupted, urgency written all over his face.

"Alison, please get some rest. We'll be back. What you've told us is very important. Thank you." She gave Alison a hug, and raced out of the room with Gabe.

Once they were seated in his car, Carly asked, "What are you thinking?"

"I need to go through every profile with the call name Anthony attached to it in Teen Chat with a profile photo that looks like me.

Then we'll be that much closer to our killer."

Cameron sat in Brody's office detailing the meeting he'd just had with Deputy Ryder.

"I just terminated Jim Ryder. I explained to him how his poor performance at the meth bust put lives at risk, and he blew up. He said neither of us would know good performance if it hit us in our faces. I have never seen anyone so angry. He turned in his service gun, his badge, and the keys to his patrol car. He insisted his performance was not bad and that we're making a big mistake that we'd live to regret."

"Not bad? If he had fired his gun, when I specifically gave orders not to shoot inside that house, he could have killed us all," Brody insisted. "And I haven't forgotten that he was the one who cleared the room the meth head was hiding in. Ryder could have shot me or that tank of anhydrous ammonia and blown us all sky high."

Carly appeared at his office doorway and Brody waved her in.

"What's going on?" he asked.

"Alison's awake. I just talked with her at the hospital, and have some important new information."

"Come in and sit down. What did you find out?"

Sitting down in the chair next to Cameron, Carly said, "The killer's house is located next to the wooded area Alison used to get to the farmer's house. Facing the front of the house, the thicket of trees is on the left side of the property. In addition, there is a garage and red barn. A field lies before and next to the barn."

"I can print a map once I get into the online property map and records site," said Cameron.

"There's more," Carly interrupted. "Alison said she'd fallen in love with someone online named Anthony, and he was the reason she took the bus to Morel. When she saw Gabe in the room, she nearly had a heart attack."

"Why?" Brody asked, obviously confused.

"Alison said that Anthony could be Gabe's twin, except Gabe is older. Anthony is supposedly sixteen."

"Where is Gabe?" Brody wanted to know.

"When we got back here, he picked up his laptop and went to his office. He said he needed to be near all of his equipment as he searches for Anthony's specific call name and real identity."

"If anyone can find his identity, it's Gabe," said Cameron.

"What time are we interviewing Ron Tyler today?" asked Brody, changing the subject as he pulled up his Outlook calendar on his computer.

"About Ron Tyler," Carly began. "Gabe found communications between Ron and the underage girl in Bloomington, and yes, Ron planned to hook up with her in Morel. But other than that, his emails were to and from family members and friends."

"That sounds good. Why do you sound so hesitant?" asked Brody, his dark eyebrows raised inquiringly.

"Gabe found hundreds of kiddie porn photos on Ron's laptop."

"Hell, yes!" shouted Cameron. "We've got him. Were there

photos of our victims?"

"No, Gabe didn't find any photos of our victims," Carly responded. "The thing about the pornographic photos is that they were uploaded between four-thirty and six o'clock this morning. If you recall, we were still at Ron Tyler's house at that time. Remember? We'd arrested Ron, cleared the house, and the hazmat team was ventilating it by then. Ron Tyler couldn't have uploaded the images."

"Who in the hell did?" demanded Brody.

Arriving at the hospital, the Master smiled to himself as he slipped by the front desk, completely unnoticed as a tall hospital security guard flirted with a pretty, young receptionist. Walking past the bank of elevators, he entered the stairwell where he took the stairs at a leisurely pace. No need to hurry, no one was going to stop him. He figured since Alison Brown was in a coma, she'd undoubtedly be in the ICU on the third floor.

Slowly opening the stairwell door to three, he peered down the hall and spotted a Shawnee County deputy sitting outside a patient's room that was undoubtedly Alison's. Closing the door, he leaned against the stairwell wall as he called the nurse's station in ICU.

"Hello, this is Sheriff Chase. I need to talk to the deputy who is posted outside Alison Brown's room. I've tried his cell phone, but he's not answering and he has a family emergency. I really need to talk to him."

"I'll go get him now," offered a nurse.

He watched as the nurse got the deputy's attention. Hearing the words "family emergency", the deputy raced to the nurse's station. The Master would have to be quick, but he was sure he could make it to the girl's room without being stopped. Taking advantage of the confusion caused when the deputy found the phone line dead, he rushed down the hall to Alison's room, visualizing all the while how he'd put a pillow over her face and suffocate her.

Reaching her room, he realized she was not alone. A woman in scrubs was washing Alison's face with a wash cloth. As he reached for the gun he'd strapped to his ankle, he debated whether he had time to take them both out. Too late. He'd run out of time. The deputy was running toward him, shouting for him to freeze.

Unable to backtrack without getting captured, he hurried toward the exit sign at the stairwell at the other end of the hall. Taking the steps two at a time, he was on the second floor when he heard the stairwell door above him open. The deputy yelled, "Stop!" Doing the opposite, he raced down the stairs until he reached the first floor exit which led to the parking lot. Soon, he was in his car, speeding out of the lot.

For the first time since he'd implemented his plan, he became alarmed and anxious. Things were not going according to plan, and maybe his sister was right when she said things were unraveling.

His only option was to kill the girl. She was the only one who could lead the police to his door. Awake now, she must be talking to the police. Maybe she couldn't figure out where he lived. Otherwise, his place would have been crawling with cops by now. That must be it. He'd come back later with a silencer on his gun and shoot the deputy, then Alison, and anyone else who tried to interfere with the Master's plan.

In his office, Gabe frantically tried to find Anthony's call name. He'd discovered twenty-one call names that included the name

"Anthony" that were being used on the Teen Chat site. It was tedious work, but he had to go through each profile and photo in order to target the Anthony who was communicating with Alison Brown. He'd gone through eighteen profiles and profile photos when he came to @Anthony16. What Gabe saw on this profile made him shake his head in disbelief, and push back in his chair. He was shocked and angry. What the hell?

He copied and pasted @Anthony16's profile image into an email and then called Brody. As soon as his brother answered, in a rush of words, he said, "Brody, do you have your computer on? Go to your email. I just sent you an image."

"Now's not a good time, Gabe. I'm meeting with Carly and Cameron."

"Move your computer screen so that they can both see what I sent. Turn your phone on speaker so Carly and Cam can hear me. Open the email, Brody."

Hearing the urgency in Gabe's voice, Brody pulled up the email and opened it.

"Tell me what you see," Gabe demanded.

"What the hell is going on, Gabe? This is the picture I took of you in your football jersey when you were sixteen. Why are you sending it to me now?"

"That's the photo that Anthony is using on his Teen Chat profile. He used it when he started romancing Alison Brown online. Our killer is using *my* fucking photo, Brody!"

"Oh, my God," said Carly. "The killer knows Gabe."

Cameron remarked, "Well, if he knows Gabe, he probably knows all three of us."

"Exactly," said Carly. "Keep in mind, our killer likes to hang around cops. It is not farfetched to think he may be a law enforcement officer for Shawnee County. That would be the perfect job for him. He would know firsthand how close the police were in identifying him as the killer."

"No way," insisted Brody.

"Why would this guy use Gabe's photo? Cameron asked.

"For some reason, he dislikes Gabe. Why else would he use Gabe's photo on his fake online profile? He's thinking if law enforcement should discover his online profile, he can divert their attention to Gabe instead of himself."

"Who would have access to Gabe's photograph?"

Gabe answered, "Since my high school yearbook is online, your guess is as good as mine. But I can tell you this. I won't stop searching for this bastard's identity until I find it."

When Cameron went to his office to look at property records, Carly said to Brody, "There were only four officers certified to go into Ron Tyler's house during the meth bust, Cameron, Blake, Deputy Ryder and you. You and Blake didn't enter the home because you were dealing with Ron Tyler, who had crashed through the back sliding glass doors, and the meth head with the gun. Cameron came out back as soon as he heard the gun go off. That leaves Deputy Ryder alone in the house for at least fifteen minutes, before the hazmat team went inside. That is more than enough time to upload those photographs onto Ron's computer."

Covering his face with his hands for a moment, Brody said, "That the serial killer we've been looking for is one of my officers is just unthinkable. One of my deputies uploading porn onto a suspect's computer and killing all those girls is quite a stretch."

"He fits my profile, Brody. Think about it," Carly began. "He's a white male in his thirties who is physically fit. Ryder would have no problem carrying his dead victims to the shallow graves he'd dug. If you check his work hours, I bet you'll find Ryder works a five-day-week and his day off is consistently on Saturday. He lives and works in Shawnee County, which is why he lures the girls here. Hanging around crime scenes is something he likes. Since he's an officer, Ryder can hang around crime scenes all he wants and no one would be the wiser. It's no coincidence he was the one alone with Ron Tyler's laptop. He uploaded those pornographic photos."

Deputy Sawyer knocked on Brody's door, and then peeked in. "Sheriff, the coroner is trying to reach you. He says it's important."

"Thanks, Deputy," said Brody.

Putting a call in to Bryan, Brody asked, "What's so important?"

"Do you remember that piece of duct tape we pulled off one of the victims we found in the car fire?" Bryan asked.

"Yeah. I recall you said it was a long shot that CSI could get a fingerprint from it."

"Well, it took a while, but Cheryl Davis got a print!" Bryan exclaimed. "The fingerprint belongs to a woman by the name of

Erin Ryder. We had her prints on file because she applied to work in the county school system."

Brody disconnected the call and said to Carly. "We have a fingerprint on duct tape found on one of the victims. It belongs to Jim Ryder's sister, Erin."

Cameron had just printed a map from the property records of Hal Locke's farm, adjacent woods, and a property that appeared to match Alison Brown's description. Curiously enough, the property belonged to Jim Ryder, the deputy he'd just terminated hours before.

In a rush to get to Brody's office, he'd snatched the map from his printer, just as Deputy Sawyer entered his office. "Is your phone on vibrate again?"

"What are you talking about?"

"I'm transferring a call to you in a second. It's Deputy Walker at the hospital and he says it's important."

Cameron answered the second the phone rang. "Detective Chase."

"Sir, this is Deputy Walker, I'm at the hospital, assigned to cover Alison Brown's room."

"Hello, Deputy. Is everything all right?"

"It is now, sir. We just had a guy try to get into Alison Brown's room. I think he called the ICU nurse's station, pretended he was the sheriff calling with a family emergency for me. When I arrived at the nurse's station to take the call, the phone was dead. I turned around in time to see him entering Alison's room. When I yelled at him, he ran down the hall and I lost him in the stairwell."

"Is Alison okay? Did he hurt her in any way?" Cameron wanted to know.

"No, sir. She's in her room, talking with her mother right now."

"Don't leave your post again for any reason, Deputy," Cameron warned. "I'll talk to you later."

"Don't hang up, sir," the deputy pleaded. "There's more."

"What?" asked Cameron, his tone reflecting his annoyance.

"The man was wearing a Shawnee County deputy uniform."

"Can you identify him?"

"No, sir. He had his back to me when he ran down the hall. I didn't get a clear visual of his face."

Cameron disconnected the call, and pounded his fist on his desk in frustration. An intruder at the hospital trying to get into Alison's room was wearing a Shawnee County deputy uniform and the property in question belonged to one of his deputies. It didn't take Sherlock Holmes to figure this one out. Cameron was more certain than ever that their killer was Deputy Jim Ryder.

Deciding it was time to move Alison to the safe house, Cameron picked up the phone, and called Deputy Walker back at the hospital. The girl was no longer safe there, especially since Ryder was furious about being fired. His behavior could escalate. After he talked to Walker, he emailed a photo of Ryder to hospital security. Cameron needed to talk to his brother, then get Alison out of that hospital.

Cameron raced down the hall and into Brody's office and said, "Our killer is Jim Ryder."

"Sit down, Cam. We've got to calmly discuss what evidence we have that Ryder is our guy. Why do you think it's Ryder?"

"A man wearing a Shawnee County deputy's uniform just tried to get into Alison Brown's room at the hospital. I pulled the property records and the house from which Alison escaped belongs to Jim Ryder. Is this a coincidence, or could Ryder be our killer?"

"Cameron, there is more information that implicates Ryder," said Carly. "At Ron Tyler's house, you came out back as soon as you heard the gun go off. That leaves Deputy Ryder alone in the house for at least fifteen minutes before the hazmat team went inside. That's more than enough time for him to upload those kiddie porn photographs onto Ron's computer."

Brody added, "Besides that, Bryan just called me. One of our techs was able to lift a fingerprint from a piece of duct tape taken from one of our victims the day we discovered the burning car. The fingerprint belongs to a woman by the name of Erin Ryder."

"That's Jim Ryder's sister!" exclaimed Cameron.

"I'm not sure we have enough to arrest the bastard, but we damn well have enough to bring him in for questioning," said Brody. "Cameron, hand me that map. Then get a search warrant for Ryder's property to Judge Carlson's office. Get a BOLO out on him. Carly and I are going to see if he's at his house."

Cameron stopped at Deputy Sawyer's desk before going to his office. "Would you please type up a search warrant?" Ripping out a piece of paper from his notebook, he handed it to her. "Here is the property address as well as a list of what we're searching for."

"But, this is Deputy Ryder's address."

"I'm aware of that. Keep this confidential until I can get a BOLO out to the deputies for him."

"No problem," she said as she looked for the search warrant template on her computer.

"Once you get it typed, get it over to Judge Carlson for her signature. Then once she signs, call me. We need to move fast on this."

Alison lay awake in her hospital bed, watching her mother, who was standing at the window looking out. Her mom was quietly weeping, her arms crossed and her shoulders trembling. It was Alison's fault her mother was so upset and experiencing this trauma. It was her fault one hundred percent.

She'd seen her mother's face moments before, when Deputy Walker raced in the room to see if they were all right. Instinctively, they both knew exactly what had happened. The Master had made his first attempt to kill Alison. Her mom's face turned dead white, and the sheer terror in her eyes was unmistakable. But soon she masked her emotions and sat on the bed to comfort Alison, when it was she who should be comforting her mother. Alison had experienced a living nightmare, but she understood that her mom's experience had not been much better. Her only daughter had disappeared. She must have felt helpless and frightened as she had to rely on others to find Alison. There must have been moments when she thought she'd never see her daughter again, just as Alison had felt she may never see her mother.

Running away was one of the most important decisions of her young life, and the choice Alison had made was the worst possible. She'd failed miserably. It had turned their lives upside down and she didn't know if they'd ever recover.

What flaw in her character made her run into the arms of a predator? Was it cowardice? Did she fear her stepfather and the wrath of her bullies so much that she ran, instead of facing her problems head-on? Was she becoming the kind of person who ran from her challenges?

Her mother was the most important person in her world. Why didn't she trust her mom enough to share what was going on in her life?

Wiping her face, Margaret turned from the window. "Are you awake? I thought you were getting some rest, Alison?"

"I want to talk," said Alison. "There are things I need to say to you."

Sitting in the chair next to the bed, Margaret asked, "What things?"

"It's my fault all this is happening. I'm sorry, Mom, and I wish I could make it up to you."

"Don't let me off the hook. I share a healthy portion of any blame that's being assigned for this mess. If I hadn't brought Raymond Brown into our lives, or been more aware of what was going on with my daughter, all this might have been prevented. So if there's blame being passed around, I claim a big chunk of it."

Alison pulled her mother's hand into her own and held it tightly. "There is something I have to tell you about my stepfather."

"I already know that you used to push your dresser in front of your bedroom door to keep him out in the evenings when I was working. The police told me he'd served time in prison before I met him for sexual misconduct with a twelve-year-old girl. I had no clue. I married a monster who molests little girls, and moved him in with my thirteen-year-old daughter. Not only did I do that, I worked nights, giving him every opportunity to get to you. But why didn't you tell me, Alison? Why didn't you trust me enough to tell me what he was doing?"

"He said he would hurt us both. I was so afraid of what he might do..."

Margaret cut in. "There's no need for you to be afraid of him ever again, Alison. Raymond is no longer living with us. I've filed for divorce. I plan to do everything in my power to see that he's punished for what he did to you."

"So when we move back to Indianapolis..."

"*If* we move back there," said Margaret, squeezing her daughter's hand. "We're going to start over, make a brand-new life, and it doesn't necessarily have to be in Indianapolis. I put the house up for sale. We can live anywhere we want. I can find a position as a nurse anywhere."

"Really?" Alison asked.

"Yes, Alison, we can decide together where we go. You were unhappy living in Indianapolis. I wish you'd told me," Margaret began. "Edward Webb is the name of the older man who lives next to the empty lot where those girls beat you. He visited me and told me everything. I'm so grateful that Mr. Webb stopped them from hurting you any more than they did. Why didn't you tell me about them?"

"There was never the right time, Mom. Besides, if you had gotten involved, they might have been even more cruel."

"I need for you to make some promises to me, Alison. Promises that you cannot break, no matter what."

"What are they?"

"Promise me you will never run away again."

"I promise."

"Now promise me that you will confide in me like you used to. I want to know everything that's going on in your life. I'm your mom. There is no one in this world who cares more about you than I do."

Alison nodded and said, "I promise."

"Trust me to do my job, Alison. It's up to me, as your mother, to protect you no matter what the cost. I'm stronger than you seem to think. Trust me to keep you safe."

"Yes, Mom."

"Sweetheart, you don't have to look online or anywhere else for someone to love you or listen to you. That person is sitting beside you right now." Throwing her arms around her daughter, Margaret squeezed Alison tightly. "I would do anything for you. Anything. I'd lay down my life for you in a second. I love you more than life itself. Don't you ever forget that."

At the hospital, Cameron reached the third floor intensive care unit and rushed into Alison's room, and saw that Deputy Walker and the nurses had the girl and her mother packed and ready to go.

"You look familiar. Have we met?" Alison asked Cameron.

"We have, but I'm surprised you remember. You were in a coma when I visited. I'm Cameron Chase. I'm a detective with the county sheriff's office."

"Why did you come to see me?"

"We'd been searching for you for a long time. I guess I needed to see for myself that you were really okay. I wanted to see in person the brave girl who escaped from the man who hurt her."

"He was here at the hospital, wasn't he?" Alison asked. Fear, stark and vivid, glittered in her eyes.

Cameron glanced at Margaret who nodded her head as if to tell him it was okay to tell her daughter the truth.

"He was in the hospital earlier and outside your room, but Deputy Walker stopped him." said Cameron. "We're moving you to a safe house where he can't find you. I have deputies scheduled to watch the house every minute of the day. You'll like it there, Alison. You'll love Jenny Lynn, who runs the place. She can't wait to meet you. She has a room for you and your mom."

Deputy Walker and a nurse entered the room to tell Cameron the ambulance that would transport Alison to the safe house was ready.

In the car, Brody turned to Carly, "When we get to Ryder's

place, you stay in the car."

"No way," said Carly defiantly. "Not going to happen."

"Damn it, Carly. Do you have to be so damn stubborn?"

"Stubborn has nothing to do with it. That meth bust made me realize two things. When I saw that drug addict with his gun pointed at your chest, I realized how much I love you and that I didn't want to think about my life without you in it," said Carly.

"Baby..."

"Let me finish. The second thing I realized is that if we are going to make a go at a relationship, we have got to cope with the other person facing danger at work. I love being in law enforcement as much as you do, Brody. Danger comes with the territory. You've got to stop being so overprotective of me, and I have to stop worrying about what might happen to you."

Silently, Brody focused on the road. They were out of the downtown area, and he'd turned onto the county road that led to Ryder's place about twenty miles away.

"Aren't you going to say anything?" Carly asked.

Pulling off the road, Brody dragged her across the console onto his lap and into his arms, and kissed her soundly. "I've lost both my parents, Carly, so I'm well acquainted with loss. I don't know if I can stop being overprotective toward you. I love you so much, I don't know if I can deal with losing you, too."

Kissing him, she said, "This is so *not* the appropriate time, but if we keep talking like this, and kissing like this, I'm going to jump your bones right here in broad daylight in your clearly marked sheriff's office SUV."

"Sex maniac," Brody said, his face breaking into a grin, as he helped her into the passenger seat. "Let's go get our killer."

Gabe paced back and forth in front of his office window. He couldn't get to Anthony's identity. Gabe tried to trace the killer through his IP address, but found that Anthony was either using a firewall to deny traffic, or he was using multiple proxies around the world that masked his original IP address. He called his contact at Teen Chat and was given a name and address for @Anthony16 that he researched, and discovered neither existed.

At the end of his rope, he thought about what Brody told him about going outside the box. His brother was adamant about doing everything by the book. But then, Gabe thought, Brody was referring to instances where he had a search warrant for the subject's computer and the computer was in his possession. This was a different scenario, he reasoned, because he didn't have a warrant or the subject's computer in his reach. He wasn't searching for evidence. Gabe needed Anthony's identity.

Stumped, he called Frankie Douglas-Hansen, a fellow private investigator he'd met at conferences, with whom he'd become good friends. They talked for about twenty minutes, as Frankie filled him in on her pregnancy, and gave him some advice for hacking Anthony's computer.

Gabe went back into Teen Chat and waited thirty minutes before @Anthony16 joined the chat room. Well, hello serial killer.

He initiated a chat acting as an interested preteen. After a short conversation with @Anthony16, he asked for a photograph. Gabe was more than happy to oblige. Using Carly's sex sting photo, he attached a backdoor Trojan Horse virus that would report directly to him @Anthony16's real IP address, which would enable him to get Anthony's real name and address.

Before long Gabe tracked @Anthony16 to his correct IP address, thanks to his Trojan-infected bait photo, just as Frankie had advised. He now had the killer's real name. Jim Ryder? The deputy? Thinking there must be more than one Jim Ryder, he looked up employment history. The only Jim Ryder in Shawnee County was a deputy on his brother's team. He was the same guy who'd ridden with the others in the back of the van he drove to Ron Tyler's house.

He had to get to Brody right away with this information. Calling both Brody's office and cell phone, he got no answer. Finally, he dialed Cameron's number.

"Cam, I know who @Anthony16 is. It's your deputy, Jim Ryder. He's the killer."

"We just figured it out, too. I'm getting a search warrant for his place signed by Judge Carlson right now. Brody and Carly are driving to his house to pick him up for questioning."

"They went without backup?" Gabe asked.

"I'm heading that way as soon as I get Alison to the safe house and Gail has the search warrant signed," said Cameron.

"I'm going now!"

Brody slowly drove up to Ryder's house. Cameron made Ryder turn in his county patrol car, but Brody knew he had an old Ford truck. There was no vehicle in the driveway, but it could be parked in the closed garage. Pulling into the driveway, he stopped a short distance from the side door of the house. He and Carly jumped out of the vehicle.

"Are you armed?" asked Brody.

"Aren't I always armed?" replied Carly, pulling her jacket back to reveal her Glock in its holster.

"Okay, you check the garage, while I knock on the door."

Brody knocked several times, and then peered in through a window. It seemed no one was home. Carly appeared at the front of the garage and signaled it was empty.

"I'm checking the barn," she said.

"I'll walk the perimeter and check more windows."

The barn was dark, so Carly pulled a small flashlight from her jacket pocket and flipped it on. The air was thick with dust, and smells of straw, manure, and something yet-to-be-identified filled her lungs. There was an eerie quality about the shadowy barn that made her skin crawl. She had a bad feeling about the barn, and her intuition was usually right. Spotting a couple of rough wooden stalls at the back of the barn, she checked out each one and found nothing.

Carly was heading back to the barn's entrance when her foot became entangled in something metallic and she slammed onto the dirt floor, knocking the wind out of her. Collecting herself, she crawled on all fours to identify what had tripped her. The area where she'd stumbled was covered with a thick layer of hay. Brushing it aside, she discovered a metal latch. Getting to her feet, she cleared away the layer of hay until a trapdoor revealed itself. Judging from the sawdust in its cracks, the door had been built recently.

Grabbing the latch, she pulled until the door opened, and saw an old wooden ladder leading into a pitch-black room below. That's odd, she thought. If one was going to all the trouble to make a new door, why is this ladder so old? Pulling out her flashlight, Carly swept the light back and forth and realized the room was larger than it first appeared. She backed onto the ladder, and rung by rung descended into the dark room. The ladder's fourth rung gave way when she put her weight on it, and she fell to the floor below, landing with a thud.

Suddenly, the trapdoor above her slammed shut, leaving her in total darkness. Where was her flashlight? She'd dropped it when she fell. Getting on her hands and knees, she swept her hands around the dirt floor, until she located the flashlight. She got to her feet and turned it on. It didn't work. She shook it. Had it broken in the fall?

An overwhelming odor in the room assailed her nostrils and she knew exactly what it was. Carly would never forget the dense, sweet and putrid stench of human decomposition. Covering her mouth and nose with her hand, she felt nauseated, and stepped backward in an effort to escape the odor. She tripped, falling through sticky spider webbing that covered her face and hair. Blindly, she did a wild dance, clawing at the webbing and swiping at the creatures skittering through her hair. Fearing spiders since she was a kid, Carly remembered Brody telling her that poisonous Brown Recluse spiders could be found all over Indiana. Just what she needed, a fatal spider bite.

Stepping down on her flashlight, it flickered on, creating a beam of light that illuminated the face of Jasmine Norris, her body in the early stages of decay. Carly shrieked in shock, and backed into something soft. Picking up her flashlight, she focused its beam on yet another body. It was Erin Ryder, with a gaping hole in her forehead.

Accidentally, Carly had discovered one of Jim Ryder's body dump sites, and the up-close-and-personal nature of the discovery was a little hard to take. Feeling sick to her stomach, she didn't want to spend another minute in the foul-smelling, dark hole. She aimed the flashlight toward the wooden ladder, from which she'd fallen.

Before she had a chance to approach it, she heard loud voices above her. Stepping on each rung slowly, testing it to see if it would hold her weight, Carly inched her way to the top.

"Drop your gun, Ryder!" She heard Brody demand.

"Go to hell," growled Jim Ryder. "If you don't have a search warrant in your hand, you're trespassing."

"It's over, Ryder. We know everything."

"I doubt that very much, Sheriff."

"What you did to Alison Brown and how she witnessed you killing Jasmine Norris is no longer a secret. We also know about all the other girls you lured to Shawnee County, tortured, and murdered. It's over. Put down your gun."

"You don't have anything solid and you know it. Alison Brown? It's the word of a trusted law enforcement officer against a teenaged twit. Any good defense attorney will take her down. Got any forensic evidence? Didn't think so."

"Put down your gun, Ryder!" Brody roared.

Pushing on the trapdoor, Carly created an opening about six inches high that enabled her to see Jim Ryder, just as he fired his gun. Holding the trapdoor in place with one hand, she used the other to whip out her Glock and screamed at Ryder to "freeze". Instead, he fired a shot at her that glanced off the trapdoor. Carly returned fire, hitting Ryder in the chest. Blood blossomed and spread across the front of his shirt as he sank to the ground. Throwing the trapdoor open, Carly rushed to him and kicked his weapon far from his reach.

Checking his pulse, she found it was weak, but his heart was still beating. Hearing movement behind her, she whirled in place with her gun extended.

"Don't shoot, Carly. It's me!" shouted Gabe, his hand grabbing her wrist with surprising force. Putting his hand gently on her shoulder, he said, "It's over. It's okay, Carly."

"Where's Brody? I heard his voice."

A moan at the back of the barn answered her question. Brody lay on the other side of the trapdoor, bleeding profusely from his arm. Carly rushed to him and Gabe called for help on his cell phone.

Carly ripped off her jacket, folded it, and tied it around Brody's arm to make a tourniquet.

"Brody's been shot. Tell them to send an ambulance, Gabe.

Tell them to hurry!"

Once they reached the hospital, Brody was whisked off to surgery and Dr. Ford promised Carly he'd take good care of him. With Cameron and Gabe, Carly stayed in the waiting room until someone notified them about the outcome of Brody's surgery. Cameron and Gabe took turns teasing Carly about the stench emanating from her filthy clothing. Carly ignored them. She was too worried about Brody to have much of a sense of humor.

When watching television and pacing back and forth didn't help, Carly searched for the cafeteria to get coffee for the three of them.

Upon her return, she saw Dr. Ford at the nurse's station and rushed to him.

"Is Brody okay? What happened in surgery?"

"I was just about to find you, Carly. The surgery went well and Brody is in the recovery room two doors down. You can see him, but just for a minute."

Placing the three coffees down on the counter, Carly hurried to Brody's recovery room. When she reached the doorway, she froze and her jaw dropped open in surprise. Mollie Adams sat on Brody's bed, holding him in her arms, stroking his face and kissing him as she wept. Had she imagined an attraction between Mollie and Cameron? Was it Brody all along for Mollie?

She felt like such an idiot. This was just as devastating as finding her ex-lover Sam Isley screwing his trainee on his desk. How many times would she find men she loved in the arms of other women?

Was she really that naive and stupid in her personal life that she couldn't see the signs?

Carly thought of Mollie's daughter, Hailey. Usually blunt and direct, why hadn't she asked Brody if the girl was his daughter?

Her eyes filled with tears, Carly backed out of the room, raced past the waiting room, out of the hospital into the parking lot.

Carly got into Brody's SUV, started the engine, then headed toward the cottage. As much as she loved Brody, she could not commit to a forever kind of relationship with him. She would not be the one to stand in the way of his happiness with Mollie and Hailey. Carly loved Brody and needed him to be happy, even if it wasn't with her.

At the cottage, she ran upstairs, packed her things, then threw her bags in the trunk of the SUV. She left a message inside the cottage that it would be parked at the airport. On her way to Indianapolis, she booked a flight to Orlando. She was going back home.

During her first two weeks in Florida, Carly threw herself into a consulting job with the Bureau. One of their witnesses in a sex trafficking case Carly had worked refused to talk to anyone but her. So Carly stayed with the witness in protective custody and supported her through a difficult two-week trial.

After the trial ended, Carly moved back home. The loneliness for Brody hit her like a ton of bricks. There were a dozen messages from him on her answering machine, but she deleted each one.

Insomnia took the name of Brody Chase and stole her sleep. Even her steady supply of caffeine wasn't working to alleviate her exhaustion during the day.

Her mother showed up in the middle of the third week to whisk Carly off to a spa. They had facials, massages, pedicures, and sipped iced mint tea, and Carly felt a little better — until she walked into her empty house that evening, loaded down with shopping bags, and had time to think.

Why had she fallen so hard for Brody Chase? Maybe because he wasn't a bad boy as all her past lovers had been. He liked her intelligence, and wasn't threatened by it. He hadn't cheated on her like Sam Isley. At least she didn't think he had.

What is it about first loves that make them so hard to forget? She had no chance of competing with Mollie Adams. Their history spanned years. If Brody had really been in love with her, Carly wouldn't have had to vie with anyone for his affection.

Pulling on her new red bikini, Carly grabbed a fluffy, white towel as she went outside to the pool. She loved to swim at night under the stars. If anything could make her feel better, swimming would. Carly did a breast-stroke for the first lap, and for the second lap she flipped to her back and gazed at the million glittering stars in the night sky. After a while, she did another couple of laps, and then swam toward the pool ladder to get her towel.

Pulling herself up onto the ladder, she'd climbed a rung when she realized, her white towel was being handed to her by a tall and very handsome sheriff named Brody Chase. Her breath caught on a surge of yearning so abrupt and intense it felt like pain.

Once she was out of the water, he wrapped the towel around her and hugged her against his hard body so tightly, she could barely breathe. He crushed his mouth to hers and she felt the surge of sexual electricity all the way to her toes. The kiss went on and on until finally, she pulled out of his arms and said, "Brody, what are you doing here?"

"I figured if you didn't want to live in Indiana, then I'd move here."

"What are you talking about?"

"Just what I said. I tried living three weeks without you, and I can't do it, Carly. I can't. So I asked for a leave of absence to talk to you about my moving in with you."

"Have you lost your mind? What about Mollie? You two have a lengthy history. What about your daughter, Hailey? You and Molly should be together."

"That's the thing, Carly, Mollie is not the woman for me and I'm not the man for her. There's another Chase brother that should be with Mollie. And if Cam has a brain in his head, he'll make it happen. Another thing, what gave you the idea Hailey is my daughter? She's not. Her father was killed in an accident years ago. I love you, Carly. I should be wherever you are. So here I am."

"But at the hospital that night, I saw..."

"What you saw were two old friends embracing each other, after one of them just got out of surgery."

"If that's true, why did it take you three weeks to contact me?"

"Didn't you listen to any of my messages? I was miserable without you, but I couldn't leave until Jim Ryder's case was wrapped up so tight our prosecutor can get a guilty verdict. He's seeking the death penalty. I met with him this morning before my flight. After that, I met with the commission and asked for a leave of absence, which they gave me. Cam is in charge while I'm gone."

"So you're here to..."

"I'm here to find out what you want. If you love me, like I hope you do, then I want to make things permanent."

"You would give up your job for me, Brody?" she asked. "You love your job."

"I love you more."

Carly backed up a step. "Well, there are a couple of things I'll need before we talk permanent."

"Negotiating again?"

She nodded. "I need to hear the words."

"Will you marry me, Carly?"

She shook her head. "Not those words."

"What about these words? I've never loved or wanted anyone like I do you, Carly Stone. It's one of those forever kinds of things, like the love I think my parents had. I love you, Baby."

Her fingers gripping his shirt, she pulled him to her and kissed him the way she'd kissed him in her dreams. "I'm thinking a pre-wedding honeymoon, lasting approximately six months to a year in the Honeymoon Cottage, with a 'do not disturb' sign on the front door at night might work for me."

"Does that mean you'll marry me?"

"Eventually, big guy, but for the next six months to a year, I'll be in your bed every night so I imagine that's enough time for you to do some impressive persuading."

Brody's face broke into the widest smile as he said, "Let's go inside, sweetheart. I don't procrastinate when it comes to showing off my impressive persuasion abilities."

Dear Reader:

If you liked *Profile of Evil*, I would appreciate it if you would help others enjoy this book too by recommending it to your friends, family and book clubs by writing an honest, positive review on Amazon, Barnes and Noble, Kobo, iTunes, Goodreads, Smashwords, etc.

If you do write a review, please send me an email at **alexagrace@cfl.rr.com**. I'd like to add you to my e-newsletter list so that you can get updates about upcoming releases first, be eligible for drawings for prizes, and get free ebook alerts.

Thank you.

Alexa Grace

P.S. If you should find a mistake, please notify me. I always strive to write the best book possible and use a team of beta readers as well as an editor prior to publication. But goofs slip through. If something slipped past us, please let me know by writing to me at **alexagrace@cfl.rr.com**. Thank you.

The Profile Series by Alexa Grace

Spring 2013 *Profile of Evil*

Carly Stone is a brilliant FBI agent who's seen more than her share of evil. Leaving the agency, she becomes a consultant for Indiana County Sheriff Brody Chase, who needs her profiling skills to catch an online sex predator who is luring preteen girls to their death in his community. A life hangs in the balance, and the two rush stop the most terrifying killer of their careers — and time is running out.

Summer 2013   *Profile of Terror*

Social media sites are the playground for twin sexual predators and are the last stops for three young women. When an ex-girlfriend goes missing, Private Investigator Gabe Chase is obsessed with finding her. Once her lifeless body is discovered, her gorgeous and accusing older sister is the distraction Gabe doesn't need as the body count increases and he hunts down the killers.

Fall/Winter 2013 *Profile of Fear*

A dismembered body found by a trash collector takes Detective Cameron Chase into the unspeakable world of human sexual trafficking. His county is the last place anyone would consider for sex trafficking, and that's just what the traffickers are counting on.

When his lover's teenaged daughter is abducted by the traffickers, the clock ticks as Cameron searches for her. Will he find her before the traffickers sell her abroad — or worse?

Other Books by Alexa Grace

From bestselling new author Alexa Grace, *The Deadly Trilogy*, three books with non-stop suspense and a healthy dose of toe-curling passion will have you holding your breath from the first page to the last. You can find them at online retailers: Amazon, Barnes & Noble, Kobo, iTunes, Diesel, Sony, Smashwords, and more.

Deadly Offerings - Book One - Anne Mason thinks she'll be safe living in the Midwest living on a wind farm left to her by her ex's mother. She may be dead wrong. Someone is dumping bodies in her corn field and telling Anne they are gifts—for her! And how can she be falling in love with the hot attorney who represented her ex-husband in their divorce proceedings?

Deadly Deception - Book Two- Enter the disturbing world of illegal adoptions, baby trafficking and murder with new detective Lane Hansen and private investigator Frankie Douglas. Going undercover as husband and wife, Lane and Frankie struggle to keep their relationship strictly professional as their sizzling passion threatens to burn out of control. Can they keep passion in control long enough to take down two murderers?

Deadly Relations - Book Three - Detective Jennifer Brennan, still haunted by her abduction five years before, devotes her life to serve and protect others. Love is the last thing on her mind, but will it find her after three young women go missing and are found murdered on her watch and she vows to find the killer — or die trying.

Deadly Holiday - If you liked the books of *The Deadly Trilogy*: *Deadly Offerings*, *Deadly Deception* and *Deadly Relations*, you'll LOVE this nail-biting, holiday-themed novella where the characters return to search for a lost boy, fight breast cancer, deal with the personal financial impact of a bad economy, and seek a Christmas miracle.

With more than 1,000 five-star reviews, it's time for you to discover *the Deadly Trilogy books*: *Deadly Offerings*, *Deadly Deception*, *Deadly Relations and Deadly Holiday*. For more information, go to http://www.alexa-grace.net/.

About the Author — Alexa Grace

Alexa Grace's journey started in March 2011 when the Sr. Director of Training & Development position she'd held for thirteen years was eliminated. A door closed but another one opened. She finally had the time to pursue her childhood dream of writing books. Her focus is now on writing riveting romantic suspense novels.

Alexa earned two degrees from Indiana State University and currently lives in Florida. She's a member of Romance Writers of America (national) as well as the Florida Chapter.

Alexa Grace is listed in the top ten of Amazon's Top 100 Most Popular Authors in the categories Romantic Suspense and Police Procedural. In 2012, she was named one of the top 100 Indie authors by *Kindle Review*. A chapter is devoted to Alexa in the book *Interviews with Indie Authors* by C. Ridgway and T. Ridgway.

Her writing support team includes five Miniature Schnauzers, three of which are rescues. As a writer, she is fueled by Starbucks lattes, chocolate and emails from readers.

Visit her online at: - http://www.alexa-grace.net/
Friend her on Facebook -
https://www.facebook.com/AuthorAlexaGrace
Follow her on Twitter - @AlexaGrace2

CPSIA information can be obtained at www.ICGtesting.com
Printed in the USA
LVOW08s0918010315

428810LV00019B/1028/P